INDEPENDENCE

INDEPENDENCE
Book One of the Legacy Ship Trilogy

Nick Webb

Copyright © 2016 Nick Webb

All rights reserved.

www.nickwebbwrites.com

Summary: We hoped, desperately, that they came in peace. We were wrong. Thirty years after the Second Swarm War devastated Earth and its colonies, a powerful, mysterious alien ship has invaded our space. Entire planets are ravaged, whole moons shattered. Any starship sent against it never comes home. But Admiral Proctor, a war hero from our last brush with annihilation, is called out of retirement to take the reins of humanity's newest starship. The ISS Independence and her crew, with Admiral Proctor at the helm, will stand as Earth's last defense. Somehow, against all odds, they will save us, even when our enemy is not just an unstoppable alien ship, but a ghost from humanity's past bent on its utter destruction. And if they fail, we fall. For good.

Text set in Garamond

Designed by Nick Webb

Cover art by Jeff Brown

http://http://jeffbrowngraphics.com

ISBN-10: 1539389340
ISBN-13: 978-1539389347

Printed in the United Sates of America

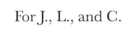
For J., L., and C.

Prologue

Irigoyen Sector, San Martin System, Asteroid belt
Asteroid Hauler Magdalena Issachar

SIGNAL RECEIVED. 5/12/2680 23:48.25
MESSAGE DECRYPTED:
It's time.
END MESSAGE.

Danny had been waiting in deep space for the signal for six days. Nearly an entire week of half sitting, half floating on his ass, the gravity plates only at one tenth power to conserve fuel, water, and food supplies dwindling down to near nothing —one more ancient, stale granola bar and he knew he'd vomit —and suffering through the constant banter of his two crewmates.

Thankfully, they'd gone to sleep hours ago. Only Danny had seen the message come in from their mysterious client— just as he'd hoped—passing it through the ten-odd levels of decryption, only to discover the text itself was only two enigmatic words. *It's time.* Damn—these guys were paranoid.

There must be a ton of platinum bullion in that giant crate down in the cargo hold. Or fluff-coke. Was he a drug-runner now? Shit. Or maybe a handful of Rigellian mail-order brides in stasis. Whatever it was, it couldn't be within the law. Law-abiding citizens didn't send hyper-encrypted messages to clandestine asteroid haulers this far out on the fringes of United Earth Space.

He had only sneaking suspicions of who the client was, but it didn't matter. The money was good, and the bonus hourly pay from the GPC was icing on the cake. The job had been high-priority—he wondered if the Secretary-General himself had approved the job. The Galactic People's Congress wasn't big enough yet to preclude the old man himself from giving the thumbs-up on even standard delivery missions.

That would change, though.

And this was no standard delivery mission.

With gravity still at one-tenth, he pushed off from his bed, launched through the air of his cramped living quarters, and landed on both feet in front of the door a few meters away. As queasy as he got in low grav, he loved the feeling of being a superhero.

A hero. Isn't that why he'd signed up with the GPC in the first place? The fight against tyranny and oppression and greed and all that shit? United Earth thought it could bully everyone into line, but it hadn't counted on people like Danny fucking Proctor. *Watch your mouth!* His aunt's voice automatically echoed in his mind.

Or was it the freedom of piloting his own asteroid hauler at only twenty-one years old? If he'd entered IDF academy like his aunt had urged him to, he'd be rotting in classrooms for the next five years. Promotions there would only happen if he learned how to kiss his commander's ass with enough tongue. The Integrated Defense Force of UE had become a behemoth in the three decades since the decisive victory of the Second Swarm War, but bureaucracies were bureaucracies, and if bureaucracy was the noun then ass-kissing was its verb. On the other hand, if he'd signed on to the merchant marine, he'd be mopping gravity deckplates for the next ten years before they'd let him even breathe on any flight controls.

But *this*—this was freedom. This was *life*. His own ship—even if he didn't own it, he *flew* it, and that was just as good. He trailed his hand along the old corridor walls as he bounced his way down to the operations center. Ridley and Taggert would be asleep, or still having sex—it seemed like they never *stopped* having sex. A week of floating next to a giant rock in the middle of empty space was conducive to breaking down inhibitions, and his two crew-mates had succumbed to the flesh spectacularly. Either way, he wasn't about to wake them. This was *his* mission. *His* ship.

This was freedom.

Once across the threshold, he jumped up a few meters and sailed across the operations center, landing cleanly in the navigator's chair with the ease that came from months at lowgrav. He entered in the coordinates for their next stop, Sangre de Cristo, the fourth planet in the San Martin system. Just a colony, really. A million or so religious fanatics had tired of the oppressive hand of a distant UE and its tin-eared government on San Martin, and had set off on their own. Shovik-Orion Industries had been only too happy to provide the domes and contract out the rest of the building effort. And the GPC was far enough in bed with Shovik-Orion that he assumed plenty of wallets were embiggening with each shipment to the fledgling colony.

His own included, so no complaints.

The main drive activated with an ear-deafening roar—one irritating quirk of the ancient freighter—and the inertial cancelers struggled to keep up with the three g burn. He could q-jump in and save half a day, of course, but the client had specified no q-jumping. Harder to track that way—q-jump signatures could be seen half a system away with the most basic sensor packages.

Luckily, Sangre de Cristo wasn't *that* far from the asteroid belt. They'd be there in four hours, and with any luck, Ridley and Taggert would still be asleep, or having their morning coffee. Or their morning screw.

He dozed off after setting the nav computer to autopilot. The ship would swivel one hundred eighty halfway out to Sangre and automatically start the decel burn. And he'd need to be awake and alert for the actual delivery—planetary re-entry on an old rickety freighter like the *Magdalena Issachar* was like trying to screw a discount mutated whore on Rigel Three while half-drunk—it required a certain amount of concentration, but not so much concentration that you realized with horror what the hell you were doing.

It had only seemed like his eyes were closed for a few minutes. The alarm was persistent, and it took him several shakes of his head to realize that that particular flavor of alarm was a proximity detector.

Shit. Something was close. Close enough to trigger a proximity alarm. He scrambled to activate the external video feed and brought up the view on his screen.

They were nearly there. Sangre de Cristo glistened far below, its massive oceans reflecting the distant sun's weak blue light. Only internal mantle heating kept the water liquid. He could barely make out the massive kilometers-long cylindrical domes dotting the rusty-colored eastern island, each transparent city-wide window keeping the noxious carbon dioxide atmosphere at bay while letting in enough light to sustain photosynthesis in the genetically modified plants that could survive on such minuscule solar irradiance.

But what caught his eye was the ship less than a kilometer away, coming in fast. It was smaller than the *Magdalena Issachar*, but even at this distance he could see it was armed to the teeth. He didn't recognize any hull markings at this distance. It was obviously human—Dolmasi or Skiohra ships looked unmistakably alien—but their transponder was running silent—a flagrant violation of United Earth law. And Russian Confederation law. Hell, *every* human government required active transponders, even the GPC. Some in the UE might consider the Galactic People's Congress a terrorist organization. *But at least we keep our transponders running.*

"Unidentified ship, this is the *Magdalena Issachar* out of Britannia on a delivery mission to Sangre. Mornin' fellas. Please respond, over."

He tried to keep his voice level and conversational. He felt anything but. Other ships never flew right up to you close enough to wave through the window. Not unless you were intentionally docking with each other, or, Danny feared, being forcefully boarded.

"Unidentified ship, please respond."

Nothing. Whatever they were playing at, the other ship was getting uncomfortably close. He toyed with the idea of making a break for it. Would they fire on him? The closer they got, the tighter the knot in Danny's stomach pulled.

He flipped on the navigational controls and started adjusting the *Magdalena*'s course. The other ship matched his movements, and moments later, another alarm started flashing on his board.

They were targeting weapons.

"Come on, fellas, let's not get carried away here…."

The message was clear. Don't move, or you're dead. From the sleek lines of the other ship, the heavy armaments, and general lack of scuffing and micro-meteor impacts, it was clear this was no pirate ship trying to relieve him of his cargo.

Someone knew about that crate down in the cargo hold. And whatever was in it was worth shooting at his ship.

It was worth his life.

A docking tube began to extend out from the other ship's port, and on instinct Danny leapt out of his chair, soared across the operations center, and landed in the corridor at a bounding run. Running at one-tenth g meant a series of powerful, one-legged jumps, and by the time he reached the cargo bay he'd only touched the floor five times.

Inside the bay he ducked into the auxiliary airlock just as he heard the ominous metallic sounds of the two ships mating together at the main docking port. At a touch to the wall panel he closed the door most of the way shut, leaving just enough of a slit for him to see out into the space beyond, and part of the walkway that circled the upper part of the cargo bay.

And just in time. The docking port opened with a groan,

indicating something on the other side was forcing it. Through the slit he could see several figures in vacuum battle armor launch through the hatch, brandishing guns. Big guns. One motioned to another and pointed towards the giant crate in the center of the cargo bay. The indicated soldier let his gun hang at his shoulder while he pulled out a hand terminal and started working the controls as the other two stood guard around him.

"Hey, Danny, what the hell is going on? I thought I heard —"

Through the slit he watched as Matt Ridley, who'd apparently just woken up, padded barefoot onto the catwalk surrounding the bay, still rubbing his eyes. He wore only underwear, which didn't do much to conceal his raging morning wood. His mohawk had lost some of its usual stiffness and seemed to flop like a rooster's comb.

A loud crack echoed through the bay, and Danny had to bite down on his fist when he realized what had just happened. A hole blossomed in the middle of Ridley's forehead, and a fine pink mist had sprayed out behind him. He still looked confused as hell as he collapsed.

The one-tenth g seemed to take forever to pull the dead young man to the deck.

Danny's stomach rose up into his mouth, and he fought the watery feelings of nausea beginning to overtake him.

He had to get out.

He had to get out.

The locker nearby held a vacuum suit. All he had to do was put it on without drawing the attention of the soldiers, open the auxiliary airlock, and jump out. Easy. He could do this.

He had to get out.

And then what? Didn't matter. All that mattered now was getting away from those guns.

He had to get out.

The image of the pink mist spraying back from Ridley's head, of him jerking back as the bullet pierced his brain, forced itself back into his thoughts, and to avoid retching he set himself to work.

He pushed the door closed all the way, locked it, and frantically started pulling on the suit, finally clamping the helmet on less than a minute later. Luckily, the data connection to the ship was working, so he brought up the heads-up display, and navigated over to the video feed from the cargo bay. Two of the soldiers were pulling the front panel off the crate, and then one of them retrieved something from a bag hanging from his shoulder. Some sort of electronic device. He attached it to the contents of the crate with a magnetic lock.

Holy shit. The contents of the crate. There was only one thing in there, resting on the center of a pallet.

It looked remarkably like an atmospheric-reentry nuclear missile. Square tail fin and all.

A gentle sway in the ship's gravity field told him that the engines had cut out and the inertial cancelers compensated for the change in the acceleration vector. They'd arrived at Sangre.

And just in time. He worked the airlock controls with one hand while trying to get the comm open to Taggert. Silence. Either still asleep, or….

He shook the thought, and initiated the airlock sequence. The air cycled out of the chamber, and the outer hatch opened, and not looking back, he pulled himself out.

Sangre de Cristo's oceans glistened below, and he could just make out one of the vast cylindrical domes on one of the peninsulas. He clung tightly to the handholds lining the hull, and started climbing around the *Magdalena*, away from the view of the other ship.

A whisper crackled in his ear. "Matt? Where are you? Matt? Danny? I hear people out there. Matt? I—"

He was about to key in a response when the sound of a door opening came through the comm, followed by a sudden sharp intake of breath by Taggert and a whispered *oh god*. And a second later, a loud crack, identical to the one that had emptied Matt's head.

Danny tried to cover his mouth, pawing at his face shield, putting up a valiant effort to stem the flow of vomit. The rancid smell pierced his nose, and he swore as he realized the contents of his stomach now covered the face shield of the helmet, obscuring his view.

Below him, he felt the maneuvering thrusters of the ship burn. He hadn't programmed that. The intruders were moving the ship. The *Magdalena Issachar* slowly turned to point straight down to the planet below. He looked back. The other ship had retracted its docking tube and fired its own engines.

The *Magdalena* started accelerating. The pull of his own inertia nearly broke his grip on the handhold.

With a dull ache in his roiling stomach, he realized he had a choice to make. The soldiers, whoever they were, had clearly set the ship on a course that would take it down into the atmosphere, and crash on Sangre de Cristo. Bail now? Or try to re-enter the ship and override whatever course the soldiers had set?

And that missile—there was no question what they were trying to do. He made his choice, pulling himself back towards the auxiliary airlock. There was still time. He touched the exterior control panel. Not operational. He yanked on the manual override, which didn't budge.

He'd been locked out. Whatever tech the soldiers had, they'd been able to override the manual override's controls, which he thought was technically impossible.

That left the only alternative. He crouched down on the side of the ship, perpendicular to the horizon, and with a grunt he jumped as hard as he could. The ship fell away from him, and now that he was free of its acceleration, the *Magdalena Issachar* shot forward, speeding towards its doom. He wondered if he'd jumped clear in time to make orbit, or if he'd similarly fall to his death. Would the atmosphere burn him up first, or would he get to at least enjoy a few minutes of free-fall? Why was he thinking of enjoying a free-fall? He'd just watched one friend get his brains blown out, and heard it happen to the other friend.

He was fucked.

Danny! Language! His aunt's sharp voice cut into his thoughts. If he wasn't about to die, he'd have laughed at the absurdity of hearing her scolding in his head, even as he drifted through space in free-fall.

Time seemed to elongate, stretch out past all recognition of seconds or minutes, and he could have sworn that at one point he fell asleep, though he granted that he may have been hallucinating. Either way, the small engine exhaust plume that was the *Magdalena* burned faster and faster towards the surface, until it was just a tiny dot set against one of the habitation domes.

"Goodbye, Mags," he whispered.

And then the nuclear missile detonated.

Danny's eyes automatically closed, his hands covered his helmet, and even through the hands, his eyelids, the face shield, and the vomit, the intense glare of the piercing radioactive light made him cry out.

A minute later, a mushroom cloud. And a minute after that, he started to feel the faint roar in his suit that announced he, too, was entering the outer fringe of the atmosphere.

And strangely enough, rather than focus on his own impending death, all he could think about was the cargo, the mysterious customer, and the equally mysterious boarding party that had killed his friends, and killed his ship. Killed his future. As the roar intensified and his arms and legs began to feel the drag of the rarified air, another thought struck him as he watched the mushroom cloud billow up to the upper atmosphere.

Whoever they were, they were trying to start a war.

CHAPTER ONE

Oxford Novum University, Whitehaven, Britannia
Curie Building, Lecture hall 201

Professor Shelby Proctor paused her lecture mid-sentence to glance at the monitor on her lectern. A text box had popped up, flashing red. *Priority One—Integrated Defense Fleet CENTCOM.*

Priority one? Bullshit. IDF could wait. *I retired ten years ago—I'm not their lap-dog anymore.*

She clicked the message off with a wave of her hand and turned back to the chalkboard in the front of the packed auditorium. She was the only professor that she knew of at Oxford Novum University that used a chalkboard—the only professor on Britannia for that matter. But she was sixty-eight years old, a decorated former fleet admiral, a friggin' war hero, and, most importantly, an expert in xenobiology. She'd use whatever the hell she wanted.

"So you can see that the mere presence of the mitochondrial DNA structure within the Skiohra cell walls suggests not only a similar evolutionary pattern to species native to Earth, but also implies that primordial prokaryotic cell union into eukaryotic structures is not only one *possible* basis for advanced life, but perhaps the only basis. Especially given that similar structures are seen in Dolmasi cells, and every other fossilized remains of now-dead civilizations that we've happened upon in the power vacuum left behind by the Swarm—"

"Is it true that you fought the last Swarm carrier twelve years ago, Professor Proctor? Destroyed it? The only living Swarm matter left in the galaxy?" An interruption. *Damn kids.*

She turned around from the chalkboard to face the rows and rows of university students. They were getting younger by the year, it seemed. And if she wasn't mistaken, stupider. Or was that just the cranky old fleet admiral talking? Stupider? She could almost hear her proper English-major mother berate her.

"That is not only incredibly off-topic, young man, but also highly classified. I could tell you, but then I'd have to kill you where you sit." Her eyes drilled into him like anti-matter beams, and she could tell the student wasn't sure if she was joking or not. "And don't assume that I'm kidding."

The kid blushed. Good. Proctor struggled to keep a smirk off her own face.

"Oh. Uh, I mean, everyone talks about it, so I assumed … I mean, I thought that since you were *there*, fighting the Swarm over Earth and Britannia and stuff, I mean, I thought you could tell us a little…."

He trailed off as her eyes drilled into him again, and he

started squirming. "You know what happens when you assume? You make an ass out of you, and … only you—I'm a horrible speller." Some of the class laughed. For the rest of them, she added, "normally, assuming makes an ass out of *you and me*. But today the monicker belongs exclusively to the young man in the back row." The rest of the class laughed.

He flustered even more. "But … uh, I mean, I was just thinking that the genocide of the Swarm might, you know, be helpful to talk about and…."

"Just because you're able to open your mouth and dribble verbal diahrrea, forming barely-intelligible phrases which I assume are English, spilling sensitive, classified information out for all our enemies to hear and take advantage of, does not make it *unclassified*. This may not be a military college, young man, but that does not mean that we won't strictly observe security protocols while I am your teacher."

The kid was clearly embarrassed—his face turned red and he started playing with the dozens of piercings hanging off his ear. He was just like all the other kids in this generation. Oblivious to the sacrifices made by the ones before him. *Her* sacrifices. Blithely throwing around words like *genocide* that he hardly understood the meaning of. Proctor grimaced as she saw him begin to open his mouth again.

"Damn, prof, it was just a question. No need to get snippy or—"

Snippy?

Proctor dropped the chalk, and it clattered into several pieces when it broke on the floor. "Listen, young man, I realize your hearing must be completely shot, what with all the nano-dildos sticking through your earlobes, so I'll repeat it once more for you. We don't talk military shit in this classroom. We talk science. Got it?"

The auditorium was as quiet as space itself. The student started packing up his things. "Professor, this is a micro-aggression. Your words are incredibly hurtful and I'm going to file a report with the Committee for Respect and Inclusion and get you reprimanded for speaking hurtfully to a student who only asked—"

"Oh *please*," she began, picking up the pieces of chalk. "We both know what you were implying. That I'm some kind of genocidal maniac for finally destroying the last remnant of the race that terrorized our civilization for decades. Let me tell you, young man, you have no idea what it was like out there." No idea. None of them. How could they? How could anyone? But now that the stopper was released, there was no holding back. "No idea. Never knowing when death would find you, wondering if your next engagement with the Swarm would be your last. So unless you want to see what a macro-aggression looks like, I suggest you high-tail it out of my classroom and get your ass into Dick Knitting 101."

The look on the kid's face was priceless, and well worth the official reprimands she knew would trickle down from the administration. Same as the last time she'd lost her cool and went to town on the previous unsuspecting clueless student. So far there hadn't been any investigations or committee hearings, just the university president taking her aside at the last senatorial reception and giving her a stern, but deferential talking-to. She was the former fleet admiral of IDF, *after all*. She fought alongside the frickin' *Hero of Earth* himself, Captain Timothy Granger.

He got up and left in a huff, and the faces of the remaining students seemed to be evenly split between looks of worshipful adoration and distasteful sanctimony. But she was too old to care what people thought about her. All that mattered now was the science, the teaching, and kicking back with a glass of the finest cabernet at night.

"Now, where were we…. Yes, mitochondrial DNA. One interesting facet of the most recent knowledge exchange with the Skiohra generational ship *Magnanimity* is that their cell structure is—"

The door to her right creaked open, revealing two burly military MPs in IDF fatigues escorting some top IDF brass, followed by a face out of her past. He strode in purposefully, as if he owned the place. The overhead lights gleamed off the white fleet admiral bars on his shoulders.

The old man nodded once, and, glancing at the rows of students, said, "Admiral Proctor, I'm sorry to intrude, but I'm afraid it's urgent."

The jackass. She could see his subtle grin at the students as rustling whispers spread through the auditorium like wildfire. Everyone recognized the head of IDF—Integrated Defense Force, United Earth's interstellar military organization. He always loved performing in front of a captive audience, occupying the center of attention, and being fawned over by adoring civilians.

"Class dismissed," said Proctor, waving them all off. When the last student had gathered her things and closed the door, Proctor turned back to the man. "Fleet Admiral Oppenheimer. To what do I owe … the *pleasure*?"

"Shelby," he began. "It's good to see you." An extended

hand.

She ignored it.

"I wish I could say the same, Christian." She wanted to say worse, but even so his face cringed slightly. He'd replaced her as fleet admiral of IDF ten years ago, and the parting had not been amicable. They hadn't clashed when they first met, years ago, during the emergency of the Second Swarm War. The derelict *Constitution* had been sacrificed to hold off the Swarm during one of the last violent skirmishes, and the *Warrior* was destroyed by overwhelming Swarm anti-matter beams. Granger and Proctor had mustered their surviving crew aboard the *Victory*, where Oppenheimer was serving as XO. He'd been level-headed and down-to-earth then, not the political showman he was today. There were three things that could fundamentally change a person: time, alcohol, and managing a bureaucracy. And Oppenheimer suffered from at least two of the three.

"We have a situation," he said, withdrawing his hand and beginning to pace across the front of the auditorium. The two MPs accompanying him stepped out the door, as if by previous arrangement with him. "Something is happening in the Irigoyen sector, and in the Dolmasi sectors near it—the Dolmasi would never admit it to us, but our intel is unmistakable—something has them reeling."

Her heart skipped a beat.

"Swarm?"

"No."

She relaxed a hair, though she considered what her reaction meant. She was responsible for their complete and utter annihilation, years ago, and even though she'd taken umbrage at the sniping from the micro-aggressed student suggesting that she was responsible for genocide ... well, it was half true. She felt it, the ... guilt? Was she a monster? No. She was following orders. Saving Earth. Saving civilization. And she slept well at night. But half true all the same.

Oppenheimer continued, "Not that we can tell, anyway, which is very little. But the attack signatures are definitely not Swarm. It's something else." He stopped pacing and faced her. "Something new. Something ... *big*."

She shrugged. "Not my problem anymore, Christian. Give an old woman her retirement. Why don't you send the *Chesapeake* out there? Captain Diaz is more than capable. He served with me on the *Constitution*, the *Warrior*, the *Victory*, and even the *Chesapeake* itself. It's the friggin' flagship. If anyone can handle the situation, it's him."

Oppenheimer nodded, stroking his chin. "We did, last night." A pause. He leaned against the chalkboard, and seemed almost reluctant to continue. Dammit—she knew what he was about to say before he even started. "We just received word this morning that Captain Diaz is dead. The *Chesapeake* is destroyed."

CHAPTER TWO

Oxford Novum University, Whitehaven, Britannia
Curie Building, Lecture hall 201

"Destroyed? How?" Proctor groped for her chair, and collapsed into it. Diaz was an old friend. Served as her XO for years aboard the *Chesapeake* before she'd left starship command to become the fleet admiral and lead all of IDF.

Worst decision of her life.

"We lost meta-space contact with the *Chesapeake* early this morning after they reported engaging a ship of unknown design and origin out in the Irigoyen sector. A scout ship was sent to pick up their trail, and all it found was debris and signs of an intense battle. No sign of the unknown ship."

Proctor couldn't believe it. Captain Diaz was the best officer in the fleet, as far as she was concerned. And the *Chesapeake* was IDF's flagship. There were other ships that were more powerful, others that were larger, and every single ship in the fleet was more modern by far. But *Chesapeake* was the last of the Legacy Fleet—the handful of ships whose thick tungsten armor and ability to sustain massive amounts of damage helped save Earth not once, but twice, from Swarm incursions.

And now it was gone. The last of the Legacy Fleet. Gone forever. An era had officially passed.

"Did they send back any visuals?"

"Negative. There was just no time between when they engaged it and when they were destroyed. We literally know nothing about this threat, other than the fact that it handily destroyed our flagship in less than five minutes."

"What about the terrorist action on Sangre de Cristo? Is this related? Same sector."

Oppenheimer shook his head. "Not that we can tell. We still have no idea who did it. The GPC claims it was us. Our intel points to a radical faction of the Russian Confederation. The RC claims it was Grangerite fanatics. The Grangerite Patriarch announced on the news this morning that he suspects the CIDR, which the Chinese, of course, vehemently deny. CIDR think it's us, too. Just a massive, fucking headache—"

"Watch your language," she replied automatically. But she was lost in thought, trying to make connections between the two incidents.

The admiral ignored her. "Whoever dropped that bomb will pay. Ever since last week we've been escorting the relief ships in the humanitarian convoys heading out to Sangre. Completely destroyed one of the habitation domes. About fifty thousand dead, and the rest of the domes are in a state of pandemonium—they all think they're next. Riots. Food shortages. The works. And with all the political bullshit going on—everyone pointing fingers at each other, half of them aimed at us—we get *this*. An unknown ship. Completely foreign design—not human, not Dolmasi, not Skiohra. And not responding to any of our hails. And now, the *Chesapeake*...." He trailed off.

Professor Proctor stood up and grabbed hold of the lectern, using it to steady herself. The news came as a shock. And she suspected why Admiral Oppenheimer had come. Given her lifelong expertise with not only the Swarm, but all things alien, be it Dolmasi, Skiohra, Quiassi, Findiri, or the handful of long-dead civilizations destroyed by the Swarm in their ten-thousand year scourge across the galaxy, he was most likely going to ask for help understanding the new threat. To study up and as the old adage said, science the shit out of it.

"Fine. Send me everything you've got. I'll make my recommendations to the Joint Chiefs once I've had a chance to go over the material. And I'll even set up a rapid-response science team if you manage to bring back any samples or recordings of the new threat. I imagine that—"

"Shelby, I'm not here asking for your help in a lab. We don't have time for science."

She turned to face him. "Then what the hell are you here for, Christian?"

"I'm here because I need you back. I need you to take a ship, and go figure this out before it destroys us all."

She laughed out loud.

"Christian, you can't be serious. I'm almost seventy years old. I teach xenobiology 101, and I just bought a condo down on the beach. Only twenty kilometers away. Do you know how long I waited for one of those properties to free up? Do you realize what the real estate market is like on Britannia? Beach properties have a ten year waiting list, at least. It's insane, Christian, they tried to charge me over—"

"Shelby," he wasn't buying her change of subject. "We need you."

"*I* need me. My baby brother and his wife and kids need me. My students need me."

"United Earth needs you."

No. She was done. She'd played the puppet, she'd acted the part. She'd let her military career be run and manipulated by aspiring and conspiratorial admirals, generals, and worse, unscrupulous and greedy politicians, always responding to the next politically manufactured crisis rather than addressing the real threat.

That real threat: the galaxy was an unthinkably large place, and humanity surely hadn't discovered all its perils. There were other Swarms. Other civilizational threats. And what had United Earth's administration and the Joint Chiefs had her do during her tenure as captain and later as fleet admiral?

Maneuvering the fleets for maximum political posturing. Against the Russian Confederation, against the Caliphate, against the Chinese Intersolar Democratic Republic. Against whatever internal enemy-du-jour the United Earth politicians wanted to impress or intimidate with a few starships.

"United Earth? Pfft. The Administration can go to hell."

Admiral Oppenheimer grunted and bent over to pick up a stray piece of chalk that had escaped her notice. "The government? I'm not talking about the government, Shelby. President Quimby can go finger his own asshole for all I care.

I'm talking about our civilization. The hundreds of billions of children, women, and men that call our worlds home. *That* United Earth needs you."

She sat down, flicking off her lesson plan, and stared at the blank monitor screen.

She'd heard it all before. It was the same speech every administration figure and every senator had thrown at her when she was fleet admiral.

And the answer was still the same. "No," she said, and stood back up, picked up her briefcase—she hated calling it a purse—and opened the door. "Find another hero, Christian. This one's ship has sailed."

"There's one more thing, Shelby."

She paused at the threshold. "Yes?"

"I understand your nephew, your brother's son, is living on San Martin."

"Yes?" she repeated.

"San Martin is in the Irigoyen sector, Shelby. And Sangre de Cristo is in the San Martin system. And just two hours ago I received … reports."

Her stomach clenched. Danny was her brother's oldest, and had just started college on San Martin the year before. "What kind of reports?"

"IDF intel has been trying to put the pieces together on this terrorist … *incident*."

Fifty thousand people incinerated, and he calls it an incident.

He continued. "I can't go into all the details because your security clearance has lapsed, but … there's been social unrest recently on San Martin. Stuff that hasn't made it onto the news. GPC related."

"Yeah, I knew that. Everyone knows that."

He shrugged. "But what you might not know is that IDF intel has been tracking Danny for about a year now—"

"Tracking *Danny*? Why?"

"—and three weeks ago, he disappeared. Gone. And ... we have reason to suspect he might be involved in the Sangre incident."

She turned, and shut the door again. "Impossible. Danny's a good kid. He'd never, *ever*, get involved in anything like this. Period."

Oppenheimer shrugged. "I'm only passing along what I've heard. Just consider it: the *Chesapeake* is destroyed by an unknown enemy, Captain Diaz is dead, and just twenty lightyears away in the same sector, a colony gets hit by a nuclear terrorist attack, and in the same system you have widespread social and political unrest. The events are not obviously related, but ... well, I'll let you connect your own dots. It's your family, after all."

Yes. Danny was family. And so was Diaz. Before he'd been captain, he was her XO. *Dammit, Oppenheimer knew exactly how to ensnare her.*

"Fine. Just this once. Just this mission. After it's done and we've sorted it out, I'm gone for good."

Oppenheimer flashed a half-smile. "I knew you'd come around. Good." He pulled a small datapad out of his pocket and tapped on it. Moments later, the door opened and the officers who'd accompanied him reappeared. "We've got you a ship, and the crew is mostly in place—I'll give you the luxury of choosing your own senior staff. Your pick of anyone in IDF, of course."

"What old clunker of a ship did you requisition away from some hapless captain somewhere?"

Oppenheimer's half-smile bloomed into a full grin. "Old? Hardly. This time, Shelby, I think even you'll be impressed. If you'll follow Commander Yarbrough here, he'll familiarize you with the *Independence*."

The ship name stirred a vague memory of some classified conversations long ago. "Why does that sound familiar?"

"Because IDF engineering conceived the project under your tenure. It was, and is, *highly* classified."

"Why?"

Oppenheimer walked out the door, calling behind as he left. "You're about to find out."

CHAPTER THREE

Oxford Novum University, Whitehaven, Britannia
Curie Building, Lecture hall 201

"If you'll follow me, ma'am," said Commander Yarbrough, holding an arm out towards the door. Proctor eyed him with unease before picking her briefcase back up and retreating out of the classroom. Yarbrough followed close behind—he was young, and already struck her as hopelessly overeager. "I think you'll be very pleased with what we've been doing in ship design the past few years, ma'am," he said with a bounce in his step that she found almost nauseating.

"I'm sure."

She followed him to the shuttle parked on the landing pad and slid into the copilot seat next to him. "We headed to Scotland Yard?" she asked, referring tongue-in-cheek to the dry-dock shipyards on the outskirts of town. The citizens of Whitehaven—Britannia's capital city—were known for their quirky sense of humor.

"No, ma'am. This ship has far too high a classification for that. We couldn't have everyone in Whitehaven look out the window and see our Little Bird hovering in the distance."

"Little bird?"

"That's our nickname for the *ISS Independence*. The lead designer thought it fitting. You'll meet her soon—she'll be the chief engineer on the mission."

"I thought I got to choose my senior staff?" said Proctor. "Are we already pulling the bait-and-switch? Shit...."

Commander Yarbrough shook his head as he maneuvered the shuttle out to IDF's Whitehaven base near Scotland Yard shipyards on the outskirts of the city. "No, ma'am. You're of course free to replace her at your whim, though I would think with her expertise in the design of the ship you might want to keep her on. The new tech we've built into her is ... well, *impressive* is not a terribly impressive word, but it's all I've got."

They landed, debarked, and climbed aboard an orbital transfer shuttle that would take them up through the atmosphere and out to Wellington Shipyards in orbit around the gas giant Calais, past the asteroid belt, just one q-jump away. As she passed through the hatch, she nearly jumped when a booming voice greeted her.

"Shelby! Damn good to see you."

Sitting in the pilot's seat was a middle-aged man who seemed like he was stuffed into the uniform of a recently graduated cadet. In spite of the tight-fitting flight suit, his face sported a fashionable, well-groomed goatee, and of course a broad, friendly smile.

She smiled back. "Good to see you too, Ballsy," she said,

using his old callsign from when they'd served together on the *Constitution* and the *Warrior*. Captain Tyler "*Ballsy*" Volz—though what he was doing here and not on his own ship escaped her for a split second before she remembered his ship had been decommissioned the year before. "Did Oppenheimer suck you into this too?"

"Suck? Hell, I asked for it. Rumor was going around last night that he was calling you back into service, and I wasn't going to let some snot-nosed kid be your CAG."

Proctor gaped at him. He was pushing sixty himself, and should have had a cushy desk job as a rear admiral somewhere with a beach. "You're *volunteering* to be my Commander of the Air Group?"

"Do European politicians smell like cheap prostitutes?" He turned in his seat to smirk at Commander Yarbrough, whose face had wrinkled up at the improper reference. "That's a yes, son. They do."

"But you've got the rank of captain, Ballsy—"

"Which made it a whole lot easier to pull the strings necessary to get here. Hold on," he added as he pushed the accelerator to maximum. The buildings flew past in a blur.

"Captain Volz, please keep the flight parameters within normal range," said Commander Yarbrough, gripping his armrests.

"Kindly unclench your sphincter, Commander. I've been flying one of these things since before you were born." He angled the nose skyward and the shuttle leapt through the clouds.

Proctor smiled—Tyler Volz was one of the senior staff she would have chosen anyway, if she'd known he'd say yes. As deeply uneasy as she felt about this mission, having him along took the edge off her apprehension.

"So tell me, Commander Yarbrough, what kind of new tech does this baby have?" she said.

Yarbrough nervously tightened his seat restraint as the craft blazed up towards the atmosphere. "Oh, various new offensive and defensive capabilities, as well as a new experimental propulsion system. We call it trans-quantum-jump technology. Basically lets us do an unusually long standard q-jump. About fifty times as far."

Proctor puffed out a surprised breath. "Five lightyears per jump? Holy shit…."

Yarbrough nodded solemnly. "Indeed. I've been doing preliminary tests with the skeleton crew we have aboard—our navigator calls them tranny-jumps, though I've asked her repeatedly to stop," he added with a pained expression. Apparently the schoolyard humor was wasted on him, though Proctor smiled on the inside at the term. *Tranny-jump*. Best not to say that one in front of Oppenheimer.

"Tranny-jumps?" Ballsy smirked. "I'll have to remember that one."

Yarbrough fiddled with the co-pilot controls in an attempt to compensate for Captain Volz's gut-churning maneuvers through the atmosphere—the old fighter pilot simply couldn't help himself as he spiraled them up to space. "I've devoted quite a bit of thought to this, actually. At first I thought we could stick with q-jumps, for continuity's sake, but then I leaned towards t-jumps for disambiguation. But once I realized that t-jumps could be confused with transmission dumps from the comm station—t-dumps—I came up with q-t-jumps—"

"Cutie jumps?" Volz made a face.

Yarbrough shrugged. "But then I decided a more formal approach might be needed so I came up with a list of possibilities that might—"

Proctor rolled her eyes—this Commander certainly dotted his 'I's. "We'll just stick with t-jumps, Commander." She watched out the viewport in front of them as the atmosphere blazed past. Yarbrough had engaged the inertial cancelers. She was pleasantly surprised—inertial canceler technology must have also improved since she resigned from IDF, as the turbulence during their ascent was hardly noticeable. "How big is this beauty, anyway?"

Ballsy smirked again. "That's what she said."

"You never grew up, did you?" Proctor feigned a frown, but truth be told, she missed the banter, the crude jokes, and the joy of serving with fellow irreverent officers, in spite of having her strings constantly pulled—yanked, usually—by top brass and politicians. Academia never filled that void for her. How could it?

"Now why the hell would I want to do that?"

Commander Yarbrough pulled out a small datapad, unfolded it, and started reading. "Five hundred and one meters long, powered by a fifty terawatt direct-injection dual fusion-antimatter plant. Central computer is infinitely-cored and non-localized, distributed throughout the walls and decks of the ship, standard propulsion is rated at over ten g's with quad-stabilized and phase-shifted graviton-emitting inertial cancelers. The tranny drive's cap banks recharge in under a minute, enabling a maximum long-range cruising rate of over three hundred light years an hour. And over fifty—"

Proctor held up a hand. "Three *hundred* lightyears per hour? That gets us to the edge of known space in less than two hours!"

"Yes, ma'am. Like I said, it's highly classified. IDF has been sitting on this tech for three years now, and is eager that it not become common knowledge quite yet."

Proctor did the math, and figured they could get the *Independence* to the Irigoyen sector in less than ten minutes. *Hell, this thing is on as soon as I gather my crew.*

As if on cue, Volz announced, "Hold on tight, boys and girls. We're about to make the q-jump to Calais." A few seconds later he pressed the initiator button, and the view out the windows suddenly changed from the blue-tinged atmosphere of Britannia to the red-and-orange-dappled clouds of Calais, one of the Britannia system's two gas giants. A few dozen kilometers away floated Wellington Shipyards, where dozens of ships in various stages of assembly or maintenance were connected to giant, sweeping construction nacelles. It had been mostly destroyed during the Second Swarm War, but in a fit of post-war construction, IDF had rebuilt her even larger than the first, keeping with humanity's defiantly stubborn tradition of *you knock down my toy, I build an even bigger toy.*

Tucked underneath one of the nacelles, like a little bird nestled under its mother's wing, was a ship unlike any Proctor had seen. While the old Legacy Fleet ships she'd served on during the last half of her military career were old, bulky, and built for punishing combat, this one seemed like a work of art.

"There she is, Admiral," said Yarbrough. "Ready to leave space dock at your command."

Volz whistled. "She's a beauty all right. Nothing like the

clunkers we're use to. Then again, those old clunkers saved our lives more times than I can count. You sure this thing is up to it? Any tricks up her sleeve?"

And after over an hour of constant frowns, furrowed brows, and worried consternation, Yarbrough finally smiled. "You'll see."

CHAPTER FOUR

Irigoyen Sector, Bolivar System, Bolivar
Watchdog Station, High orbit

Lieutenant Ethan Zivic knew, beyond a doubt, that his posting aboard the defensive platform *Watchdog* over the far-flung colony world of Bolivar was a punishment. Retaliation for insubordination. Well, "insubordination" in the eyes of his former dickweed of a commander. In essence all he'd done was tell the truth.

That uniform does *make you look fat, ma'am.* That was all he'd said. Was there anything wrong with that? She'd asked him for his unvarnished, truthful opinion, and he'd given it.

Sure, it could have been the time he'd shown up drunk for duty, but it seemed like half the officers on the *Farragut* did that anyway. The XO was a fat bastard fluff-coke-addict herself, so she tended to look the other way with the sorts of violations that would make her a hypocrite if she called her crew on them. But insulting her appearance? Even when she looked like a massive over-grown stoned toad?

Heresy.

He pressed a few buttons, on mental autopilot, running through the regular hourly sensor scans that would ostensibly warn him of any unexpected ships in the vicinity Bolivar. Due to the recent emergency on Sangre de Cristo, and the even more recent disappearance of the *Chesapeake* about ten lightyears away, he even paid some attention to the scans. Usually he played solitaire or jack's doozies while the scans came in, confirming the negative reading by the soft beep that always accompanied the lack of any intruders.

Intruders? Heh. It had been years, *decades*, since there'd been any intruders. The Swarm was dead. The Russian Confederation had withdrawn into a state of inward-looking hermitage, the Caliphate had elected a Mullah that, for once, was preaching not only peaceful co-existence, but cooperation with United Earth, and the Chinese Intersolar Democratic Republic, as usual, only wanted to profit from the West. But profit peacefully. War was bad for business. Unless that business was armaments and ships, in which case the CIDR profited almost as handsomely as when there was peace.

He looked out the window.

And fell out of his chair.

He never usually fell out of his chair—at least not while sober. But even so he found himself on the floor—he'd tried to leap to his feet so fast that his knees had collided with the cramped console in front of him and sent him sprawling down again, painfully.

"Emergency action," he called upward towards the auto-comm. "Defensive ops on full alert! Intruder approaching!"

Why hadn't he heard anything? If the scan came back clean, there would have been the usual beep. If the scan came back with a contact, there would have been a raucous klaxon, just like in drills. He'd have to have a stern talking-to with the boys down in maintenance.

To his eyes, the ship was nothing much to look at. Bulky, but with no discernible surface features indicating weaponry. Covered with small pod-like protrusions. But an intruder was an intruder. He'd received no notice from IDF to expect any unknowns ships or foreign vessels, so that made this a red-alert event.

Except all he wanted to do was drink. A lot. He reached down to his knee, fumbling with the top of his boot, loosening the strap and reaching inside for the small flask just below his knee. He usually never started drinking until just before getting off duty, but today was *special*. Why it was special, he couldn't fathom. It just *felt* special, dammit. And everyone knows you drink on *special* days.

The little ship erupted with a red beam which pierced the defensive platform. *Well that's a problem*, he thought, and seriously considered getting on the comm to alert the mag-rail crews. Instead, he tipped the flask back and downed the whole thing. *Damn, I need more of this shit.*

The door to his little command center burst open, and Commander Dipshit strode through. At least, that was what Zivic called him in his mind. His mustache bounced up and down when he talked, and his comb-over tended to stick upright when he was agitated, and now was one of those comb-over erection moments. He supposed the ship firing at them was the cause, but was it really something to let one's comb-over stick up like that? Honestly, he looked like he should be driving an old-style darkened-window hovervan past a school, slowly, waving candy out the window.

"What the hell is going on, Zivic? Why weren't we warned?"

Blow it out your hole.

He stifled the rude response, allowing a slightly less rude retort to come out in its place. "Seriously, sir, do I have to do everything around here?"

Part of him couldn't believe his ears. Was he *really* saying that? What the hell was he doing? The other part of him laughed like a twelve-year-old boy, and wanted to add a boob joke just for good measure. Honestly, the commander's man-boobs jiggled with every step. It was hysterically funny, especially when combined with the comb-over erection and the flop sweat.

The commander stopped in his tracks. He looked conflicted, alternating between a face that wanted to clock his subordinate, and a face that was absolutely, utterly bewildered.

Thankfully, the bewilderment won out. "Something's off, Zivic. Can you feel it?"

"Feel it? Are you asking me to fondle your balls again? Because that look on your face tells me—"

"Shut the hell up, Lieutenant. And listen."

Zivic forced himself to bottle up the next adolescent comment, and calm his breathing to the point that he could hear.

Shouting. Screaming. Laughing. Somewhere down the hall someone was having an *amazing* party. Or a bloody-fisted death match. Whatever it was, it was *loud*.

The commander swore. "Can't you feel that?" The man's hands shook, and his eyes grew wide. He flexed his fingers into white-knuckled fists. Under his breath, barely audible to Zivic, he muttered a foreign-sounding word, and crossed himself. "Golgothica."

Huh? And what the hell was the guy doing crossing himself? Had he always been religious? The laughs and screams down the hall sounded out even louder. "And why they're partying while we're being fired at is beyond me, Pat. Patsy. Can I call you Patsy?"

A fist sucker-punched Zivic across the face, and his mouth filled with blood. *Shit, am I going to take this? Time to muster up, Ethan. As soon as I find that next drink....*

Commander Flopsweat, rather than swing a second punch, leaned over the console, pressing the all-station comm button. "All hands, this is Commander Smith. Fight it, people. You know what I mean. You feel it. The voices telling you to do ... things, things that you know you shouldn't. Fight it. That's an order. Do your duty. Or ... or I'll come and beat the shit out of each of you. Smith out."

The voices? What the hell was the man talking about? Dammit, things always made more sense when he'd gotten a few bottles down. *Now where did I put that second one?* He fumbled at his other boot. But another voice in his head, a more reasonable-sounding, boring voice, said there was truth in his commanding officer's warning. He was *not* feeling normal. In fact, he was pulled in two directions. Half of him wanted to spring into action, be the hero, pulverize the alien ship, save the day. The other half wanted to knee his commander in the balls, take another swig from his flask, and go join the party down the hall.

"Commander Zivic, if you don't start issuing orders to return fire, I'll send you to the brig," said Commander Combover-erection. His jaw trembled, as if he were only just barely containing his rage. Zivic toyed with the idea of cajoling the man further, payback for the sucker punch. But a moment later he realized how irrational that was. After all, they *were* being fired upon by an alien ship.

Holy shit, an *alien ship*.

Commander Pot-belly continued. His trembling subsided —it appeared he'd gotten control of himself. Perfect opportunity to throw another ball joke his way. "And issue a distress call. Tell IDF CENTCOM we're under attack."

Out the window, the little ship continued firing, advancing on the *Watchdog* until it was just a few kilometers away.

Then it unleashed hell, and Zivic, in spite of the oncoming storm, continued fumbling with the clasp at the top of the other boot. *There it is*, he thought, finding the second flask.

He'd need it to cope with what he could see coming towards the station.

CHAPTER FIVE

Wellington shipyards, Calais, Britannia System
Conference room, ISS Independence

Four hours after she'd boarded the *Independence*, Admiral Proctor stood at the head of the conference table. For her, it was one o'clock in the morning, but on ship's time it was only the second hour of the second shift, so she'd need to stay up for several more hours at least—and she felt it. She hadn't had to pull an all-nighter since she was a captain. *Damn, I'm getting old.*

"Thank you all for coming. For some of you this was a long trip. Believe me, I was hoping to enjoy my retirement and my classroom in peace until I became so old and accumulated so many cats that they'd have me committed."

Uneasy chuckling around the table. They all knew why they were here, and most of them, having fought through the Second Swarm War thirty years ago, knew all too well what could be coming.

"First, some brief introductions." She held up a hand to the gray-haired man next to her. "Captain Prucha will be my XO for this mission—"

"Admiral," began Commander Yarbrough, "far be it from me to take issue with your personnel assignments, but wouldn't it be more prudent to have someone who was intimately familiar with this new ship and the crew as our XO?"

Proctor looked daggers at him. "Yes, Commander, you're right about one thing. *Far* be it from you to take issue with my personnel assignments."

Some of her old hands around the table chuckled. The chief engineer clucked her tongue several times. Yarbrough, however, continued undeterred. At least he was persistent— she could give him that. "But Admiral, IDF regulations clearly state that the choice of XO is to be guided primarily by—"

She turned to him, letting a sharp note tinge her voice. "The regulations *clearly* state, Commander, that the prerogative lies with the commanding officer as to who she wants in which position, end of story."

Yarbrough's mouth abruptly shut, and he shrugged his reluctant agreement. "However," she continued, "I want you as the assistant XO, since, as you rightly point out, you've been with the crew since they were assigned and know the ship inside and out."

That seemed to placate him. *Good—the last thing I need is an uppity Commander questioning my every move.*

"Captain Prucha has graciously agreed to return early from his sabbatical. I believe you have a ship of your own waiting for you, don't you, Jeremy?"

He flashed one of his easy smiles she always remembered him for. "The *Forester*, yes. New heavy cruiser they just finished out at Omaha Shipyards on Earth. But how could I turn down one last mission with the legend herself?"

She smirked uneasily. "Flattery will get you everywhere, Captain. Or it may just get you air-locked. Depends on my mood." She turned to the other end of the table. "I believe you all know the Chief Engineer, who apparently designed the ship from scratch." She indicated the mousy, purple-haired woman seated at the other end, who flapped a wrinkled hand up in greeting to everyone. "Commander Rayna Scott. Rayna, how the hell is it that you're not a captain yet? You're as old as I am."

"'Cause I don't wanna," came the gruff reply.

Proctor shrugged. "Fair enough."

The Chief Engineer glanced at the rest of the senior staff. "And call me Commander Rayna. Or Granny Rayna. Or just Rayna, unless you don't mind an occasional blunt hydro-wrench to your face."

Commander Yarbrough raised a tentative hand. "But regulation clearly states that—"

"You can shove your regulations up your skinny ass, Yarbrough." Rayna cackled. "I've been around the bend enough times to be called whatever the hell I want. So unless you want me calling you Commander Rectum for the rest of the mission I suggest you stop quoting regulations at me."

Captain Volz, who'd been sitting silently next to Commander Scott the entire time, put an arm around her. "I think I like her, Admiral. Can I keep her?"

Everyone chuckled—Volz and Rayna had been close since

their days on the *Chesapeake*, over twenty years prior.

"You all know Captain Volz, or Ballsy, as his friends call him. He'll be CAG. Though I'm hoping this mission will not involve any fighter battles."

Volz shrugged and his goatee wrinkled. "No fighter battles? We gotta have *some* fun Admiral. All work and no play makes Ballsy a dull boy."

Captain Prucha stuck his thumb over at Volz. "Something tells me that Ballsy will find a way to make this interesting whether we want him to or not. Let's not forget the little incident during the battle of Mao Prime—"

"Hey, I swear those holes in the *ISS Lincoln* were already there…."

Rayna snickered. "Oh, are we calling that an *incident*, now? That's not what they called it at your court martial. I believe old General Norton—god rest his cantankerous soul—called it ass-hattery of the highest caliber—"

"People, please," said Admiral Proctor, holding up her hands. The underlying tension they all felt from the emergency returned. "As much as I'd enjoy catching up on old times, we've got a serious situation here." She finished out the introductions: Lieutenant Jerusha Whitehorse as the tactical crew chief, Ensign Annie Riisa as helm crew leader, polyglot Lieutenant Qwerty at the comm—he tipped an imaginary hat—and science chief Commander Mumford, who'd have looked like a heavyweight boxer were it not for the old-fashioned black plastic-rimmed glasses on his nose.

Ballsy interrupted her. "Didn't you used to be a boxer, Commander Mumford?"

"I did."

Proctor raised her eyebrows—she hadn't expected her guess to have been right. "Really? What brought you to the dark side? Science doesn't pay nearly as well as professional sports."

"I like beating the shit out of things," he said, nodding, as if that explained everything. He pushed his glasses back up after they slipped a bit.

They all stared at him.

"Nothing beats science." He shrugged, still clearly thinking that explained everything.

"Indeed," she said, letting the subject rest. "You all know why we're here. We've got a situation in the Irigoyen sector, and it doesn't look pretty. As we speak, Fleet Admiral Oppenheimer is on Britannia preparing the main IDF defense fleet for major combat operations, but we're being sent in as soon as possible to gather intel, scout out the enemy, and hopefully stop it before it can do any more damage."

Captain Prucha stirred. "What kind of damage are we looking at here?"

"The entire world of Irigoyen Prime has gone dark. All communications are out. No ships out of the system since yesterday morning. We've also got spotty intel from the Dolmasi—turns out they've lost a few colonies, and if reports can be believed, Verdra-Dol has gone dark as well."

"Verdra-Dol? Isn't that the closest thing to a homeworld that they've got?" said Captain Prucha.

"It is their second most populous world, yes," replied Proctor. "And the latest intel report from Oppenheimer came in just a few minutes ago. Bolivar, the second largest world in the Irigoyen sector, reported sighting an unknown vessel entering the system just a few hours ago. Since then, nothing. Not a single meta-space signal has gotten through."

Silence around the conference table as they all considered the gravity of the situation. "Not a single message? From the entire world? The orbital defense platform?" said Captain Volz.

Captain Prucha whistled. "That must be some ship. Reminds me of the Swarm when they first attacked thirty years ago. Remember the first incursions? All the systems went dark —they were able to disrupt all communications with their Russian-borrowed singularity tech. Are we certain this threat is not the Swarm?"

Proctor shook her head. She almost *wished* it was the Swarm—at least that was an enemy she knew how to deal with, as deadly as they were. But she'd led the mission that had destroyed the last known Swarm carrier twenty-five years ago, effectively putting an end to their entire race. A whole species, gone, with the press of a button. The war had been over for years, and the remaining Swarm carriers were mostly dormant since Granger had closed the black hole they were being controlled through, but still, CENTCOM had insisted that each remaining carrier be utterly destroyed. So she destroyed.

"No. The threat signature doesn't match anything we ever saw from them. This is new, as far as we can tell. The ship description is unlike anything we've seen, their tech—what little we know about it—is advanced, and the worst part might be something we've never encountered before." She glanced over at Commander Mumford.

He cleared his throat. "Before Irigoyen Prime went dark, there were widespread reports of civil unrest in the cities."

"Which cities?" said Captain Prucha.

Mumford shrugged. "*All* of them. Fighting. Arson. Murders. It was like the entire surface just went up in the flames of riots and thuggery just before the unknown ship struck. And once it struck, that was the last we heard."

Admiral Proctor nodded, and continued for him. "We've hypothesized that the aliens are using some sort of EM wave —possibly meta-space enhanced—that somehow influences organic neural pathways and brain chemical structure, inducing some kind of psychotropic response."

Proctor looked around at all their faces, and saw understanding suddenly dawn on them. The un-asked question had probably been nagging them the entire time, she knew. *Why her?* Why turn to the ousted former fleet admiral, who was happily spending her retirement in the classroom and on the beach?

"Yes, that is the main reason they called me up, due to my extensive experience studying xenobiology, and my years of direct interactions with all things Swarm, Dolmasi, Skiohra, and every other alien race we've encountered."

Rayna muttered. "Like hell, Cap'n. They're calling you up for more than that. You're a god-damned hero. The closest thing United Earth has to one, if you don't mind my truth-speakin'."

Proctor smiled, but held up a hand. "Thank you, Rayna. But we all know that all the heroes are dead," she replied, using an oft-quoted aphorism of the Second Swarm War. "They died saving Earth last time around. I'm just a gal that knows a thing or two about commanding a starship, and a little extra experience dealing with aliens. Tim Granger was the real hero, god rest his soul."

Her staff, old faces and new, beamed back at her. Many of them had been to hell and back at her side. As for the others, she assumed Admiral Oppenheimer had given her the best of the best. "We t-jump out within the hour. I want final readiness reports in thirty. Dismissed."

"Don't you mean *tranny-jump*?" said Volz with a lop-sided grin. "I mean, let's call it what it—"

"Admiral Proctor, bridge." The comm interrupted him. Proctor touched the glowing indicator on the conference table.

"Go ahead, bridge."

"Sir, we just received a meta-space distress call from orbital defense platform *Watchdog*, orbiting Bolivar. They say they've, and I quote, *engaged the Golgothics*. It's not entirely clear what they mean by that, Admiral."

So, the Bolivarans have given the aliens a name already? "Golgothics?"

Lieutenant Qwerty, his voice tinged by a heavy southern drawl, raised a finger. "Ma'am, if I may. Grew up on Bolivar myself. Old Bolivaran legend, or rather, a campfire story you'd tell to scare the pants off each other. They're supposed to be a race of unholy terrors that make you feel your worst emotions. All multiplied and enhanced till you're good right batty. *Eat your supper or the Golgothics will eat you*—, my granmam always said. Of course, she was half coon crazy herself...."

Proctor snorted. "That name will do for now, I suppose." She raised her head towards the comm. "Thank you, bridge." She eyed them all. "Let's move."

CHAPTER SIX

Britannia System, Calais, Wellington shipyards
Bridge, ISS Independence

"T-jump in five, ma'am," said Ensign Riisa.

Proctor gripped her armrests in preparation. She had no reason to assume the t-jump would be qualitatively any different than the q-jump, which was basically undetectable to the senses, but her careful instincts set her on edge.

"Initiating."

The view on the screen covering the front half of the bridge shifted from a serene display of the giant red clouds of Calais to a star-speckled canvas of black—open interstellar space. It had been years since Proctor had seen it, and had almost forgotten how free it felt. It reminded her of how sea captains must have felt as they lost all sight of land, seeing only the unending swell of distant waves.

Proctor's ears popped.

"What the hell was that?" She craned her neck around to look at Commander Yarbrough.

"Normal, ma'am. The t-jump is a bit more … intense than the q-jump. We did just travel five lightyears, after all."

Proctor opened and closed her jaw to relieve the pressure differential. "But why the pressure change?"

"Just an artifact of the t-jump process. Due to the extreme distances involved, the less dense matter arrives first—in our case, the atmosphere. Just a fraction of a fraction of a second, but the individual speeds of the air molecules are high enough that when the rest of us appear the internal ship pressure has dropped by a small amount."

Proctor glanced at science chief Mumford, who shrugged. "Well that's … unnerving," she said. "There's no chance things could get out of hand and we suddenly lose all pressure on one of these jumps?"

Commander Yarbrough shook his head. "No, sir. We've run the numbers on our t-jump simulations for years, and the chances of that happening are less than five sigmas of standard deviation from the mean. If you'd like, I can run a few additional Monte Carlo simulations and determine a better regression—"

"Thank you, Commander," she said, cutting him off. She remembered being a little uptight herself back when she was a fresh commander seeking to stand out, but she already found his eager-to-please attitude tiresome. "Let's focus on the emergency at hand." She turned back to Ensign Riisa. "Time until next t-jump?"

"Just a few seconds, sir."

The same unnerving feeling washed over Proctor as her

ears popped and the starfield on the screen shifted almost imperceptibly. "Not sure I'm going to get used to that."

The jumps ticked by, and within ten minutes Ensign Riisa announced, "last t-jump."

Proctor nodded. "All hands to battle stations. Sound red alert." She motioned over to Captain Prucha to begin battle readiness operations.

"Mag-rail stations, commence loading operations. Laser turret crews, prime initiators and start auto-targeting sequences. Emergency crews, stand by to prepare for damage control and casualties...." He went down his readiness checklist while Proctor clicked the comm over to the CIC on the fighter deck.

"Ballsy, everything ready down there?"

"Yes, ma'am. Got a pretty green crew down here, but the squad leaders are veterans, at least. No one has seen actual combat. Except me, of course," he added off-handedly. "I would have thought that with a new experimental starship we'd get new experimental fighters."

"Problem?"

"Not at all. These old X-25's are solid workhorses. I wouldn't ask for anything more. Just let me know the plan when we get there, Shelby."

"Stand by, Ballsy. One t-jump left. Have all fighters ready to launch."

"All stations report ready, Admiral," said Captain Prucha.

She nodded. The old, swelling feeling of pre-battle adrenaline surged into her chest. This was the part of command that she both hated, and missed. The feeling of urgency and clarity that preceded an impending battle. The awful feeling that some of them might die, that she might lose people under her command. But it was invigorating nonetheless—nothing in academia or the rest of her experience came close to replicating the feeling. It was like a drug: she felt guilty for enjoying, yet looked forward to the next fix.

"Initiate final t-jump."

The screen shifted, and in place of a brilliant starfield appeared a blue and white-dappled world, with a strike terminator separating night and day on the surface. Bolivar.

And on the night side of the planet, the surface burned.

CHAPTER SEVEN

Irigoyen Sector, Bolivar System, Bolivar
Bridge, ISS Independence

Something inside her snapped. Something latent, and visceral. Proctor gasped—for the briefest moment, images of scores of eviscerated Skiohra flashed before her eyes, their small, alien blue bodies torn, their thousands of embryos stored within their bodies oozing red blood, as if she were momentarily transported to a waking nightmare, but the next moment her vision snapped back to the rising smoke plumes on the planet below.

What the hell was that?

She turned to the tactical crew. "Lieutenant Whitehorse, scan the surface. What the hell are we seeing?"

Something odd about the woman—the tactical officer was staring at her console, her face muscles occasionally making twitching or jerking motions, as if she were having a minor seizure. "Lieutenant?" she repeated.

Whitehorse shook her head. "Uh, yes, ma'am." The officer focused on her data console, her face still screwed up as if in intense concentration, but she finally shook herself out of whatever had come over her. "Widespread fires on the surface, mainly from the densely populated areas. The cities, towns—anywhere with a high concentration of people—lots of fires. Some have spread to the forests."

"Why?"

"No idea, ma'am."

She turned back to the viewscreen covering the front of the bridge. The fires themselves weren't actually visible on the day side of the terminator since they were orbiting over five hundred kilometers above the surface, but the sight of the giant plumes of smoke rising from the cities was disturbing, to say the least.

And she couldn't shake the overwhelming feeling of … what the hell was she feeling? Fear? Anger? Something inside of her was writhing, raging, seething to the surface, making her either want to lash out, or run, or both. She balled her fists and bit her lip in an attempt to ground herself.

"Scan all orbits. Search for the alien vessel."

"Scanning," said Whitehorse. She reached up and scratched furiously at the back of her neck—Proctor could see the hand shake. Damn—they could all feel it too. Something was *wrong*.

Proctor wheeled around to face Commander Yarbrough. "Now's the time, Commander. Where the hell are all the new fangled defensive capabilities you were talking about?"

"Admiral?" The man looked puzzled.

"We're being hit with ... something. It's affecting our brain chemistry—can't you feel it?"

Yarbrough paused, looking down at his arms as if in a moment of introspection. "I suppose I could catalogue my feelings and compare them to prior baseline feelings, though I haven't been as diligent at cataloguing my feelings lately—"

Proctor couldn't tell if the man was joking or not. Yarbrough hadn't seemed like the type to *ever* kid, and so the remark made even less sense. Whatever the aliens, or Golgothics, were hitting them with, it was clearly affecting him too—his eyes darted back and forth over his handheld datapad, and he spoke almost twice as fast as he usually did. "I suppose if I tapped into the ship's medical logs and compiled a spreadsheet of baseline neurotransmitter levels and kept a running log of—"

"*Commander*. Snap out of it. We need to block this, whatever it is. What can the *Independence* do for us?"

Yarbrough's eyes continued darting back and forth, and he was at a loss for words. Flustered, Proctor spun around to the comm station. "Ensign Qwerty—"

"Billy-Bob," interrupted the man.

Proctor closed her eyes in annoyance and struggled not to lash out. Surely *that* was a normal response to the officer's breach of decorum. "Ensign *Billy-Bob* Qwerty, are you reading anything on regular channels?"

"No ma'am," he began, his voice heavily tinged by a deep-American-south accent. He was either from Ganymede, or Alabama. "All the comm channels quieter than a hibernatin' coon."

"Broaden the spectrum. Look at the whole band. Adjust

harmonics to look for meta-space carrier frequencies."

"Yes'm. Any idea what I'm lookin' for Ad'mril?" he twanged. At least his fingers were dancing deftly over the console.

"Anything." She had to keep herself from rolling her eyes—Commander Yarbrough had assured her that Ensign Qwerty was the best of the best—polyglot, linguist, a virtual communication genius. But all she could see and hear was a redneck, and—was that *chew* bulging in his cheek? Shit. Before she lashed out at him—was that a normal feeling?—she turned to Mumford, the boxer-turned-science chief. "Can we disrupt it? Whatever it is?"

He shrugged—his massive shoulders bouncing up, mirrored by his eyebrows. "We can't block it if we don't even know *what* it is."

"We could try the new anti-laser EM shielding," said Yarbrough, apparently in a moment of clarity. "Though I'd be more comfortable if I could compile a list of failure modes and run a few Monte-Carlo simulations on the—"

Proctor snapped her finger—she remembered the new shielding back from her days as fleet admiral of IDF. In fact, if she remembered correctly, the signature authorizing the release of funding for the project was hers. The research and deployment must have finally happened. "Brilliant," she said, cutting Yarbrough off, and, pointing to Mumford, "Could it work? I mean, assuming this signal, whatever it is, is EM-based?"

Mumford, in spite of being the science chief, was built like a bull. His shoulders heaved as he lifted his hands to his terminal—damn, why was she so fixated on those shoulders?

Those huge, meaty shoulders, rippling like—

Yarbrough kept right on speaking, not even giving Mumford the chance to reply, his mousy features and flimsy mustache reminding Proctor of some old television caricature of a dopey, nameless worry-wort—someone who usually ate it when the monster or the alien or the big bad showed up. "Admiral, I strongly protest. If we want to use the EM shielding for something other than its intended purpose, we need to run tests. We need benchmarks. Baselines. Error analysis. We can't get sloppy, especially now with our lives on the line."

Proctor just stared at him. What the hell was he talking about? Running engineering tests *now*? In the middle of a red-alert all-hands-to-battlestations situation? She shook her head and glanced back at Mumford, who was himself looking skeptically—scornfully—at Yarbrough, his broad shoulders bulging underneath the too-tight uniform—

Shit. They were all going crazy, herself included. But no, not exactly *crazy*, just ... exaggerated. Whatever this was, it seemed to be amplifying whatever their basest and most fundamental mental processes were compelling them to do. Amplifying and hyperbolizing their thoughts. For Yarbrough, it was amplifying his urge to cross the t's and dot the i's, to proceed with maximum safety, to understand whatever threat they faced in gory, unnecessary detail. For Mumford, well, who knew what he was feeling—he seemed to be acting very hesitantly, at least, in spite of those beef-cake shoulders, while Proctor herself seemed overly focused on *doing* something. Anything. But that was rational, right? Was that her only tic? The *doing* something? And the shoulders?

A voice came from right behind her—Captain Prucha had crept over to the captain's chair and spoke near her ear. "We need to get the hell out of here. Now."

Leave? She turned to face him. "Are you suggesting we just turn tail and run? We're supposed to be the rescuers, remember."

Prucha's face was tightening by the second, his brow furrowed more than she'd ever seen it. He seemed on the verge of screaming at her. "We can't be rescuers if we go crazy, Shelby. Our ability to render aid is severely curtailed if we can't even trust our own judgement skills."

"But we're all these people have—"

His eyes twitched even more. "We are steering the most advanced warship humanity has ever known towards one of the most populated planets in United Earth space. Do we really want our twitchy fingers on the triggers of these new weapons?"

He had a point. And the overwhelming feelings she—and all of them—were experiencing could just be the tip of the iceberg. Judging from the thousands of fires ravaging the surface, things could get a whole lot worse.

On the other hand, they had to *do* something. They had a mission. There were people to save. A planet to save. Hell, a *civilization* to save. If what she was seeing down on the surface was all caused by the alien ship, then this was not only a threat, but an existential threat.

"Any progress locking down that signal's spectrum?" she said to no-one in particular while she watched the surface burn.

"No, ma'am," said Lieutenant Whitehorse as a new alarm

sounded in the background. "But now reading a sensor contact coming on fast." She looked up, her face flushed red—probably from holding in an outburst of some kind. "It's the alien ship. It'll be here in two minutes."

CHAPTER EIGHT

*Irigoyen Sector, Bolivar System, Bolivar
Watchdog Station, High orbit*

When Lieutenant Zivic woke up, he wished he hadn't. His head throbbed—he had no idea why, though as he lifted his head from the deckplate his cheek stuck to the surface. A probing finger revealed his face was covered in blood—likely his head too, if the pain back there was any indication.

A glance to his left told him that Commander Smith had fared worse. A hole where his face had been didn't bode well for the man's health.

"That shouldn't be there," he mumbled, gaping at the bloody space where Smith's nose, skull, and brain should have been. The gore still hadn't registered as something real to his mind—it was like watching a movie. He knew he should be repulsed, he knew he should be doubled over and vomiting at the sight of the gruesome scene, but all he could think about was trying to remember what was going on. He tried to remember what had happened before he blacked out, but failed. There was a battle. Weapons fire. But with whom? His head hurt too badly to remember.

Klaxons. Alarms. Shouting. Everything in the background was chaos—was the battle still going on? Groaning, he pushed himself to his knees and tried to stand. As he swayed, he caught sight of a hole in the bulkhead, about the same size as the hole in Smith's face. A shimmering field covered the opening, an emergency measure to prevent the loss of atmosphere. But emergency hull containment fields were energy-intensive, and if it wasn't physically patched soon the field would fail and expose the room to vacuum.

At that thought, the room spun and he doubled over again, vomiting all over his boots. He glanced to his left at the gory sight of Smith's former face, and felt his mouth water again before another fit of vomiting overtook him. Reality was starting to set in. The foul aroma of alcohol and stomach acid assaulted his nose and pierced the hazy veil over his memory. He'd been drinking. Heavily. And he was starting to remember why.

The ship.

He jumped to his feet, suppressing another wave of nausea, and slid into his chair at the command station. Where was the ship? A quick glance over the sensor data revealed no unknown contacts within hundreds of kilometers. Just a few hundred ships over Bolivar in various stages of falling through the atmosphere. Merchant freighters, cargo carriers, military patrol ships, colonial transports—all of them, almost every single one, either burned through the atmosphere or were falling quickly towards it. A few lucky ships appeared to be in stable orbits around Bolivar along with *Watchdog* Station.

The planet wasn't faring any better than the ships. Smoke billowed up from the major towns, dozens of kilometers into the atmosphere, some forming great mushroom clouds as if nuclear explosions had flattened entire cities. Did the governments of Bolivar have secret tactical nukes? Or were those from the alien ship?

Where the hell was that ship? He tapped into the planetary sensor network, giving him access to data from the other side of the planet, and, sure enough, a weather satellite confirmed the presence of the unknown vessel, orbiting slowly. The defensive satellites seemed to be all knocked out or disabled: the ship seemed to glide right on by without a single defensive shot from the defense network.

It was headed towards another ship. An IDF ship—one he didn't recognize. He keyed in a command to read the ship's transponder. *ISS Independence*. Never heard of it.

He shook his head. The earlier conflicting emotions had subsided. Fear still threatened to paralyze him, and the urge to liquor up still gnawed at him, but for the most part, his head was clear. Did those feelings … did they come from that alien ship? Luckily, it was on the other side of the planet now.

The sensor readout changed. Something was happening. The distinct signature of weapons fire, though he couldn't tell who was shooting. Perhaps both the *Independence* and the alien ship. All he knew was that the power readings from the *Independence* were starting to fluctuate.

Shit. They needed help. Otherwise they'd end up just like *Watchdog* Station, broken and bleeding. As if to punctuate his thought, another klaxon sounded in the distance. Another hull breach. The energy field over the hole in the bulkhead nearby started to shimmer and fluctuate. If there were more of those holes in other parts of the station, say, a few dozen, then the power draw to maintain atmospheric integrity would be substantial. And a quick glance at the operations console monitor nearby told him even more bad news.

The station's reactor was going critical. Whereas before he was worried that they'd be dead within the hour, now he knew he only had a few minutes if he was going to do anything at all.

And from the station he could do very little. There was really only one choice at this point, though it was the one choice he dreaded. But given the alternative, it was all he had.

He hadn't flown a ship for over a year. He'd sworn he wouldn't ever again.

Watchdog Station had a handful of fighters stationed in its bay, and a quick glance at another readout on his console told him that all of them were disabled except for two. The rest had holes in them the same size as the hole in Smith's face. In fact, the entire bay was at vacuum—the fighter pilots on standby could be dead, for all he knew.

His stomach seemed to lurch into his mouth and his head spun again, though at the sight of a coffee mug flying past his face he knew this wasn't just his queasiness again. Artificial gravity was out. The rest of life support would probably soon follow. If he was going to do this, it had to be now.

Launching himself out of his seat, he swore as he collided with the ceiling. Dammit—his zero-g training certification had lapsed earlier in the year. He hated zero-g. He hated all g's that weren't regular g. It was part of why he'd turned in his fighter pilot wings a year ago, much to the chagrin of his father. If his mother were still alive, he imagined she'd kick his ass. Flying fighters was in his blood. It was his heritage. It was the family business, it seemed, and he'd turned his back on it and on his dead mother and his living, and livid, father.

He shook his head clear of the collision with the ceiling and pushed himself towards the door. Luckily, it sensed his impending approach and slid open at the last second, allowing him to sail through into the hallway beyond, though he needed to make a last-minute adjustment to his trajectory to avoid crashing into the limp body of Commander Smith which had floated up, along with dozens of globules of his blood.

One of the floating red spheres splashed onto his shoulder as he passed, making his stomach churn again. *You can do this, Zivic, you can do this, Zivic,* he chanted to himself over and over again, like a mantra.

He flew down the ruined hallway, seeing an occasional hole in the floor. When he glanced up, he saw a matching hole in the ceiling. Beyond each he could see the chaos in the deck below or above. At one, he paused to look through the oval-shaped hole, peering through at least four deck's worth of destruction, terminating in a hole of exactly the same shape in the exterior bulkhead. Stars twinkled on the other side of the shimmering blue screen. *Shit. I've got no time.*

At the lift, he pushed the call button, but nothing happened. He wondered if the lifts depended on the artificial gravity system, but even as he thought it he realized he didn't need the lift. Keying in the emergency override code, the door slid open, but stopped halfway. With effort, he managed to push it back into its sleeve, and he pulled himself into the empty elevator shaft.

Luckily, the lift seemed to be stuck above him, though with the zero-g, he now thought of that direction as *behind* him, and he sailed forward through the shaft, counting the decks down until he arrived at the fighter bay. With another override entry and more grunting, he managed to force the door open and push himself into the ante-chamber of the bay, which, luckily, was not at vacuum.

Distant explosions punctuated his panic. Was that the core? No—if that were the core exploding, he wouldn't be here right now. Nevertheless, another explosion—this one close enough to make him instinctually cover his ears—pushed him to hurry even more.

Except that wasn't an explosion.

It was a gunshot.

Who the hell was shooting a gun, on a station whose core was about to go critical? Had that mysterious ship dropped off a boarding party?

But the questions could wait for now, since shouting voices nearby made him dash for an armaments container in the corner. He yanked it open, and swore under his breath—he'd been hoping to find at least a sidearm there, if not an assault rifle. It was completely empty.

The voices were getting louder. With no other choices left, he pulled himself into the container and yanked the lid mostly shut, leaving just enough of a space to see out into the launch bay's anteroom. He'd hid just in time. The door into corridor slid open and a man, handcuffed and thrashing, flew through and collided into the far wall, bounced off, and drifted back towards the door. He was wearing a contractor's uniform—

probably from one of the commercial vendors that regularly serviced the station.

Two other men, both in IDF uniforms, appeared at the door, and as the flailing handcuffed man sailed back toward them, one of the newcomers bashed his face with the sidearm he was holding. The handcuffed man started spinning, blood flinging off his face in all directions.

"Last chance, Underwood. Where is it? This is the last time I ask." The man with the gun leveled it at the bound contractor's head, who now was being held in place by the other IDF officer. Zivic didn't recognize any of them, though *Watchdog* Station was pretty large, hosting over three hundred IDF personnel and contractors at any given time.

The contractor struggled against the handcuffs, but it was a futile effort. "You people are freaks. This place is going to blow, and all you care about is the—"

Another blow to the face from the sidearm silenced him.

"Last chance." The man holding the gun checked the safety, and then pointed it at the man's forehead. The other officer let go of the contractor and pushed himself away—up toward the ceiling, and then back down to the door to float next to the officer with the gun.

The contractor swore under his breath. "Fine. It's already loaded onto one of the shuttles."

"So you lied to me earlier?"

The contractor was getting frantic as he watched the barrel of the gun pointed between his eyes. "I had orders. You have to understand. I was just—"

"I have orders too." But he smiled, and lowered the gun. "You passed the test, my friend. I knew it was on the shuttle already." He started to push the gun into his belt, fingering the safety on. "We may just take you with us. Save your life, you know? Pay you back for finally coming around to see reason. A reward, you see?"

The contractor breathed a little easier, and nodded vigorously.

"I need the authorization code to open the shuttle. What is it?" He peered out through the thick composite glass windows into the actual shuttle bay. "And which shuttle is it?"

"Shuttle *Fenway*. Code is Fenway-bravo-shovik-orion-one-one-two." A distant explosion shook the room, and the contractor eyed the walls nervously. "Please. Please hurry. We've got to get out of here."

The man with the gun nodded. "Agreed." He pulled the gun out, flipped the safety off, and shot the contractor through the forehead.

The body jerked once, and started somersaulting backward, blood trailing out from the head in a spiral as the corpse slowly rotated.

"Let's go." The man nodded at his companion, holstered the gun, and they both sailed over to the fighter pilots' lockers, searching until they found flight suits and helmets. "Bay's at vacuum. Be ready for explosive decompression."

Zivic tried not to gasp, but he knew what was coming. And before he could even breath deeply a few times to prepare, the whole room exploded in a rush of air as the thick doors opened into the shuttle bay.

CHAPTER NINE

Irigoyen Sector, Bolivar System, Bolivar
Bridge, ISS Independence

"It's firing at us, sir!" yelled Lieutenant Whitehorse.

Proctor spun around to face the screen, her eyes darting back and forth across the other vessel, searching for the expected energy beam or whatever the Golgothics used for their weapons.

"With what?"

The entire deck jolted under her feet.

"With that," said Whitehorse. "They've got mag-rails. But … holy shit…."

"Spit it out, Lieutenant."

"These are mag-rail slugs all right, but they're bigger than anything I've ever seen—at least a hundred kilos each and solid iron—and they're going faster than, well, anything I've ever seen. Fifty kps, at least."

Proctor's eyes bulged. A hundred kilos accelerated up to fifty kps in the space of a few milliseconds? The power required to achieve such a feat was ... formidable. Terawatts at least.

"Damage?"

"Blew a hole clean through the *Independence*, Admiral," said Captain Prucha. "Receiving reports of casualties on several decks. Hull containment is compromised, but backups are in place."

"It's firing again!" yelled Whitehorse.

The deck lurched and bucked. Proctor grabbed her chair and pulled herself into it, fastening the restraints to keep herself from flying out. For the last dozen years or so of her career as an IDF captain she'd served aboard Legacy Fleet ships—*Constitution*, *Warrior*, *Victory*, *Chesapeake*—massive behemoths that didn't, couldn't, shake so much. The *Independence* was far smaller, far lighter, and she could feel it in the tremors in the deckplate.

"All mag-rail crews, target the vessel and open fire. Laser crews, same. Open up hell on that thing."

"Aye, ma'am." Lieutenant Whitehorse signaled to her tactical crew, coordinating firing patterns. "All mag-rails engaged. Lasers...." she frowned. "Lasers having no effect, sir. They're just bouncing right off."

Proctor snapped her head towards Captain Yarbrough. "You said those are terawatt lasers."

"They are!"

"Then how the hell can that blasted thing out there repel a terawatt beam?" She watched her video feed, and indeed the laser beams, rather than turn the other ship into glowing slag or a rapidly expanding cloud of vapor, just bounced off like the *Independence* was shining handheld pointer lasers at the other ship.

"And the mag-rail slugs?" She watched the video feed, but she knew she'd never see the damn things going over ten kilometers per second.

"They're, uh, also bouncing off, ma'am." Whitehorse's brow furrowed. "I don't understand—they shouldn't do that. Ever."

Impossible. "Are the mag-rail calibrations off? Are they moving at the right speed? The only way a slug bounces off is if it's only moving very slowly—"

"No, ma'am." Whitehorse pounded the console in frustration as another burst of slugs shot out from the *Independence*, and bounced off, faster than they could see. "I don't understand it, sir. It's almost like there's different physics governing that hull over there. Terawatt beams of photons and slugs of tungsten don't bounce off any surface, no matter how well engineered it is."

An explosion tore through the rear of the bridge, sending Captain Prucha flying forward, along with two ops technicians. They landed in a crumpled pile after hitting the front wall. Proctor ripped the seat restraint away and ran towards them, but she could see immediately there was nothing she could do. Prucha bled profusely from his neck, and it seemed his head was only half attached. All three officers were completely scorched.

Admiral Proctor's breath caught in her throat. It had been decades since she'd seen such visceral gore and violence, and with the sight of the erupting blood came the memories of the

Second Swarm War, rushing back to overwhelm her. "Ensign Riisa, get us out of here."

"Ma'am?"

It was a retreat, but there was no choice. They'd be picked apart without so much as touching the mysterious ship.

"Now! Any heading!"

Proctor supposed that the inertial cancelers were damaged because she nearly fell down as the *Independence* started speeding away from the Golgothic ship, shooting eastward above the upper atmosphere of Bolivar. *Smart move*, she thought. If they were to lose engines, orbiting in the same direction as the planet's spin would make a crash landing that much easier.

"Pursuit?"

Whitehorse shook her head. "None. The alien ship is proceeding along its heading as if we'd never met it."

"Course?"

"Looks like its heading out towards Ido. Bolivar's moon."

"Ido? What the hell would it want with Ido? A billion people on Bolivar … and how many on Ido?" She looked over to Commander Yarbrough with her brow raised in a question.

"A few hundred. Tops. It's only used as a ship supply depot and transfer point."

Proctor turned back to look at the dead Captain Prucha. They'd served for years together on the *Chesapeake*. He was her confidante, her rock during the most difficult days of that assignment. But she forced the tears back and swallowed the growing lump at the back of her throat. *Mourn later. Survive now.* At the back of her mind she thought it was remarkable how the old survival instincts she'd developed during the Second Swarm War thirty years ago came back so readily. Like riding a bicycle.

Except this bicycle was on fire, made of dynamite, and she was speeding over a cliff—her ship status schematic on her command console was a sea of flashing red.

"Does IDF have any defense assets out at Ido?"

Commander Yarbrough shook his head. "Barely. Just a single orbiting defense platform. A couple mag-rails. Crew of twenty, tops."

"Madam Ad'mril, think you should see this, ma'am." The comm chief, Lieutenant Qwerty, was waving her down. The urgency of the situation was exacerbating his southern twang. "Pickin' up a shit-load of comm chatter on IDF frequencies."

"What is it?"

"Sounds like Admiral Mullins down in CENTCOM Bolivar finally managed to muster his planetary defense fleet. They had been dispersed throughout the sector helping with relief operation for Sangre de Cristo. But there's a slight problem…."

What could possibly make this situation worse?

"I'm sure we can handle it."

Qwerty nodded. "Much of Bolivar's defense fleet has mustered at Ido to face the Golgothic ship, but from the sound of things, several of the captains have … uh, declared for the GPC, and are threatening to shoot any IDF vessel that intervenes."

CHAPTER TEN

Irigoyen Sector, Bolivar System, Ido
Bridge, ISS Independence

"Are they crazy?" Proctor asked, turning to look at the schematic map of the fleet layout, which showed the ships arrayed at Ido. Several of the blue icons had turned red, indicating which ones had supposedly declared for the GPC.

Commander Yarbrough came up behind her. "They actually could be crazy, judging from the ... effects from that alien ship. I confess, when that ship was close to us, I half wanted to take over the helm and get us out of there, and half wanted to grab the nearest gun and blow my own head off I was so scared."

She looked back at him and nodded. "I agree, it was harrowing, but this is different. I didn't sign up to reign in a bunch of separatist malcontents." She turned back to the screen. "I don't care what that alien ship is doing to their judgment, they'd better stand down now or face a very angry former fleet admiral," she added under her breath.

"Do we have time to babysit a bunch scared IDF captains?" Yarbrough asked.

"Or fight a civil war? Because that's what this looks like—you don't take over an IDF warship and think United Earth is going to come after you with kid gloves." She approached Ensign Riisa at the helm. "Get us out there. T-jump. Put us right in the middle of the ships that haven't declared for the GPC."

"Aye, aye, ma'am."

Moments later she felt the now familiar vertigo from the t-jump, and the viewscreen shifted to reveal Bolivar's planetary defense fleet, with the gray regolith of Ido behind them.

Almost immediately, the earlier feelings of raw fear, rage, lust, and terror returned. The Golgothic ship was near.

"Open a channel to the whole fleet," she said.

Qwerty nodded. "Open, Admiral."

"All IDF ships, this is Admiral Shelby Proctor, acting under the direct authority of Fleet Admiral Oppenheimer. As you're all well aware, we're under attack." She clenched her jaw, weighing her next words carefully, which was ten times more difficult under the influence of the Golgothic's emotion-disrupting broadcast. "I'm under the impression that several captains have chosen this moment to declare their … political leanings. This is unacceptable, especially in the face of an existential threat that we face in the form of that alien ship. While we don't understand yet its intentions, I think we can assume—"

The comm erupted with a booming voice that interrupted

her. "Admiral Proctor, please spare us your speech. We've suffered under the oppressive regime of United Earth for too long to have to suffer through the empty threats of a washed-up former wannabe war hero."

Proctor's face flushed red with anger. On the split screen she saw the Golgothic vessel was approaching the moon, and their fleet. They had minutes at best to prepare themselves. And here she was arguing with a political idealist who was under the influence. She glanced at the fleet layout schematic and noted the captain's name, and ship.

"Captain Shee, I presume? Look, Captain, we can discuss your political grievances later. But what matters now is that you bring the *Davenport* with us into battle with the alien ship. Our very survival depends on it."

Lieutenant Whitehorse called from the tactical station. "Admiral, they're arming mag-rails and laser turrets. Targeting computers are locking onto us."

"Oh, for the love … Riisa, move us away. Get us in orbit around Ido on a course that won't pass us anywhere near these assholes." She motioned towards the comm station for Qwerty to open up the channel to the entire fleet. "All IDF ships who are willing and able, follow the *Independence* to Ido to intercept the alien ship. Any IDF vessel that chooses not to engage with us will face severe repercussions when this is over. Proctor out."

On the screen the intransigent IDF vessels shrunk to small white dots as the *Independence* accelerated away, accompanied by over half of the Bolivaran fleet. They started swinging around the moon, passing the terminator and into the darkness of Ido's night. After a minute or so, the sense of rage and dread induced by the Golgothics dissipated to just a background murmur, like shadowy fears in the corners of her mind.

"Riisa, increase speed to ten kps. We're going to slingshot around the moon and hit it with a barrage of mag-rails slugs." She sat down in the captain's chair and fastened the restraints. "Granger's favorite move," she muttered.

"I thought his favorite move was hurling other starships into Swarm carriers," said Yarbrough.

She shrugged. "They did call him *the bricklayer* for all the bricks he sent through the Swarm's windows. Starships were expendable to him. To me they're not." She glanced up at Yarbrough. "Yet."

But the memory of Granger's … *unorthodox* tactics gave her an idea. If Captain Shee and his cohort were going to get in the way of her tactical operations….

"Ensign Riisa, adjust our heading. Come up on the alien ship from the direction of the rebels. Reduce speed until we're right up under their noses."

"Ma'am? That's going to expose us to their fire," said Whitehorse.

"Yes," she said, gripping her armrests. "But it will also let us use them as a shield."

CHAPTER ELEVEN

*Irigoyen Sector, Bolivar System, Bolivar
Watchdog Station, High orbit*

Zivic gripped the storage locker so hard that the edges dug into his palms, but mercifully the maelstrom of air, debris, and the contractor's blood ceased soon after it began as the bay doors shut behind the two officers. He counted to ten before launching himself out of the container. The station was going to blow any second. He had to balance that impeding death with the possibility of being seen by the two unknown assassins, who would surely kill any potential witnesses to their crime.

What were they looking for? Why was it worth killing for?

He didn't have time to think about it. He ripped one of the fighter pilot lockers open. Empty, except for a few personal effects. The next three lockers also showed no signs of a flight gear, or any other kind of emergency environmental suit that would let him survive the hard vacuum of the bay.

The last locker, marked *Johnson*, bore fruit. He wondered where Lieutenant Johnson was as he pulled the man's suit on, locking the seals in place and struggling to squeeze into something that was obviously meant for a slightly smaller man, a situation made worse by the fact that he was floating in the air, pulling the suit on without any leverage from gravity. He rammed the helmet onto his head. Stickers, insignia, and graffiti covered the exterior of the well-worn helmet, but it looked serviceable—the oxygen indicator suggested the reserves were full, and the power backups were at full charge. Thank god for the diligence of maintenance crews. And Shovik-Orion, military equipment supplier extraordinaire.

He hadn't even locked the helmet seal in place when the pressure in the ante-chamber blew again, this time because of a hull containment force field that had failed. The air in the room flooded towards a hole in the wall separating him from the bay, and any object in the room not nailed down suddenly became a deadly projectile.

But projectiles weren't his immediate concern. He gasped as the air thinned, and he struggled against the fierce wind to seal the helmet. At the moment he felt like his lungs were about to burst into his mouth and his eyes pop, he managed to crank the seal shut, and the oxygen system automatically engaged as it sensed the near-vacuum condition of the suit.

"That was *too* close," he told himself, pushing away from the locker towards the door to the bay. The override code unlocked the door, but it didn't even move. Emergency power reserves were probably completely drained, as evidenced by the lack of a shimmering blue screen over the hole in the bulkhead. He managed to wedge some fingers into the opening and forced the doors open inch by inch, though these were far heavier than the lift doors he'd forced earlier.

Finally, twelve inches later, it was open just enough to let him squeeze through. Debris, hydraulic fluid, ordnance, tools, and bodies all floated in the bay, obstructing the path in between him and the two operable fighters at the end of flight platform. He didn't know if the surrounding chaos was the result of the two mysterious assassins, or the earlier bombardment from the equally mysterious ship. But a quick glance at the giant bay doors that opened out into deep space told him that the two murderers had left; the shuttle they piloted careened out the doors, which started to close behind the small craft. Before it darted out he just barely caught sight of the nameplate affixed to the rear. *Fenway*.

As another explosion registered in the background he launched himself straight through the debris—in the back of his mind he realized he didn't actually hear the explosion, but holding onto the bay doors he'd felt it, and feeling the vibration through the metal seemed to create the perception of sound in his head.

From the state of the bodies it was clear the emergency had taken them completely by surprise: none of the techs were wearing the environmental suits that would have saved their lives, and the pilots were all helmet-less, their partially donned flight suits insufficient to save them from the vacuum. He tried not to look at their bloated purple faces as he passed.

Except for one, which had a helmet on, and was flailing and trashing around, several meters off the deck. She was terrified, and calculating the risk in his head, he decided to take it. Better die with honor than live with the shame. He bounced off a tumbling barrel full of lubricant grease and used the collision to redirect himself upward towards the woman. They collided, he grabbed her upper arm, and as they hit the ceiling he pushed off with a grunt, aiming for one of the remaining craft, and prayed that his aim while maneuvering in zero-g was as good as it was with the fire controls of a fighter.

It was. They nearly bounced off, but at the last second he grabbed the small handhold near the hatch with his free hand, wrenching the flailing woman towards the fighter with his other.

The hatch to the fighter opened far easier than any of the doors he'd opened so far, and a quick glance over the controls told him the craft was in good shape. Whatever had barraged the station had fortunately missed this particular bird. He pushed the woman into the space behind the seat, secured her as best he could with the auxiliary restraint, strapped himself in, fired up the engines, and pulled away from the deck with a quick burst from the maneuvering thrusters, tapping the button that would have opened the exterior bay doors.

They didn't budge. *Of course*, he thought, *that would be far too easy.* He keyed in an override code for the doors, but they still didn't move. After all that work, he was stuck in the bay.

An alarm sounded from his helmet's headset, and he glanced at his console to see what the new emergency was.

The core. It was going critical. He had maybe fifteen seconds. Twenty tops. Soon, the entire station and everything inside would be nothing more than a glowing cloud of molten radioactive slag.

He gripped the firing control, aimed the guns at the bay

door, and fired with everything the little bird had.

Out of the corner of his eye, he saw something move. One of the floating bodies. A pilot.

His helmet was on, and the man was struggling to maneuver in the debris field floating over the bay's deck, unable to get enough leverage to launch himself towards the remaining fighter.

Zivic glanced at the console, even as he continued pummeling the doors with shells.

Ten seconds.

He caught sight of the other pilot's face as he rotated into view. Contorted in sheer terror.

But there was no time. Either Zivic got them out of there now, or he stayed and tried to help the other man, and probably kill all three of them in the process.

He could only be so much of a hero.

Zivic squeezed the trigger of the fighter's guns and the doors blew outward, revealing the safe embrace of empty space beyond. He breathed deep—he hadn't flown in two years. Not since.... *Don't think about it.* He kicked in the accelerator. Two g's thrust him back in his seat and his vision went momentarily dark as his body struggled to keep up. The broken bay doors sailed past and he shot out into space.

Two seconds later, *Watchdog* Station exploded.

CHAPTER TWELVE

Irigoyen Sector, Bolivar System, Ido Bridge, ISS Independence

"Coming up on the mutinous ships, Admiral," said Lieutenant Whitehorse, though there was no need to say it. Everyone felt it. They felt the distance between them and the alien ship shrink with every passing second. The calm, cool, rational part of Proctor's brain wondered at the science behind it, how amazing it was that whatever field the Golgothics were broadcasting it was somehow perfectly tuned to be able to influence their actual brain chemistry.

The cavewoman part of her brain, strengthening by the second, could only say, *Run! Fight! Have sex! Beat the shit out of that ship! Punch Yarbrough! Rub Mumford's beefy shoulders! No— RUN!*

She shook her head and tried to think through the oncoming rush of confusing thoughts and emotions. "Steady, people. Use your brains. You know what is rational, and what is crazy." Her jaw was clenched so hard her teeth hurt. This was going to be some battle. If they were fighting themselves, and the mutinous ships, and the alien vessel, things would get interesting—and deadly—very quickly.

"In weapons range, Admiral," said Whitehorse.

"Are the mutinous ships in between us and the alien? Perfectly aligned?"

"Yes, ma'am."

Proctor nodded, as calmly as possible. Was this rational? Was using the ships as cover the right thing to do? The moral, ethical thing to do? The cloud was too thick to rationalize either way. The only course she had was action.

"Fire. Ballsy, standby to deploy fighters."

The *Independence*, and the rest of the fleet accompanying it, opened up with a barrage of mag-rail fire and pulsed laser beams that, under normal circumstances and against a normal enemy, would have torn any ship to shreds within seconds. The mag-rail slugs and beams shot past the mutinous IDF ships and slammed into the alien ship, which had slowed down and seemed to be holding over Ido.

"Any effect?"

Whitehorse shook her head, far more quickly than was probably normal for her. "No, ma'am." She whirled to one of her mag-rail crew officers. "You're out of sync! Get it together, Ensign!" She slammed her fist down on the tactical console. The ensign swore under his breath, but to his credit, kept it together and relayed instructions to his gun crew.

They were all going to lose it soon if they didn't either win, or get the hell out of there.

"Maybe we can weaken one spot if we concentrate our fire." She brought up a schematic of the Golgothic ship. "All ships, concentrate fire on…" she tapped on a random location on the ship's hull, "these coordinates." The computer automatically broadcast them to the tactical station and the rest of the fleet. "Ballsy, deploy fighters. All ships, deploy fighters and engage that location on the ship."

She held her breath, waiting for the concentrated barrage of mag-rail slugs to finally break through. Dozens of fighters from the *Independence* and her fleet swarmed out, targeting the chosen location on the alien ship.

Nothing. Every slug, every round from every fighter, all just bounced off. Every. Single. One.

"Impossible," she breathed. The primordial rage and terror boiling under the surface was starting to surge up.

"Admiral, the *Davenport* is firing. On us!" yelled Whitehorse.

The deck shook. Klaxons rang out. "Captain Shee, cease fire immediately or your vessel will be destroyed," she said as calmly and yet urgently as possible.

Commander Yarbrough called out from the XO's station. "Damage on decks seven and eight, forward sections. Evacuating section one."

The barrage from the *Davenport* continued, while the *Independence* and her fleet continued pounding the alien ship, to no avail. *Dammit.*

"Fine. Alter targeting to the—"

"Admiral! The Golgothics are firing. Reading energy levels completely off our normal scales!" Lieutenant Whitehorse's hands were a blur on her tactical console. On the viewscreen, past the mutinous IDF ship, the stationary alien vessel had initiated some sort of pure energy beam. Shimmering purple-white, it lanced out, not at any ship….

But towards the moon below. It bored down through Ido's surface, digging deep into its crust. Debris, dust, and explosions blasted out from the drilling zone in a hellish maelstrom.

"What the hell…?" Proctor leaned forward. "What is it doing?"

Commander Mumford shook his head. "The beam is an ultra-high-energy composite mix of anti-gallium, boron ions, gamma-, x-, and ultraviolet rays, along with pure anti-proton ions. Adjusting sensor scales now…." He looked up at her, his face draining of color. "One hit from that beam and any ship is a goner. Instantly. I'm reading billions of terawatts coming off that thing."

The deck shook again. The *Davenport* was still firing on them, and now a few of the other mutinous ships had joined in, shooting mag-rail slugs at her own fleet.

Rayna Scott's voice boomed over the comm. "Shelby, can we tone it down some? Those bastards are hurting my engines."

"Sorry, Rayna, we're in the thick of it. How are we holding up?"

Rayna grunted. "I'll keep her together. But one more well-placed rail-gun slug and the core starts getting fussy. Rayna out."

Proctor nodded. "Target the *Davenport*'s weapons systems. Fire."

The deck pulsed with the regular thumps of mag-rail fire,

and the *Davenport*'s surface was peppered with tiny explosions as the slugs tore into the hull.

"The alien ship is opening fire with their rail gun again," said Whitehorse. "Their drilling beam is still on, but aimed at the planet."

"So they can walk and chew gum at the same time," murmured Proctor. "Who's getting hit?"

"Mainly the *Davenport*. A few of the other mutinous ships. One of our ships, too. It's basically targeting every ship it has a clear shot at."

"So our shield is working," she said. *God help us.* "What's the status of the *Davenport*? Are they still firing on us?"

"No, ma'am. Their laser turrets are dead. Mag-rail tubes destroyed. Reading power fluctuations all over the ship. I think it's going to—" Lieutenant Whitehorse didn't even get to finish her sentence.

The *Davenport* erupted in a blinding explosion as its core went critical.

CHAPTER THIRTEEN

Irigoyen Sector, Bolivar System, Ido
Bridge, ISS Independence

When the glow diminished, the expanding cloud of molten slag that had been the *ISS Davenport* dissipated enough that Proctor could see through to the other side, where the alien ship still drilled into the little moon. Ido now sported a hole the size of the *Independence* on its surface, and the purple-white beam continued to plunge into it.

"Sir, something's happening," said Whitehorse. "Detecting movement on the ship. A port is opening."

Proctor snapped around to the tactical station. "Scan it. All bands. We need to see inside that thing, or we'll never know how to beat it."

"Scanning." Whitehorse bit her lip. "The opening is still covered by some kind of dampening field—similar to our atmospheric containment fields. Except this one is blocking all

EM bands."

"Neutron scan, then."

Whitehorse shook her head. "Same."

Proctor did a double take. "They have have an EM field that's blocking a neutron scanning beam?" She glanced over at Commander Mumford. "How?"

The scientist shrugged. "Unknown, Admiral. Apparently their technology far exceeds our own," he deadpanned.

Proctor's eyes stayed locked on the viewscreen image of the Golgothic ship drilling into Ido. "Commander, you win the understatement of the year award." She scratched her chin. "No change in its offensive stance?"

"No, Admiral. The other mutinous ships have finally all withdrawn to a distance that appears acceptable to the alien ship. At least, it's not firing on them. Or us."

"So what the hell is it doing, then?"

As if in answer, something shot out the port that had opened on the ship. Too fast for Proctor's eyes to track, she glanced at her command console. "What the blazes was that?"

"A small tungsten sphere. Contents unknown. It's heading straight down into the hole on the planet." Whitehorse glanced up at Proctor. "Shall we fire, Admiral?"

"Negative. As long as the ship is not attacking us, we just watch." She noticed Commander Yarbrough eye her with surprise. "For now," she added.

On the viewscreen, they all watched the sphere arc down towards the surface of the moon. The purple-white beam shimmered briefly, pulsating in its last gasps, then disappeared right as the sphere entered the hole that had opened up on Ido's surface.

The entire bridge waited with bated breath. Waiting for the inevitable explosion, or moonquake, energy spike. Or whatever massive destruction the alien device would cause on the small moon.

Nothing happened.

"Lieutenant?" Proctor said to Whitehorse. "Anything?"

"Sensors are quiet, sir."

"So what the hell did that thing do?"

Whitehorse shrugged. "Nothing on any bands. Just faint tremors, but that looks normal considering the bastard just drilled a hole down to the moon's core. I can scan using—"

Yarbrough interrupted them. "Look!"

The ship was moving. Away from the *Independence*, away from the small, battered mutinous IDF fleet huddled in the background. And moments later, with the tell-tale flicker of a q-jump, it disappeared.

Instantly, the intense, overflowing surge of emotions dissipated. Her heartbeat slowed to something normal. Everyone on the bridge breathed a little calmer.

Lieutenant Qwerty called over from the comm station. "Receiving messages from the captains of the mutinous ships, Admiral. They're … uh, apologizing. Profusely and all sincere-like."

"Well," began Proctor, swiveling around to face her bridge crew. Her eyes drifted over the spot on the deck where Captain Prucha's blood still stained it, then back up to the viewscreen which still displayed the tiny moon Ido. "This certainly qualifies as the oddest alien invasion I've ever seen. Still no changes from the moon?"

"No, ma'am." Whitehorse's brow furrowed. "Unless you

consider a point zero zero zero zero zero one percent increase in its mass to be a significant change."

CHAPTER FOURTEEN

Irigoyen Sector, Bolivar System, Bolivar
High orbit

When Zivic woke up, his first thought was to wonder at which point he'd passed out, and why. Must have been the sustained high-g thrust. Or maybe they'd run into something on their way out of the station and he'd hit his head. Or maybe the expanding apocalyptic sphere of the exploding station had caught up with them. Whatever it was, something was tugging persistently on his arm. And, distantly, he could hear a similarly persistent voice.

The woman. She was pulling at him, and yelling something, which of course he couldn't quite make out since they both had their helmets on. But he didn't need to hear her to understand what she was saying, since with her other hand she was frantically pointing up through the cockpit.

He looked up.

Oh shit.

Bolivar loomed up above them, or below them, since they were technically falling. Falling very quickly, judging by the orange shock wave of compressed atmosphere taking shape between them and the planet.

He grabbed the controls and pushed on the accelerator. It was dead.

"Oh, *hell* no," he said, punching buttons on his console in a vain attempt to restart the engines. But they were dead. Cold out.

The distant voice suddenly magnified a thousand fold. "The reaction chamber is fine. I think it's the plasma conduits." He nearly jumped out of his seat hearing the bullhorn sound in his ears. She must have figured out what comm channel his helmet was on.

"What? How do you know?" He still fumbled with the controls, his hands trembling now that that the cockpit was shaking from the reentry. He wasn't sure if they were trembling from fear or momentum transfer.

"We hit something a few minutes ago. I think it cut through the main plasma line, and the auxiliaries are notoriously unreliably on these birds."

She sounded oddly confident in her diagnosis and assessment of the little ship's idiosyncrasies. "Mechanic?" he said.

"Yeah." She was breathing heavily, rapidly. Unless she slowed down she was going to hyperventilate. Not that the imminent fiery death coming for them wouldn't quickly solve her breathing problems.

"I'm Ethan. What's your name?"

She gulped, and panted into her helmet's microphone. The shuttle shook even harder. "Sara."

"Look, Sara, we can pull out of this, but I need your help. Can you fix it?"

"I—I think so. I don't know. If I were down underneath the fighter and had all my tools, maybe."

"Not the main plasma line. I mean the auxiliaries. You sound like you know all about them. Can you get them working? We have access to them right there in the back of the cockpit."

She nodded. "Oh yeah. I—I should have known that. Sorry."

It was obvious that she was in shock. Her hands trembled, and her eyes kept darting around the cockpit, up through the transparent cockpit windows overhead toward the glowing shock wave and the icy blue planet beyond.

"Look, Sara, we're going to pull through this. Just get back there, and work your magic with those auxiliaries."

She nodded vigorously, again. Her restraints fell away and she squirmed her way back into the rear of the cockpit, and he could hear the access panel fall away. "Ok, I see the auxiliary lines. Backed up, just like I thought."

"Can you ... *unback* them?"

"If I had my tools—"

The roar from reentry was getting loud enough to hear through the helmet, and almost loud enough to make it difficult to hear her voice.

"Look, Sara, we don't have time. We're dead in twenty seconds unless you do something. Anything."

Her breathing grew calm. Finally, she said, "Well, here goes nothing."

She started pounding on the plasma line with her fist.

"What are you doing?" He started to hyperventilate a little himself.

"Being persuasive," she grunted, in between blows.

Oh my god, we're going to die.

She pounded harder. He tried to breath regularly. "Are you sure that's going to do anything? It only works in the movies—"

But the shuddering whine of the engine cut him off, and she laughed triumphantly.

Holy shit, it actually worked.

"Hold on to something…." He pushed the accelerator to maximum—as high as it could go while running off auxiliaries, which was still capable of producing a dangerous amount of thrust if one was not properly secured.

She grunted as the fighter started to swivel. Zivic managed to get the belly of the craft aimed at the planet, and then point the nose, slowly, toward the horizon, and then above it. The roar from the engines overtook the roar of reentry, and the plasma lines began to whine in protest.

"Those things going to hold?" He risked a glance back at her.

"Yeah. If they don't I'll beat the shit out of them again," she said.

I think I like this one. "Ok, here we go. Things are about to get really rough."

"Rougher?"

"Touché." The accelerator depressed to maximum, and three g's of relentless force thrust him back into his seat. He heard her swear up a storm as she was mashed against the rear of the cockpit, and he prayed she managed to keep her limbs from falling down into the access plate or her bones would snap in an instant.

Ten seconds later, it was over. The red compression wave dissipated, and his instruments informed him that they'd achieved a stable orbit.

"Well," he began. "That's a supposedly fun thing that I'll never do again."

"You call that fun?" She pulled herself up to a sitting position from where she'd fallen after the thrust had cut out.

"If it means we get to live at the end, then yes." He looked all around the fighter at the area of space they were in. Bolivar appeared peaceful and blue below them, in contrast to the still expanding glowing wreckage of the former *Watchdog* Station. There was nothing salvageable. The reactor going critical was enough to heat every remaining particle of the slag cloud up past a few thousand degrees, and even through the thick composite glass of the cockpit windows he could feel the radiated heat from the debris. It was like a small, diffuse sun.

The woman, Sara, stared transfixed out the window, up at the glowing wreckage cloud. "I knew people there. It was my home." She murmured the words in a flat, monotone voice, as if still in shock and not believing what she was seeing. "They're all dead, aren't they? No one else made it out but us."

He frowned, his last memories of the escape from the station flooding back to him. "No, we weren't the only ones. There were two others. Two IDF guys, like me." He glanced back at her uniform. "Contractor, right?"

"Yeah. Shovik-Orion."

He nodded. That was the main commercial supplier of equipment to the station, especially the high-grade military stuff. The fighters, some of the station's armaments. The massive multi-world conglomerate had a few competitors, Howe-Wang Enterprises, Luminaris Corp, Blue Sky Development, but none of them were quite the "one-stop-shop" like Shovik-Orion.

That man. The one killed, execution style, by the murderers….

"Did you know a guy, another contractor there at the station, who was—" He tried to remember the man. Luckily, the adrenaline rushing through his brain at the time had etched every detail into memory like dynamite-proof stone. "Short, balding, a little goatee, talked like he was from Britannia—"

"Jerry Underwood? Yeah. Did you know him? Was he—" she paused, glancing up at the glowing slag set against the peaceful backdrop of stars.

"He's dead, yes." He wondered how much he should tell her. What he'd seen had the hallmarks of organized crime, or a large political-military-industrial conspiracy, or … something. Did he want to draw her into that? Did *he* want to get drawn into that? He followed her gaze up to the expanding cloud. Damn. He was already drawn into it. Both of them.

"He was shot." Zivic turned to her, watching the horror begin to spread over her face. "The two IDF guys I was talking about. They shot him point blank, right in the forehead, just a few minutes before I picked you up."

"Jerry," she began. "No. Why would someone do that? Are you sure you saw what you—"

"I'm sure. Look, Sara—" he paused, waiting for her last

name.

"Batak."

"Look, Sara Batak, I'm Ethan Zivic. IDF's in my blood. My mom was a fighter pilot before she died. Fought in the Second Swarm War. My dad too. He's a big shot IDF guy now, and knows lots of people high up. I think we need to go find him. I don't know who we can trust right now, after seeing those two officers blow away Underwood. They might be expecting to be the only survivors of that place, and wouldn't take kindly to, you know, witnesses."

Her face hardened. "You don't suppose there are more of them in IDF? Do you think they were lone wolves, or is this something bigger?"

He shrugged. "What with Sangre de Cristo a few weeks ago and the GPC insurgency? This could all be a part of that. And if they found out that there were witnesses to … whatever it was I witnessed … let's just say I think we should keep a low profile until we can figure out who we can trust."

"You don't think we should go down to CENTCOM Bolivar and report in?"

He shook his head. "I don't. I think we should go find my dad. Like I said, he's well connected—really high up at IDF, like probably an admiral by now, and … I trust him."

She eyed him with what he guessed was mild suspicion. "*Probably* an admiral? Trust him? You don't sound terribly convinced…."

That's because I'm not, he wanted to say. But that would be silly. Just because he had a bad relationship with his pops didn't mean the guy couldn't be trusted. *Bad* relationship wasn't quite the right term. *Nonexistent* would be better, though that would imply they hadn't had enough contact for the old jackass to disapprove of his son's career choices and general lack of turning out just like him.

"Nah, he's ok. He's an old war hero, and everyone trusts him. We need to find him, and tell him what happened. He'll know what to do with it. I just … after seeing Underwood get blown away by two guys in IDF uniforms, I'm not sure I trust anyone in an IDF uniform right now."

She was still in too much shock to argue. "You think he'll know what to do?"

He nodded, and pressed on the accelerator, aiming for one of the civilian rescue ships that had deployed into orbit, hard at work responding to the hundreds of civilian vessels that had been affected by the mysterious alien ship, and the subsequent blast of *Watchdog* Station. "He always knows what to do. Especially when it's someone else's problems."

Like mine.

CHAPTER FIFTEEN

Irigoyen Sector, Bolivar System, Ido
Bridge, ISS Independence

Flashes of the Second Swarm War erupted into Proctor's memory. All those artificial singularity devices the Swarm carriers launched at Earth, and dozens of other United Earth planets, devastated cities and killed hundreds of millions. Four months of horror, sacrifice, and unthinkable numbers of dead. And through it all, the fear that at any moment a Swarm fleet would appear suddenly over the next UE world, launching dozens of singularities towards the surface. Sucking billions of tons of matter in, then blasting outward, consuming entire cities in seconds. Even the most destructive thermonuclear weapon humanity had ever tested couldn't hold a candle to a single Swarm singularity device.

Which meant it was time to leave. Whatever was increasing the mass of Ido was … well, whatever it was, it was suspiciously and dangerously like what the Swarm had thrown at them before.

But the Swarm is dead, isn't it? I killed the last ship myself.

"Get us out of here. Now. Signal a general retreat. Everyone regroups at Bolivar."

Whitehorse looked up at the screen suddenly, as if expecting to see a new deadly threat. "Ma'am?"

Commander Yarbrough, who'd remained mostly silent throughout the engagement ever since the gruesome death of Captain Prucha, took a few steps to the center of the bridge. "What now?"

"Is the mass still increasing?" Proctor asked, without acknowledging the question.

Whitehorse nodded. "Another point zero zero zero zero one percent increase."

"Could the sensors be miscalibrated?" Yarbrough asked. "We did sustain heavy damage. There might be a trickle power buildup along the sensor array that could explain the readings."

Proctor shook her head and stood up, jabbing a finger towards the moon on the screen. "No. It did something to Ido. The moon's going to blow, and I want to be as far away as possible from it when it does. Ensign Riisa, now, please. Take us back to Bolivar." She punched the comm button on her armrest. "Ballsy, are the fighters in?"

"But how do you know that, Admiral?" continued Yarbrough, before Volz could respond from the fighter deck. "There's no indication whatsoever that Ido is going to explode. Is this just a hunch?"

She shot him through with a withering glance, full of annoyance. "Yes, Commander, it's called a friggin' hunch. You know how many battles I lived through thirty years ago? How many times Captain Granger and I had to rely on our hunches to get us through to another day? Twenty-three. Twenty-five if you count that first battle for Earth as three separate battles, which it sure as hell felt like. And I saw enough of those artificial singularity bombs to know that any time you see something's mass increase—especially in an inexplicable way like we see down there, then you get the hell out. Fast."

Volz's voice pierced through the conversation. "Yeah Shelby, we got everyone."

Proctor glanced one more time sidelong at Yarbrough. "We done?"

From his frustrated expression, it was clear he wasn't, but he gave a quick, exasperated nod. He apparently dealt with stress by fretting over numbers and specifics. But anal retention was not going to win them a war.

"Ensign, now please," said Proctor.

"Course, Ma'am?"

"Back to Bolivar. At least there we can watch and see whatever the hell is going to happen to this moon."

Ido continued rotating slowly beneath them, and then it was gone as they t-jumped away, replaced by a starfield, until the camera shifted towards Bolivar, and the wreckage of the IDF station that had just been slagged in orbit. Proctor let out a long, slow breath. *Safe for now.* "Now the damn thing's probably moved on to another system."

Ensign Riisa, young as she was, breathed deeply now that the immediate danger had passed, looking around the bridge erratically. She fixated on the stained ring of blood on the deck where Captain Prucha had fallen. "What do they want?" she murmured.

Proctor stared at the ring of blood along with her. "I don't know. But if it's the Swarm, or anything similar to the Swarm, then the answer is clear."

"They want us dead."

CHAPTER SIXTEEN

Irigoyen Sector, Bolivar System, Bolivar
High orbit

The intra-system comm traffic was a mess, with literally hundreds of ships disabled or underpowered from the havoc caused by both the mystery ship, the ensuing battle, and the explosion of *Watchdog* Station, and Zivic had a hell of a time getting through to the civilian rescue vessel *Miguel S. Urquiza*—a massive old colonial transport ship with a dozen cargo bays meant for moving large amounts of goods to sustain new colonies that hadn't reached self-sufficiency yet.

"That's what I'm telling you, ma'am, our inertial motivators are out, and we need to dock with you folks since we'll never be able to make it down to the surface—"

The traffic coordinator on the colonial ship interrupted. "I understand that, sir, but what I'm telling you is that space here is at a premium right now on the *Urquiza*, and that all military ships unable to reach the surface are advised to wait for the Bolivaran defense fleet to return, or hitch a ride on one of the other IDF ships in the vicinity."

She sounded snippy and curt, and Zivic imagined a boring administrator in a drab gray business suit in a drab gray bureaucratic office with drab gray furniture and ugly bare walls. "Look, Mrs....?"

"Chalmers. *Miss* Chalmers."

"Look, *Miss* Chalmers, we're not going to make it over here. Besides the motivator being out—" he glanced at Batak, with a questioning look, but she only shrugged. "Besides the motivator, ma'am, our life support is on the fritz. I'm not entirely convinced we're going to make it here...."

She sounded like a comm broadcast on auto-repeat. "I understand that, sir, but what I'm telling you is that space is at a premium, and strictly reserved for damaged civilian craft, of which we have quite a backlog, some in worse condition than you. You'll just have to hold on until—"

He rolled his eyes towards Batak, who rolled hers in return. She shared his disgust, apparently. And then it hit him —he'd been staring at the answer without realizing it. "*Miss* Chalmers. I neglected to mention that my shipmate here is a civilian. A contractor that was working at *Watchdog* Station. Surely *that* qualifies us to land?"

A pause.

The traffic coordinator's voice stayed the same—neutral and bland. "Landing approved. Stand by for approach vector and landing coordinates."

"Thank you," he said, with a tad more sarcasm than he intended, and flipped the comm off.

Batak rolled her eyes again. "All I could imagine was some drab gray business suit lady in some drab gray office with boring inspirational posters on the wall."

In spite of the shock of what they'd just gone through, he grinned—they were clearly on the same wavelength. "Marry me?"

She shook her head and held up a wagging finger. "Sorry, I only marry boring assholes. And then I divorce their asses when they don't buy me shit."

"Sounds like you've had a fun life." He eyed her again, she couldn't be older than twenty-five, tops. "Married already?"

"Twice. Divorced twice. Yeah, I know how to pick 'em." She shifted around on the floor behind the seat, trying to find a more comfortable position. "In all fairness, the second divorce was twenty-five percent my fault."

"Oh?" He pushed the fighter's controls along the approach vector that the civilian transport beamed to him.

"Well, I figure I was fifty percent responsible for the wedding, and zero percent responsible for the divorce, so that comes out to an even twenty-five."

"I'm not sure that math works out…."

She sighed in mock exasperation. "It never does."

The fighter settled into its approach vector, and Zivic switched it over to autopilot, letting the computer coordinate the details with the transport's computers. In spite of their lighthearted conversation, all he could think about was that poor contractor. Jerry Underwood. His body tumbling gently in the zero-g, blood streaming out of his forehead, forming a spiral as the corpse rotated. He knew he'd have nightmares about it the rest of his life.

"Look. We've got to figure this out. Until I know what's going on, I don't know who we can trust." He pulled up the computer and linked to the civilian network through the data connection with the transport. "Do you know what Jerry was working on?"

She shook her head. "He was one of the supervisors. I was just a grunt working on the shuttle bay deck."

"Hmm," he began, "I can't even find my pops. His location is classified. Hold on, let me switch over to the military network…."

She kept shaking her head intermittently. Damn, she was still in shock. "I just can't imagine why anyone would want to kill Jerry. He was such a nice guy. Never snapped at me. Was always helpful. Cheery. Smiling." She finally looked up at him. "Why? Who would do this?"

"Bad guys." He connected to the network and repeated the search. "Ok, looks like dad's location is even classified on the military network. Which means it's actually classified and not just protected info. He must be up to something big."

"You said his killers were wearing IDF uniforms?" she asked.

"Yep. That doesn't necessarily mean they were IDF," he paused, considering. "But … it probably does. No idea. Let's … let's just get over there, collect ourselves, maybe grab a drink, and then huddle."

"Huddle?"

"Yeah. Old football term. Something I did a lot—old pops loved making me play football."

"You don't like your dad, do you."

"Was it that obvious?" The fighter sailed past the shuttle

bay doors on the transport. "Ok, here we go. Prepare for landing. Might bump a little."

It did bump a little, but she looked like she weathered it ok. Once the fighter's engines powered down, he finally realized that his entire body had been tense, so he focused on relaxing. No sense in passing out once he jumped down from the hatch.

He hit the deck, and reached up to help Batak down. "There you go, watch your head there. That's it."

She landed with a grunt—she might be injured, so he made a mental note to get her to the transport's sickbay. In fact, she looked dazed. She'd probably need help checking in with the deck staff on duty. He turned to lead them to processing, and immediately stopped in his tracks.

Two security officers blocked his path. One of the men unholstered a gun, while the other brandished handcuffs. He heard Batak mumble under her breath. "It don't rain, but it shitstorms."

The man with the gun eyed him warily. "Lieutenant Ethan Zivic. You're under arrest. Please come with us immediately."

CHAPTER SEVENTEEN

Irigoyen Sector, Bolivar System, Bolivar
Bridge, ISS Independence

Damn. She'd been out of IDF for too long. Out of leadership and away from the requirements of being a leader. Away from the spotlight. Away from the need to inspire one's people, and to present a steady hand and firm guidance in the face of danger. Her people needed her.

And she needed them. She needed them to be their best, and they wouldn't be their best if they thought she was some old batty woman about to lose it. She rose slowly, confidently, out of her chair and turned to face her bridge crew before unleashing a rapid-fire list of orders. *Like riding a bicycle,* she thought, with an inward grin.

"Commence orbital scan. Look for survivors and dispatch shuttles to bring them in. Lieutenant Qwerty, get me the local IDF brass down on Bolivar. I need to know who was giving orders to the Bolivaran defense fleet, and if they were somehow connected to the mutiny. Commander Yarbrough, get the damn ship fixed. Stat. All crew are to be assigned to repair and recovery duties until further notice, with emphasis on *repair*—I want to be ready if that turd-waffle of a ship comes back. Ballsy," she rose her head to the comm microphones listening in, "I think you know what to do, Captain. I want you analyzing that ship—everything we've got on it—and hunker down with your boys and girls and figure out some combat strategy against that thing."

"You got it, ma'am," Ballsy said through the speakers.

She continued rattling off a list of commands, and she was heartened to see her crew spring into action as she gave them direction. None of these people had seen battle. None. Half of them weren't even born yet when Earth and its colonies had nearly been wiped out. She supposed she and Ballsy were the only ones who had been around during the Second Swarm War thirty years ago. Well, them and Captain Prucha, for all the good it had done him. *Dammit Prucha, you left me with a boat full of kids.* They had better be more mature than her classes full of snot-nosed pre-teens in post-teen bodies.

"Ma'am," began Lieutenant Qwerty, the single word drawn out into two syllables, "got Ad'mril Mullins on the line for you. He's the ranking IDF officer at CENTCOM Bolivar."

"Thank you, Lieutenant. Patch it through to the ready room," she said, retreating to a door off to the side of the bridge. She'd only spent a few minutes in there since stepping foot on the ship. She hadn't even packed any of her belongings to decorate the walls or desk, so the space was rather stark and bare. Not that she was the sentimental type for knick-knacks and odds and ends that just got in the way, but still, she supposed it was something a normal ship captain would do. Hell, she hadn't even had time to bring a picture of her brother's family to hang on her wall. She considered them her own family and had essentially adopted her brother's kids, even though he'd been happily married for decades. She could have at least brought a picture of them.

The thought reminded her of her main reason for being out there, at least, the main *unofficial* reason. "Danny," she murmured to herself. "Where the hell have you gotten yourself to?"

She sat down at the desk and waved the video comm on. "Admiral Mullins?"

A heavy-set middle-aged man flashed onto the screen. His gray mustache rested on his upper lip like a dead snail, his brow furrowed and wrinkled like a man who'd lost a lot of sleep. "Admiral Proctor, I see they've dragged you out of retirement, which I suppose means that IDF thinks we're fucked."

"Language, Admiral."

The other man snorted a quick chuckle, but became serious within seconds. "Proctor, you engaged the ship. Notice anything ... odd, about your crew when you did? About yourself?"

She nodded. "We're analyzing that now. Must be some sort of high-level EM interference with a modulation that was somehow able to couple with our ... well, with our brains." She shrugged, acknowledging the improbability of it all. And yet she'd felt it. They'd all felt it.

"Is that even possible?"

"We have several hundred witnesses up here that say it's possible, Admiral. And you've half a planetary defense fleet that went rogue on me. I think that speaks for itself."

He nodded, and his mustache bristled as he frowned. "And we've got about twenty million people down here that can back them up. Proctor, ever since that ship entered orbit a few hours ago, we've had massive social unrest. Riots. Violence. Arson. On a planet-wide scale. It's like something just ... exploded, in the minds of everyone down here, all at the same time. Even I was feeling it. Nearly bit the head off my chief of staff...."

"Is everyone ok? Looks like the effect is highly localized."

Admiral Mullins looked off-camera as if to receive a report, and nodded curtly at whoever was speaking to him. He turned back to Proctor. "A few thousand deaths across the planet—all told, it's remarkable that's all there were. And yes, I can confirm that the effect was localized. The areas most intensely affected were directly under the orbital path of the ship. But Shelby, riots happened everywhere. Bolivar isn't the most ... stable planet. Politically, I mean."

She frowned. "What *do* you mean?"

"Bolivar is a hotbed for GPC activity. Half of the Bolivaran Planetary Senate are GPC loyalists, and to be honest," he looked to his left, as if to check who was in the room with him, "I think half the ship captains of the planetary defense fleet are too."

Well that made sense, she thought wryly. Information that would have been far more helpful an hour earlier.

"GPC loyalists in IDF? Are you sure?"

"Well, no, I'm not sure. But there've been rumblings. Whispers. Not exactly of an uprising or mutiny or anything like that. But ... rumors. Messages I've seen that the senders weren't planning on me seeing seem to suggest that there's widespread discontent with UE's central authority, even among some of the IDF officers at CENTCOM Bolivar."

That was troubling. Why had Oppenheimer not told her anything about that? She'd remembered ten years ago that there were rumblings in the lower officer corps about the GPC, but nothing in the open. Especially not among her top admiralty and ship captains. "Do you think there's a deeper problem here? Or is it really just grumbling?"

Mullins shrugged. "A few weeks ago I'd have said it was nothing. But ever since Sangre…."

"The situation's inflamed," she finished for him.

"That's being generous. Sangre blew the lid off the pot. It changed everything. Where before we had simmering tensions between GPC separatists and UE loyalists, now we've got … well, not open fighting, but *tension* is too naive. Nine officers have been found dead in the last week, either in their quarters or some back alley in the city or on some hiking trail out in the suburbs. Violence against both sides is skyrocketing. This world is a powder keg, Admiral, along with half a dozen other worlds in the Irigoyen sector, if my sources are right."

"San Martin?"

He nodded. "That's basically the epicenter of the GPC organization. Bolivar is probably the second biggest, but the GPC's Secretary General lives on San Martin, they say, and half his shadow cabinet."

"Curiel? I'd heard he was dead. Assassinated by his own bodyguards."

Mullins chuckled. "Rumor. Probably spread by Curiel

himself to confuse IDF Intel. But my source swears she saw him two weeks ago, alive and well."

Proctor shook her head. She didn't have time for this—she wasn't a politician, and she wasn't an intelligence official. She just wanted to save her civilization from an existential alien threat, and hopefully find her nephew in the process.

She didn't have time for humans being humans.

"Admiral, while this is all very interesting, I think I'm the wrong person to be talking to. You need the chief of IDF intel out here. Get your heads together. But as for me, the *Independence* is out of here as soon as repairs are done, and I've completed a little mission of a personal nature planetside."

"Oh?" His eyebrows rose, questioning.

"My nephew. I think he's got a few friends down there I want to question. The thing is … he's missing."

He nodded. Almost as if he'd been expecting her to say it. "I know."

Her eyes narrowed. "How do you know?"

"Because, you know that source that told me she saw *Secretary General*—" he held up two sets of fingers as air quotes, "Curiel two weeks ago? Well my source happens to be Danny Proctor's girlfriend. I'm sorry, Shelby, but it looks like your nephew is a GPC pilot."

She opened her mouth, and closed it again, grasping at something to say. "Fuck," was all she could settle on.

"Watch your language, Shelby," he deadpanned.

CHAPTER EIGHTEEN

Irigoyen Sector, Bolivar System, Bolivar
Rescue ship Miguel S. Urquiza, High orbit

Zivic's mind was racing—staring down the barrel of a gun tended to have that effect.

"And ... you are?" He flashed a wide smile. *Nothing to see here, folks. Move along....*

"Bolivaran Intelligence Service," one of them said, pulling his badge out and flashing it too quickly to see. "We've been monitoring your movements and communications," he added, as if that answered everything, as if that automatically made Zivic guilty of whatever they were implying. "You'll come with us now, sir."

They advanced towards him, slowly. Zivic realized his hands were already in the air, automatically. It's amazing what one's body automatically does in response to threat, he thought.

Wait a minute ... Bolivaran Intelligence Service? What the hell is that?

To his surprise, someone moved in front of him, stopping their advance. It was Batak. Her arms were folded, and her face said *don't mess with me.*

"Bullshit," she said. "I know you. I seen you around the offices and warehouse, even up on station. You're Shovik-Orion. Security, right?"

The man with the gun looked taken aback, but quickly regained his footing. "Switched jobs a few months back. Come on. Let's go." He motioned with the gun towards one of the exits. Several people nearby had noticed the standoff, and were rushing away, making the man with the gun glance at them with what was clearly apprehension. They clearly did not want to be seen.

Thankfully, the deck officer of the transport approached. "Is there a problem here?" he said, angrily—as angrily as he dared to be with someone holding a gun. "Gentlemen, may I see your badges?"

While they were fumbling for their IDs, Zivic glanced around the giant cargo bay which had obviously been refitted in a hurry to serve as a shuttle hold for a rescue operation. Frightened people were stumbling out of their ships—merchant freighters, pleasure yachts, tourist corvettes, orbital transfer shuttles—and moving quickly towards the exits, ushered by flight deck staff to make room for the steady stream of newly arriving ships.

One particular shuttle stood out to him.

Holy shit.

It was the shuttle from the *Watchdog* Station. *Fenway*. The one the two murderers had escaped in. It was unmistakable.

The deck officer looked up from the IDs the "Intel officers" had handed him. "Everything looks to be in order. Mr. Zivic I suggest you cooperate. Don't give us any shit. Not on my deck." He took a few steps back, and seeing another commotion from the passengers of another merchant freighter he left.

The man with the gun smiled. "So, Lieutenant Zivic. Do we do this the easy way or the hard way? I'd greatly appreciate prefer the easy way, I don't want to see anyone else here get hurt. You're already responsible for enough death today."

Zivic's eyes darted to the shuttle again, and back to the gun, his mind racing furiously. Obviously, something was up. Not just *something*. This was conspiracy theory level shit here. The two men on board the *Watchdog* in IDF uniforms. These two guys in the uniforms of what was probably a completely fabricated organization. Batak claiming that at least one of them was a Shovik-Orion employee. The deck officer taking their side, though he supposed in his shoes, seeing the gun and not wanting a gunfight to erupt in the middle of a desperate rescue operation Zivic would probably do the same.

And the shuttle. *Fenway*.

His hands were still up, and he nodded. "The easy way, if you don't mind. Sara, if you'll excuse me—"

"No. Her too. She'll be investigated as an accomplice," said the man with the handcuffs.

Zivic allowed them to cuff him. They shoved him ahead, and Batak followed close behind, with the two men bringing up the rear, corralling them towards one of the exits.

Luckily, that exit lay just beyond the shuttle *Fenway*. As they passed it, he rammed into Batak with his shoulder, pushing both of them around the corner of the shuttle. "Open it and get in—FAST."

She was quick on the draw—he'd give her that. Without waiting even half a second, she'd punched the hatch controls. It was going to take at least five seconds for the hatch to open completely, so he needed to do something incredibly stupid to stall for time.

The gun, and the hands holding it appeared around the corner of the shuttle, and Zivic did his best imitation of a karate kick.

To his complete surprise, the gun went flying. *Holy shit, that only happens in the movies.*

But he didn't have time to pat himself on the back. The man who'd been holding the gun dashed for it as it slid away on the deck, and the other leaped to tackled Zivic. They both went down in a tangle of thrashing arms and legs.

He heard a solid thud, and his opponent went limp. Batak grabbed his arm, yanking him up the ramp, just as gunshots rang out, hitting the hatch next to his head in a hail of sparks. He dove in and rolled out of the way of the entrance as the door started to close—apparently Batak had managed to hit the controls again.

More gunfire, striking the opposite wall from the closing ramp, and then hitting the backside of the ramp itself as it sealed shut. He finally risked a glance back up at Batak, who stood there trembling, still holding the plasma welding torch she must have used on the other man's head.

"You keep that in your pocket?" he said with a lop-sided smile.

Damn, Zivic, now's not the time for flirting.

"I—" she began. She was trembling even more now.

He stood up, which was decidedly more difficult with handcuffs on than without. "Hatch locked?"

She nodded vigorously, eyes wide. He saw that her fingers were gripping the plasma welder so tight that her knuckles were white. He turned around and presented his handcuffed wrists to her. "Will that work on these?"

"Yeah," she said, snapping into the moment as she brought the torch to bear on his wrists.

"Don't cut my hands off, please, they're actually my best fea—"

The cuffs dropped onto the floor. Damn, she was good. "Wow, I hardly felt what you were doing." He rubbed his wrists.

"That's what she said."

He did a double take—she still looked half in shock, but the comment, combined with the slight wink, told him she'd be just fine. Maybe. Her hands were still trembling.

Freed from the cuffs, he ran for the navigation station cockpit. The shuttle was small, only a cockpit, three tiny crew quarters, a mess, and the cargo bay, which was little more than a glorified trunk. He'd only flown one a few times before—it was the last thing he flew before he lost his wings. He took a deep breath to ground himself before he slid into the pilot's seat. *You can do this, Zivic.*

"Hold on, we're making what you might call a quick getaway. Strap in."

He fired up the engines and skipped the pre-flight checklist, rather, he grabbed the controls and immediately lifted the shuttle off the deck, soared up high towards the ceiling to avoid hitting any refugees standing nearby, and shot through the shimmering blue field that held the atmosphere in.

"What the hell just happened back there?" she said.

He steered the shuttle away from the *Urquiza* and angled up towards the north pole of Bolivar. He had no idea where they were going, but he figured the fewer people that knew where he was, the better, and there was no better place to hide than over a magnetic pole of a planet. Especially one with such a strong magnetic field like Bolivar. It had been wreaking havoc with his regularly scheduled sensor scans aboard the *Watchdog* ever since he'd started his tour there. Now it was finally working in his favor.

"I don't know."

"What did you do on the *Watchdog*? Why are they trying to arrest you?"

He shook his head. Jerry Underwood spun helplessly in his mind, flinging blood in a slow spiral. It was a like a video on repeat. Spin, spin, blood, spatter, spin.

"I don't think it's what I did. I think it's what I saw."

CHAPTER NINETEEN

Irigoyen Sector, Bolivar System, Bolivar
Shuttle, Bolivar's stratosphere

A GPC pilot. Her little nephew. The one she'd bounced on her knees and played with on the beach and changed his diapers while she was stationed on Britannia as the fleet admiral of IDF. A pilot for the god-damned Galactic People's Congress. What the hell did people see in that gang of miscreants?

"Dammit, Ballsy, what the hell do people see in that gang of miscreants?" She stared fiercely at the screen on her hand unit. Volz looked back at her, shrugging. She puffed air out in frustration and glanced out the window of the shuttle as the compressed atmosphere glowed red with reentry.

"Freedom's a powerful word, Shelby," he began, before she cut him off.

"Freedom? How in the world is United Earth not free?

How can anyone possibly think that? Are they mistaking us for the Russian Confederation? The Caliphate? The CIDR?"

"I'm sure the Chinese would dispute your insinuations. But that's not the point Shelby."

"How is it not the point, Ballsy? Enlighten me." She was agitated, and treating him harsher than she meant, but he took it in stride, seeming to understand that the source of her consternation was not him, or even the GPC thugs, but that little boy she'd bounced on her knees.

"There are GPC people in all four nations. Not just UE. They're sick of us. They're sick of the international tensions and disputes. They see themselves as *the people*." He rolled his eyes as he put air-quote around *the people*.

"People my ass." The shuttle bounced in the upper atmospheric turbulence, and she glanced at the ETA timer on the pilot's dashboard. Five and a half minutes to Shovik-Orion City, Bolivar. *Shovik-Orion City*. Idiot corporations and their idiotic naming and branding schemes.

Her executive assistant, a young red-haired ensign with a noticeable bump on her lower abdomen, entered the cabin from the tiny galley, offering Proctor a steaming cup of tea. "Thank you, Ensign Flay."

Volz continued. "Have you been in a mining colony before, Shelby?"

"This isn't the twenty-second century anymore, Ballsy. Sure, humans did awful things to each other. Sure, the mining colonies out on Ceres and Vesta and all the other Asteroid belt settlements were scandalous, ugly affairs. But that was five hundred years ago."

Volz shrugged again. "Uh huh. But tell that to people

living in mining colonies today. Yeah, they're not necessarily starving, or growing up with chronic bone deformities because of the low-g. But you ask any iridium miner whether he actually wants to be there, guess what you're going to hear? You ask some farmer out on Cadiz whether they want UE bureaucrats two hundred lightyears away on Britannia deciding the finer details of harvest equipment certifications. You ask Russian merchants on Syrene if they want a distant Russian Confederation government telling them what they should be paying in taxes just because they live on the wrong side of their own city."

"Then they can leave! They can move on and go farm somewhere else. Or sign up for IDF. Or go on the dole if they want. Seriously, my taxes are high enough that half of UE could be living like kings if they didn't throw it all away on post-Swarm War defensive posturing."

Ballsy's eyes narrowed. "Oh come on Shelby, you were the architect of half those programs—"

"Like hell. It was all President Singh. I was constantly telling him the Swarm was gone. I killed the last ship, after all, and my Skiohra contacts assured me that they could detect nothing through their mental meta-space link—the Ligature, or whatever they call it. The Swarm was dead. There was no reason to spend ninety-five percent of our friggin' galactic budget on defense if all there was to defend against was each other."

Ballsy fell quiet, looking at her intensely through the comm device on her lap. "So then what the hell was that thing out there? That ship?"

She paused, thinking. Considering. It just didn't *feel* like the

Swarm. The Swarm was relentless. Overpowering. Almost bloodthirsty. So far, the best descriptor she had for this mysterious ship was … erratic. "I don't know."

"You think it's the Swarm?"

She slowly shook her head. "No."

"Me either. Look, you go find your nephew. I've got my pilots here in the conference room and we're poring over the vids and scans, designing appropriate attack measures and defensive postures, and I've borrowed some of your bridge tactical folks and we're doing the same with them, figuring out how the *Independence* itself should respond next time. When you face them again, you'll have some options."

She smiled. "Thank you, Ballsy. I'm glad you're with me on this one. After seeing Jeremy go like that…."

He nodded. His face was taut, as if he were trying desperately not to feel. Not to hurt. "Prucha was a good man. Let's make sure no more join him. Volz out."

His face winked out from the comm, and she settled in for the rest of the descent. She prepared herself to meet this woman, this mystery person that Admiral Mullins claimed was Danny's girlfriend. This woman who'd apparently been in such a position that she'd not only seen the so-called Secretary General Curiel of the GPC, but also been in a position to report it to Mullins. What the hell was she, an intel agent? She supposed she'd soon find out—Mullins had arranged a meeting, and Proctor was on her way to CENTCOM Bolivar in Shovik-Orion City to talk to her in a briefing room. And finally get some answers about her nephew.

Ensign Flay had strapped in and was on her comm device coordinating Proctor's security with the marine office at

CENTCOM Bolivar. Eventually she shut the device down and nodded over at her. "All set, Admiral."

"Thank you, Ensign Flay." Her eyes dropped down momentarily to her abdomen. "Congratulations."

"Oh," the ensign replied, blushing slightly. "Thank you. Seven months went fast. Maternity leave starts next week, if you were wondering. Sorry you'll have a disruption in your staff—I'll train my replacement well and make sure it's as painless as—"

Proctor held up a reassuring hand. "It's all right, Ensign. Life happens. And besides, this is a short term assignment for me anyway. I won't even be here next week."

The young ensign looked relieved. Proctor reviewed a few administrative items with her, and before long the ETA timer had ticked its way down to zero. She unstrapped herself from the seat and descended the shuttle's ramp.

"I'll be with you shortly, ma'am. I need to hand off the shuttle to the guard," said Flay from the cockpit.

Proctor nodded her approval and continued down to the landing pad where she met an aide to Admiral Mullins who had come with a marine honor guard. They indicated towards the entrance to the massive CENTCOM building from the landing pad, where two more guards stood at attention.

And suddenly, the guards were no longer standing.

They were flying.

Flames gutted windows all around them and the doors blasted outward in a jarring explosion. Proctor touched her forehead and her hand came away red. She didn't realize until moments later that she was lying on the ground several meters past the shuttle from where she'd been walking.

Don't pass out … don't pass out….

CHAPTER TWENTY

Irigoyen Sector, Bolivar System, Bolivar
Shuttle Fenway, High orbit

"What do you mean, they're following us?"

Zivic eyed the sensor readout, pointing at the map of the surrounding space in their orbit over Bolivar. Transponder codes and insignia from hundreds of different ships dotted the schematic, but the main one, the biggest one, had changed course and was headed straight towards them on an intercept course.

"That's what I'm saying. The *Urquiza* is on our tail. And if those two *Bolivaran Intelligence Officers*"—he made some air-quotes with his fingers—"are any indication, there's clearly some people that want us off the board. And they're high up enough to redirect Bolivar's main emergency response ship. That spells trouble if I ever saw it."

She shook her head in disbelief. "I just don't get it. So you saw a guy get offed. I mean, that's really bad. Sure, it's murder. But let's face it, the entire station exploded. You'd think the authorities would have bigger fish to fry here."

What's the connection, Zivic?

"What?" she said.

He hadn't realized he'd murmured the question under his breath. "Sorry. Just ... what's the connection? Two IDF officers blow a guy away, on a station that's just been hit by a mysterious ship and is about to go critical, they steal a shuttle, which later shows up on the relief cruiser. Then two different guys working for a phony intel service try to kill me—"

"Shovik-Orion," she murmured.

"What?"

"That's the only connection. Shovik-Orion. Jerry Underwood was a Shovik-Orion employee. And I swear at least one of those goons back there was too. At least, I think he was. There's been tons of staffing changes lately. Lots of new people. Lots of old hands getting pink slips. New managers, same old shit."

He shrugged, eyeing the schematic map warily. It would take the *Urquiza* a while to spin up its engines enough to change course, and their shuttle had a good head start, but the massive colonial transporter had more thrust than they did, and, most likely, a few hidden rail guns.

"What the hell would a corporation want with me? Why would they kill the contractor? You don't think they have anything to do with the alien ship, do you? I mean, *you* work for Shovik-Orion, right? You'd have heard ... something."

"Well, yes and no. I'm technically with a sub-contractor. Snell Staffing corp." She pointed to a tiny name badge on her chest, which had been obscured by a rip in the fabric. It displayed her name, Sara Batak, along with a little company logo made up of two intertwined S's surrounded by a larger C.

He frowned, and brought up the shuttle's computer. "Those two IDF guys were looking for something. The contractor—Jerry—claimed it was on board the shuttle. Go check the hold, will you?"

The restraints across her chest and hips fell away as she sprang out of her seat and ducked out of the cockpit. It seemed that, with something to finally do, she had some pent-up energy. An outlet for the nervousness and stress that came from being shot at. And almost exploded.

"Nothing," she called back from the tiny cargo hold. "It's empty."

"No hidden panels or anything?"

She reappeared in the cockpit. "In a T-39? These things are built for space efficiency. No hidden panels, no compartments under the floor. Nada."

"So you're saying this thing ain't built for smugglers. Fine, so whatever was here is gone. Those two IDF assassin guys made off with it." He scanned the computer logs for the shuttle's most recent ports of call. Usually the shuttles on *Watchdog* were used to transport crew members on and off station, and it relied on the contractors like Shovik-Orion to shuttle their own supplies and materials on their own transport ships.

But there was always a chance he was wrong.

"Looks like the last time this thing left the Bolivar system it went to San Martin," he said, running through the logs.

"Makes sense," she said. "It's the center of power here in

the Irigoyen sector, center of commerce, yada yada."

"Then that's where we're going." He glanced at the schematic map to check up on the *Urquiza* trailing them. Sure enough, it was catching up. He did a scan of the ship, and just as he thought, he saw that an exterior panel had retracted, revealing the unmistakable profile of a rail gun. It was still in the process of swiveling towards them. "And there's our cue to leave."

He entered the coordinates for San Martin into the q-jump drive computer and confirmed that the cap banks were full. "Shuttle's caps are small, so should take us a few dozen jumps to get out there. Settle in for a good nap. With any luck, I can tap into CENTCOM San Martin when we get there and find out where my pops is."

"You really think he can help us? If this is some kind of IDF, Shovik-Orion, GPC, alien conspiracy thingie, what good can one guy do against *that*?"

"Don't know." He pushed the initiator button when the q-jump computer indicated it was ready. The view out the front window port adjusted. The green-blue of Bolivar disappeared along with the approaching *Urquiza*, replaced by the blackness of deep space. "But he knows people. And *they* know people." He glanced at her. She didn't look convinced. "At this point, what other choice do we have?"

CHAPTER TWENTY-ONE

Irigoyen Sector, Bolivar System, Bolivar
Hutchins Memorial Hospital, Room 1400

When she woke up, Proctor was a little surprised to see Admiral Mullins standing over her. Who the hell had let him in her quarters? She'd have to have a stern talk with her marine detachment. But not before getting something for the splitting headache.

It was the searing pain that finally jogged her memory. She was not in her quarters. She was in a hospital in Shovik-Orion City.

"What the hell happened, Tim?" she murmured, rubbing her forehead.

A wrinkled frown bloomed down Mullins's face. "Tim?"

Oh, damn, she thought. "Sorry, Ted. Old habit. Last time I was this injured, it was…."

Mullins nodded. "On the *Warrior*. With Captain Granger."

"Yes." *That blast must have hit her hard.* She forced her eyes open and blinked a few times. "Please tell me that wasn't a bomb."

"It wasn't a bomb."

She looked at him incredulously, then glanced around at the other beds in the intensive care unit, all of them full.

"Bull," she replied.

"It was a well-timed power surge, that triggered a cascade buildup and subsequent failure in the internal cap banks at CENTCOM. We rely on our own power of course, and not the city's grid, and it looks like in this case it bit us rather firmly in the ass."

"You're telling me it was an accident?"

He looked down at her gravely, slowly shaking his head. "No. I'm not."

Shit. She repeated the word in her head like a mantra. She was desperately trying to deal with a potentially civilization-ending threat embodied by a mysterious, unthinkably powerful ship, while simultaneously trying to find her lost nephew. She didn't have time to deal with saboteurs and malcontents.

"Who the hell was it then?"

He sat down in the chair next to her bed. "We're still trying to figure that out. Whoever it was, they had long-term access to CENTCOM's power systems, and the expertise to pull this off under the radar, right under our noses. *And* the expertise to keep us from immediately being able to know who it was—they've covered their tracks like regular pros."

"Speculate then." Proctor glanced around for a nurse or the attending physician—the pain was subsiding, but her back ached, and she wanted a rundown of her injuries before she duly ignored the sound medical advice and returned to the *Independence* to save civilization as they knew it.

"GPC loyalists. Who else could it be?"

"Are they that brazen already?"

"Extremists always are. What zealot ever waits until it's prudent to act? They always jump at the chance to make a big splash and catch everyone's attention."

She frowned. "Zealot? What do you mean?"

Mullins shrugged, and hesitated a moment before continuing. "I have reason to believe that this is not just GPC. There might be a Grangerite element to this."

She rolled her eyes. "Oh, you've got to be kidding me."

"You don't think some of them would be capable?"

She shook her head, and caught the eye of the doctor at another bed across the room, waving him over. "It's not that they're not capable, it's just I still can't believe that, A, there are Grangerites to begin with, and B, that any of them would leave their temples or churches or underground lairs or whatever the hell they have, long enough to plan something like this."

"You've had thirty years to get used to the idea of Grangerites, Shelby."

"And I had four months before that to get used to the idea that Tim Granger was a human being. Not some kind of goddamned prophet. Seriously, if you'd seen him like I saw him, knew him like I knew him, you'd realize the absolute absurdity of it—"

He held up his hands defensively. "Hey, no need to convince me of their lunacy. But just because we think they're lunatics for worshipping a bloke we all knew, praying that he comes back to save us all and bring us candy and unicorns, doesn't mean we shouldn't take them seriously. At least their potential threat."

"What do you mean? They're ignoramuses. The only dangerous thing about ignoramuses is when they vote for ignoramuses. And last time I checked there weren't any Grangerite candidates in any elections that matter."

"All I'm saying is that—well, I've just heard things. Rumors. That something big is going to happen, or has happened, or is happening. Something that the true zealots are excited about. And then this explosion happens. Right as you show up. Coincidence?"

"But Ted, who the hell would want to kill me?"

The attending physician finally arrived at her bed and looked questioningly at Mullins, as if expecting him to leave. He stood up, but touched Proctor's elbow and leaned down towards her ear. "I'm not sure it was *you* they were trying to kill."

Her eyes grew wide, and she knew what he was going to say before he said it.

"Fiona Liu? Your nephew's girlfriend? She's dead."

CHAPTER TWENTY-TWO

Irigoyen Sector, Interstellar space
Shuttle Fenway

Zivic wondered how anyone could stand interstellar travel in a ship with such a small q-jump cap banks, and when he thought about it too much it gave him a sense of almost overpowering vertigo.

"You never think about how empty it is out here until you're in it," he murmured, staring out the port at the endless stars.

"Huh?" Batak stirred, and opened her eyes. *Oops*, he thought, not realizing she'd dozed off.

"Space. Interstellar space. It's just so ... empty. Think about it. If that cap bank fails, we're fifty-thousand years from the nearest star at full thrust. We lose the cap banks and the meta-space transmitter in one go? Then here we are, stuck for the rest of our lives, on this shuttle."

"The rest of our very *short* lives," she said, closing her eyes again and leaning back. "Only so much food the material reprocessors could make out of our shit."

He squirmed at the thought. Luckily the console beeped to distract him. "Coming up on q-jump number three hundred and fifty-two. Eight-hundred and eleven to go. Only eight hundred and ten if we decide to stop off at El Amin."

"Huh?"

"Farthest planet out in San Martin's solar system. They might have a supply depot there," he added, looking back up through the port to stare at the abyss. "It's like walking on a tightrope. Over a bottomless cliff. One wrong step, and pow, you're falling forever, never dying until you have a heart attack or starve."

"Huh?" she repeated. "You're starting to worry me with all your morbid talk."

"I wonder if this is what it was like for Granger."

"Huh?"

He was starting to wonder if that was her only response when she was trying to sleep.

"You know, as he was falling into that black hole."

She grunted. "Falling? I thought he was aiming."

A smile tugged at his lips. "Heh. Right. Swarm never knew what hit 'em."

She shifted in her seat, eyes still closed, trying to get comfortable. "Assuming he actually hit them."

"What do you mean?"

"Well, as of a few weeks ago, he was still technically falling in. Hadn't even crossed the event horizon yet, from our perspective. So my question is, how did that actually stop the

Swarm from sending meta-space signals out of that black hole from their own universe, if Granger hadn't even fallen in yet and blew them to smithereens with the anti-matter aboard the *Victory*? And what was the plan, anyway? There's a lot the higher-ups never told us. I think they're covering up something, if you ask me."

He blew a puff of air in disbelief. "What, you're not a Grangerite, are you? Or a conspiracy theorist?"

A wry smile crossed her lips, even though her eyes stayed closed. "Right, because conspiracies *never* happen. Just ask Jerry Underwood."

He shrugged. *Touché.*

"And no, I'm not a Grangerite. Those people are a little mentally disturbed, if you ask me," she murmured. "But ... my brother-in-law is. My sister and he were Methodists. She still is, and the kids, but he started falling in for the Grangerite stuff a few years ago. But he was always a little whacked."

"I just don't understand how they can deify a guy like that. Dad always talked about him. Granger. Said he was just this regular dude. A bloke, as mom called him. And now these freaks are turning him into a god. Seriously? Welcome to the twenty-seventh century, people."

"Meh. Catholics do it all the time."

"Huh?" Now it was his turn for the *huhs*.

"You know. Saints, and all that."

"Oh. Right. Still, at least they...." He trailed off, wondering what point he was about to make.

"At least they what?"

"You know. At least they've got almost three thousand years of precedent and history behind them. They've been making people saints for millennia. And Jesus is, like, you know, ancient history. There's some historical heft there. Same with Mohammed and Buddha and whatever religion you want. But Granger? We've got video of him. People are still alive that knew him. How do you make a god out of that? Especially now? You know, in the present? Modern society, modern culture, and all that?"

"I'm sure people living around Jesus and Mohammed and Buddha thought the same thing."

"Yeah, and what happened to them?"

She shrugged. "They either all converted, or were killed, I guess."

"Well *that's* a wonderful thought."

Her eyes still closed, she flashed a devious smile. "So, would you rather lose q-jump engines in interstellar space in a shuttle, or convert to Grangerism?"

He chuckled. "Depends. Can I bring a deck of cards on the shuttle? Or at least a multi-level marketing sales presentation pamphlet? Then I choose the shuttle."

The console beeped again. "Ladies and gentlemen, prepare for jump number three hundred and fifty-three," he announced.

She grunted. "You know, I'm trying to sleep here."

"Fine, I'll shut up."

She smiled, and snuggled down further into her seat.

"But before I do—"

She frowned.

"—Help me think through this. What could be so important that someone would kill for it, right in the middle of a battle, when the station is about to explode?"

She shrugged. "Chocolate?"

"I'm serious here."

"So am I. Are you going to let me sleep, or not?"

He sighed. "Just thought it might be important to think about, seeing how someone's trying to, you know, kill us because we already know too much about it."

"Not much we can do about it now, can we? In case you hadn't noticed, we're kinda in interstellar space…."

He ignored her. It was crucial that they figure this out, and not only to save their own necks. It just … felt wrong. There was far more riding on this than just a few hired goons shooting at them. Something big was happening. Or was about to happen.

"It was either a weapon, or … or evidence about something. Evidence of some conspiracy or wrong-doing or whatever. The guy—Underwood—kept on calling it *it*. So it's a singular item, not a collection of things, unless *it* meant like a crate with lots of stuff in it. Or maybe—"

"You're not even making any sense," she mumbled.

"I wonder if its connected to Sangre."

She frowned. "I'm not good with Spanish. Blood?"

"Sangre de Cristo."

"Oh. You think it was another nuke? Aren't those, you know … conspicuous?"

He nodded. "Well yeah, especially since they're banned."

He bolted upright, then stood. She finally opened her eyes. "What? What is it?"

"If it was a nuke, we can tell." He dashed out of the cockpit, and she rolled out of her seat to follow him. As if reading his mind, she grabbed the engine diagnostic toolkit and pulled out the general-purpose scanner.

"What band?" she asked, fiddling with the handheld device.

"Gamma band. That's the one that will detect any leftover radioactive signature."

She nodded, frustratedly. "Sorry, I should know that."

"You're good." He worried about her—it was clear she was still in a little shock from the previous day's traumatic events, in spite of her show of bravado and humor.

She went into the cargo hold, and waved the detector back and forth across the floor, over the walls, up to the ceiling.

He waited. Patiently. *Dammit, hurry the hell up!*

"Ok, looks like—"

She paused.

"And?" he asked.

"Nothing. No leftover radioactive signature."

He sighed. "Well, it was worth a shot." He started heading back to the cockpit.

She wasn't moving. "Wait. I'm reading something, though."

He stopped in the doorway. "What is it?"

Her eyes went wide. "I have no idea."

CHAPTER TWENTY-THREE

*Irigoyen Sector, Bolivar System, Bolivar
Bridge, ISS Independence*

The doctor had recommended bed rest and observation for a day in the hospital, followed by a week of recuperating at home, along with pain meds and reconstructive enzyme therapy for the torn ligament in her right leg and some frightfully large orange pill as a precaution against hemorrhaging because of her concussion. Proctor had smiled, thanked her, and told her to go to hell when the doctor protested her getting out of bed and boarding her shuttle back up to the *Independence*.

"Admiral on the bridge!" called out one of the marines at the entrance as she hobbled through—*damn, was she hobbling?*

Commander Yarbrough looked up suddenly from the XO's station. "Admiral? Are you feeling well enough to continue with the mission?"

"Am I dead?"

Yarbrough's eyes narrowed slightly. His reply was slightly hesitant. "No?"

"Then we're continuing the mission. Prepare for t-jump. Any new sign of the mystery ship?"

He shook his head, then glanced at tactical, and Lieutenant Whitehorse flashed a quick thumbs-down. "No, Admiral, no sign of it. All systems in this sector are on the lookout, and have express instructions to report to us by meta-space signal if anything changes." He hesitated again. "Uh, ma'am, where exactly are we t-jumping to if we have no contact with the alien vessel?"

Proctor, trying not to limp too much, walked to her chair and eased herself into it. *Dammit, seventy-year-old bodies and torn ligaments don't mix very well.* "San Martin."

"What's on San Martin?"

She snapped her head towards him with an impatient glare. "Our destination."

Yarbrough nodded nervously. "I'm sorry, Admiral, I didn't mean to sound impudent, if that's how I came across. It's just Fleet Admiral Oppenheimer has been insistently, uh, *badgering* would be the wrong word, but he's been following our progress very closely—"

"Wait, Oppenheimer's been in touch with you?"

Yarbrough looked uncomfortable. "Yes, ma'am. Meta-space messages."

Interesting. Oppenheimer was keeping tabs on her. Through her own XO, no less. "Very well. Keep me apprised of what he says, and if CENTCOM Omaha has any new info for us on the extrapolated origins of this thing. Oh—" she turned to face him fully. "And see what you can find out on the GPC."

"Ma'am?"

"You know. What Oppenheimer and his people are doing about it. What the political climate at CENTCOM is. If their reach has extended up into the chain of command, I want to know about it. See what Oppenheimer's opinion of them is. His *real* opinion—he and I are not exactly conversation buddies."

"Yes, ma'am." Yarbrough turned back to his station, but paused as if he had more to say.

"Spit it out, Commander."

The man actually looked sheepish. "You don't suppose Oppenheimer is sympathetic to the GPC, do you?"

Proctor glanced sidelong at the rest of the bridge crew out of the corner of her eye. She could see Lieutenant Whitehorse sit up a hair straighter. Ensign Riisa cocked her head slightly. Proctor knew that gossip, especially the juicy, political kind, was the life-blood of a crew, even in wartime. Hell, especially in wartime—people just seemed to need something to distract them from the awful realities of life. And death.

"No, I don't," she replied quickly. Maybe too quickly. "Ready room. Now." She pointed to the door off to the side and grunted as she pushed herself to a standing position. Damn leg. She resented it already.

She hobbled into the ready room, making no effort to hide the limp this time, all pretense of being the picture of health for her crew forgotten. The door slid shut behind them. She turned to face the commander, her eyes flared open wide. "Commander Yarbrough, on this ship, on my bridge, we do not openly speculate about the political leanings of our commanding officers. Period. Is that clear?"

Yarbrough cowered. *Cowered.* "Sorry, Admiral. I'm … sorry. I didn't think that combat would affect me as much as … well, as much as it did."

Proctor's face softened a bit. She was being too hard on him. On all of them. None of them, save Ballsy, had actually been in combat before.

Though, neither had she, when the Swarm attacked out of the blue, thirty years ago. Swarm behavior and biology had been her doctoral thesis, and even she had been taken by surprise. She had been sure the Swarm was on a hundred and fifty year activity cycle, and that, seventy-five years after their first attack humanity was safe for another seventy-five. Humanity should have enjoyed seventy-five more years of security, time to build before the next attack.

As it turns out, the sense of safety was false, and Proctor swore to never again be lulled away into a feeling of false security. But it was one thing to live through all that, and another to be ready for it all to happen again. These people, her crew, never had that. They only had their history books. Stories of bravery. Cultural legends of heroism, loss, and sacrifice. They'd all lost relatives in the war, but it was already distant enough to be out of living memory for anyone under fifty.

"It's ok, Commander. I was the same way in your position, thirty years ago."

He did a double-take. "You were?"

No, I wasn't. I was a frickin machine.

"Yes, believe me. You're doing fine." His face told her he

still didn't believe her, so she waved him over to the desk and sat down, pointing to the other chair. She reached over to the teapot that she'd asked Ensign Flay to have ready and hot at all times, and poured them both a cup. "I was Captain Granger's new XO—"

"The Hero of Earth," interjected Yarbrough, accepting the cup of tea.

"The Hero of Earth, yes. Though you'd be surprised that the Hero of Earth had his moments. He doubted. Agonized over what to do. It was hit or miss there for awhile. Mostly miss. But anyway, I was his new XO, and my job—given to me by your grandmother by the way—was to decommission the *Constitution. With Granger still on it.* Can you imagine?"

"She didn't!" said Yarbrough, with an amused air, his brow furrowed in disbelief.

"She did. But I was up-and-coming, let me tell you. I was going to have my own command if it killed me, and I saw that as my opportunity to prove myself to old Admiral Yarbrough. I mean, if she could trust me with such a … bold assignment, then she could sure as hell trust me with my own little cruiser. And so I went aboard the *Constitution*, and I was a ball-buster, taking names, blazing a trail that would have gotten me kicked off any other ship under any other captain."

"The Hero of Earth was pretty magnanimous, then?"

She snorted. "Magnanimous? Tim? He was as crotchety as they come. I'd only been aboard a few days and he was thinking about air-locking me."

"Why didn't he?" Yarbrough leaned in closer, sipping his tea.

"The Swarm saved me, ironically enough. Once it became

clear what we were up against, my job—my only job—was to enable Tim to win. He was my captain, and, while he wasn't the greatest, most inspirational leader around, he had grit, and he had what all of us need in a situation like that. He was a survivor. He wasn't going to go quietly. He was going to do anything—*anything*—to stop the Swarm and win. I recognized that in him instantly, and so I made it my job to make his job do-able. I ran the ship. I organized the repair crews, the ordnance and reload teams, the fighter jocks, the ops teams, the science team, the … well, you name it. I slept about two hours a night for those four months, and aged twenty years in the process. And in the end, we did it. Tim did it. We won."

"Not without a huge cost, though," he added. "Granger piloted the *Victory* into the black hole the Swarm was coming through, to shut it down."

"He did. And saved us all in the process."

"Some say he's still there. That he'll come back some day." Yarbrough finished his tea and set the cup down.

"Grangerites, yes. They need their messiah, whether it's Jesus or Buddha or, in this case, a man who finished his day by collapsing onto his couch, farting up a storm, and scratching off his bunions with his thumbnail."

"Is it even possible? Can he come back? Technically he hasn't even crossed the event horizon yet…."

"Actually, he has. As of a month ago." She took a sip of tea. "The light coming off of the *Victory* finally red-shifted down into the radio waves, and once the wavelength of those waves stretches out to be greater than the width of the event horizon, then he's truly crossed it, from our perspective. At least, that's what the theoretical physicists say. No, he can't come back. He's gone. Forever."

She finished her own tea and leaned forward again, touching Yarbrough's forearm amiably. "Commander, I need you. The point of all that is to say: I need you. Granger was nothing without me. And without you, I likewise can be nothing. As captain and XO, we depend on each other, absolutely and irrevocably, like no other relationship, especially in wartime. We live for this moment, right here. The moment when our entire civilization depends on us."

Yarbrough nodded, with what Proctor interpreted as the man's best show of confidence. "Yes, ma'am. I'll do the best I can."

"Can I trust you?"

Without blinking, he nodded. "Yes."

"Good. Because this threat is like nothing I've ever seen. Twenty-five years ago, when the order came down from President Singh to go and annihilate the last trace of the Swarm, or rather, the liquid beings that the Swarm had usurped for use in our galaxy as the vehicle of their influence in our plane of existence, I was ambivalent. Torn, really. I was being asked to commit genocide. And, regrettably, I did not have an XO at the time that I could trust, that I could depend on to help me make the right decision."

Yarbrough shifted in his seat uncomfortably. "I'm sorry to hear that, ma'am. So your mission failed?"

"Failed? Of course not. It was a rousing success. I utterly destroyed the last few remaining Swarm carriers, and razed the surfaces of the planet the liquid beings called their home. And my XO was there, encouraging me to go through with it, just as CENTCOM wanted him to."

"Then what was wrong with him?"

"What was wrong with him is that, ever since then, I have the sneaking suspicion that I made the wrong choice. I committed genocide against a race that was as much a tool of the Swarm as the Russian Confederation had become. Would it have been right to utterly destroy the Russian Confederation? Every last man, woman, child? Of course not. But that's what I did to the Liquid Swarm. And I should have been able to depend on my XO to see the situation clearly, and urge me to make the right choice. He didn't. And I've lived with that decision every day since. I have to look myself in the mirror at night with that knowledge." She looked up at him. "I pray you never have to do that."

Yarbrough leaned back in his chair, seemingly at a loss for words.

"And years later, that XO succeeded me as the fleet admiral of IDF. Admiral Oppenheimer knows my views on this subject, and I've told him that, given the choice, I will not destroy our enemy if I can help it. I will stop them, but I won't destroy them. At least, not without knowing their true nature. If it turns out that they are evil personified, then fine. Bam. I'll rain fiery death on them relentlessly. But, with the exception of the Swarm, I've never encountered any being of unmitigated evil like that. And I want to know that, when the moment comes, when the time of decision is at hand, that you'll have my back, and be my conscience." She reached out again and gripped his forearm. "I need to know you'll help me make the right decision this time."

Yarbrough shook his head. Maybe a little too quickly. Oh well, he'd learn. Just like she did. "I will, Admiral. I'll do my best. You can count on me. Though, Admiral....?"

"Yes?"

"If we're going to trust one another, completely, like you've so eloquently suggested, I'd really like to know why we're going to San Martin. It's in the same sector, sure, but we have no reason to believe that the mystery ship went there...."

"Right. I'll admit, there is a personal aspect to going there. My nephew is missing."

He paused, and his brow furrowed, as if he were making quick mental calculations. "I see. I'm sorry. But is this really the time—"

"It is. I have reason to believe that there is a connection between his disappearance and the recent terrorist action on Sangre de Cristo."

He frowned. "That's all well and good, but my question stands: what does that have to do with the alien ship?"

She smiled. "Good. You're doing your job. Calling me on my shit. Good. You're right, there is no obvious connection. But call it a hunch. Terrorists managed to get their hands on a nuclear missile and destroy one of the habitation domes on Sangre de Cristo, by all accounts a peaceful world, who, in spite of their GPC leanings, have never presented IDF with any problems. At the same time, a mysterious ship appears and wreaks havoc in several systems nearby. Coincidence? Maybe. But I think there's more here than meets the eye. So we're doing what I do best."

Yarbrough smiled. "Saving Earth?"

Yarbrough puffed a breath of air in exasperation. "Figuring shit out. Saving Earth was Granger's job."

"I'm with you, Admiral. I've got your back. You figure this

out, and I'll keep the ship running for you."

"Good." She nodded, and stood up. He followed her to the door to the bridge, where she paused. "So to address the reason we came in here, yes, it's true, I don't have the best relationship with Admiral Oppenheimer. I feel like he failed me at a critical moment in my life. But he's a good man, and a good admiral. One of IDF's finest. We can't be publicly questioning his loyalty in front of the crew. Understood?"

"Yes, ma'am. Sorry, it won't happen again."

She smiled, and touched his elbow again, before striding—limping—back onto the bridge. "Ensign Riisa, are the t-jump calculations complete?"

"Yes, Admiral."

Proctor sat down. "Then get us there, Ensign."

"Aye, aye, Admiral."

"Admiral?" Commander Yarbrough had taken his seat at the XO's station and strapped himself in for the jump. "Shall I update Admiral Oppenheimer on our progress?"

"Yes, Commander, please."

She held on to her armrests in preparation for the t-jump. Her stomach quivered, a moment of vertigo came and went, and when she looked back up at the viewscreen, the view of Bolivar had been replaced with the tranquil San Martin rotating beneath them, blue and green and safe, for now, from the dangers Bolivar and Sangre de Cristo had been facing in the very same sector.

Now to find the connection.

"Where the hell are you, Danny?" she whispered under her breath, to no one in particular.

CHAPTER TWENTY-FOUR

Irigoyen Sector, Bolivar System, Bolivar
Bridge, ISS Independence

Commander Yarbrough released the seat restraint that chafed a little too much against his chest, and brought up the meta-space controls on his console. He composed a message. One that he was sure Admiral Proctor would look at, and so he composed it deliberately and transparently.

Mystery ship engaged, damage sustained to the Independence. *No apparent damage to the mystery ship, which has since disappeared after digging deep into Bolivar's moon, Ido, and depositing a strange device into the moon's core. Tracking the ship. Now at San Martin to follow up on a few leads. Will update soon.* —Yarbrough.

He prepared the message for the meta-space transmission, which operated at such a low bandwidth that it could only accommodate text messages.

But it wasn't *that* low of a bandwidth. It could handle an

underlying data stream on the carrier wave that carried the signal itself, and to this he appended another message. One he was sure Proctor would never read.

Gaining Proctor's trust. The plan continues.

CHAPTER TWENTY-FIVE

Irigoyen Sector, San Martin System, San Martin
Landing pad, CENTCOM San Martin, Ciudad Libertador

The shuttle ride down to the surface of San Martin was turbulent—far more than Proctor preferred, such that when she finally stumbled out of the shuttle at CENTCOM San Martin in Ciudad Libertador, she was positively nauseous. This time she'd told her young executive assistant, Ensign Flay, to stay up on the ship—surely Proctor could reach her own tea while on the shuttle. And Admiral Tigre, head of CENTCOM San Martin, had an entire battalion of marines assigned to her protection and was organizing her security himself. He met her at the landing pad, standing at the head of a squad of twenty well-armed men and women, with a look of studious concern on his face.

"You all right, Shelby?"

"Fine." She waved him off, and held on to the nearby

railing—the steady, unmoving railing—to center herself before trying to walk any more.

"We weren't expecting you. Oppenheimer told me you were tracking the Golgothic ship that destroyed the *Chesapeake*. But we haven't seen hide nor hair of it out here…."

"I know. But I'm following up on a few leads while we track it." She looked to either side to make sure they were out of eavesdropping range of the marine guard and his aides. "Tell me, what's the GPC activity like on San Martin?"

Admiral Tigre looked surprised. "GPC? No more or less than other systems in the sector, which is to say, it's a little turbulent. But we try not to get involved in politics here at CENTCOM."

"Good." She released her death grip on the railing, and allowed herself a few hobbling steps.

"You ok? You look awful. You're limping." Tigre held out his hand for her to take as she walked towards the doors leading into the CENTCOM building. Last time she'd done this she'd nearly died.

"I'm fine. Just a little incident on Bolivar. I ask about GPC because, well, I was almost one of the casualties of a GPC terrorist action there at CENTCOM Bolivar. An explosion took out a whole side of the building there. Killed a couple folks."

"I heard. We've raised our readiness alert level in response, and I've instituted special security measures to all critical systems within CENTCOM San Martin, just in case. But I trust my people here, Shelby. You're safe."

She eyed the aides following Admiral Tigre, and with a quick glance at him, she locked eyes and told him without saying a word that she wanted to talk privately.

He nodded. "Right this way."

Tigre led her to a conference room next to the command center. "We'll just be a moment," he said to his aides, smiling briefly before pushing the door shut. He turned to her. "What's up, Shelby? Why the cloak and dagger?"

"I'm sorry, Miguel, I just don't know who I can trust."

"Can you trust me?"

The words hung ominously, but after a moment his intense stare broke into a mischievous smile.

"Miguelito," she said, using the nickname his friends called him, "if I couldn't trust you, then we may as well throw up our hands and surrender to whatever that thing is out there, and hand the entire government over to Curiel and the GPC. Pack up the whole shop."

"You think the GPC is behind the mystery ship?"

Proctor shrugged. "No idea. But that's not exactly why I'm here. Miguel, Danny's missing."

His eyes went wide. "Little Danny?"

"Little Danny. But little Danny isn't little anymore, and is apparently a twenty-year-old GPC loyalist. And I want some bloody answers."

Tigre sighed, and put an arm around her shoulder. They'd been good friends back during her days as Fleet Admiral. He'd been her chief of staff, and had become a good friend of the family, even coming to the dinners she hosted for her brother's family. The man had taken a liking to little Danny, having been a grandpa himself.

"We'll get some answers, Shelby. We'll get to the bottom of it. Just tell me what you need, and you've got it."

She sniffed. *Damn, was that a frickin tear?* "Thank you, Miguelito. All I know is that Danny was living here in Ciudad Libertador. I need his address, and access to his apartment. Do you have a relationship with the local police force? Will they look the other way if I, well, force the lock?"

He nodded. "Yeah, I know the police chief. We owe each other favors. Give me a few minutes, and you're in." His shoulders slumped a little. "You don't suppose Danny had anything to do with the alien ship? Or with the Sangre incident?"

"I sure hope not. He's just not the type. I mean, he was always so idealistic as a teen, so I can see, just barely, that he might have fallen in with the wrong folks if their rhetoric was convincing enough. But terrorism? No. Not Danny."

Admiral Tigre looked at her long and hard. They'd been friends for a long time, and she knew he wouldn't BS her, so she braced herself for what was coming. "Shelby … this is hard." He hesitated.

"Spit it out, Miguel."

"You know that Sangre de Cristo's defense is basically provided by CENTCOM San Martin, right?"

"Sure. I set the whole situation up when they established the first colonies there fifteen years ago. But I remember that we put them on a path to getting their own defense establishment, including their own CENTCOM. Isn't that progressing since I left?"

He shook his head. "It's not up to me to divulge such high level operational affairs with a *former* head of IDF. Sorry, Shelby. But I bring it up to remind you that I'm effectively in charge of Sangre's defense, and all investigation of *the incident* has gone directly to me."

She nodded. "Go on."

He walked over to the viewscreen on the wall and input a few commands into the console. A video feed popped up, showing the grainy image of a ship making a hard burn for the surface of a planet. After a moment she recognized the planet as Sangre de Cristo.

"Is that what delivered the nuclear device?"

"It is."

She watched as it accelerated into the atmosphere, and the shock wave began to glow red. "When does it launch the missile?"

"It doesn't. Watch."

The hull started to break apart, white-hot streaks peeling off from the sturdy bulk of the craft. It was built to last, that was for sure. It was an older ship, clearly, built out of solid, heavy metal. It dove through the atmosphere, finally breaking its acceleration as the main thrusters gave out from the duress of uncontrolled atmospheric reentry.

And then it exploded in a blinding flash, the glare overwhelming the optical sensors of whatever was recording the image.

"This is the telemetry picked up by a weather satellite. Just got it a few days ago. My people have been working on it, and we've ID'd the ship." He fished a datapad out of his pocket and handed it to her. "The *Magdalena Issachar*. Cargo freighter. Out of San Martin."

She accepted the datapad and examined it.

Impossible.

"Miguel, this is … no. I can't believe it. I won't."

"It's registered to a shell corporation called Emigrant Metrics, which we've linked back to another major corporation that's backing the GPC. But the port logs are unambiguous: they list Danny Proctor as the captain of record of the *Magdalena Issachar*. He flew that bird for two whole months before this, docking at a dozen spaceports before heading back here to San Martin, and then off to Sangre. Then, for a week, nothing. He doesn't show up on any station logs or planetary spaceport customs. Nothing. It's like he just floated out in space somewhere for a week. Then, this," he waved a hand toward the viewscreen, which still showed the destruction unfolding on the planet's surface, as the hapless habitation dome imploded under the incontestable pressure from the nuclear shock wave.

"You honestly think Danny nuked a city? Our Danny?"

"Of course not. But the data says what it says."

It couldn't be. Danny wouldn't do this. Someone either put him up to it and didn't tell him all the details, or he wasn't on that ship. Or … something. Not Danny.

"You're still analyzing the video, I assume. Are there others? Surely there was not just one weather satellite in orbit around Sangre?"

He nodded. "My best people are working on it."

"I want access to his apartment. Now."

He reached over and touched a few buttons on the datapad he had given her. "There. That's the only apartment we found registered to his name. Just downtown a few kilometers. I'll let the police chief know to look the other way for the next two hours."

CHAPTER TWENTY-SIX

Irigoyen Sector, Interstellar space
Shuttle Fenway

"What do you mean, you have no idea?" Zivic reached out for the scanner Batak was still scrutinizing, but she waved him off, and fiddled with a few of the settings.

"Switching to Q-band," she said, sweeping the area of the cargo hold with the scanner, waving it back and forth.

"Sara...?" He tried looking over her shoulder at the scanner, but she kept moving around the hold, pausing every few seconds to examine a spot on the floor or wall or some other nook.

"It's ... it's not nuclear, if that's what you're wondering," she said.

"Then what the hell is it?"

"Working on it. I'm not a friggin' scientist. Just a deck lackey. I fix shit. I don't theorize shit. And this," she indicated the scanner with her free hand, "this is theory shit. It shouldn't be here."

He tried grabbing the scanner again, but she moved out of his way. "Sara, just tell me what you're seeing on that thing."

Her brow furrowed deeper. "It's … meta-space. I mean, that's not possible. You shouldn't be able to detect any meta-space signatures from anything other than a meta-space transmitter, but all the same—"

"I'll go check the transmitter. Maybe it got stuck in the 'on' position somehow." He turned and dashed back to the bridge and examined the dashboard, bringing up the meta-space controls with a few swipes of his fingers. The transmitter was off. Definitely off.

"It's not on," he called back to the hold.

"I didn't think so," she called back. "This reading isn't so much an *active* signal as it is a … signature? Ghost reading? I don't know how to explain it. Maybe go manually check the transmitter? That console might be lying to you."

He nodded, and bent down under the dashboard to remove the panel on the wall underneath. At least, that's where he assumed the transmitter electronics were. A quick glance at the tumble of wires and components told him he guessed right. "Uh," he poked around at various flashing parts of the circuit board, "how does one go about figuring out if it's actually transmitting?"

"You just—" he could hear her swear under her breath, though it was clearly audible. "Hold on."

A moment later she knelt down next to him, holding another instrument, this time just a common multimeter. She poked one of the leads at the ground terminal and the other at another spot on the board he didn't immediately recognize. She shook her head. "No. Definitely not transmitting."

She looked up at him, her brow still furrowed. He shrugged. "So? What does it mean?"

With a small grunt she fell back from her knees to her rear, and tossed the multimeter aside. "Honestly? No idea. Could be absolutely nothing. Like I said, I'm a mechanic. I don't know the first thing about meta-space theory and quantum shit."

"Is that the technical term?"

She smiled. "Basically. Look, all I know is meta-space waves are very ... finicky, I guess. Hard to produce. Low bandwidth. They pass in and out of regular four dimensional space, interacting with the background..." she waved her hand around in the air, "whatever."

"The background whatever?"

She glared at him. "You know what I mean."

He shrugged. "No, honestly, I don't. I'm a former fighter pilot turned sensor officer. I wouldn't know a meta-space signal from an fm-band signal if you shoved both up my ass and twisted real hard. I mean, I'm good at reading the console, doing some quick analysis, and parroting it back to the commanding officer. That's it."

At least, that was all he was good at *now*. He dreamed of getting back in the cockpit. Alternately wishing for it, and having nightmares about it.

"Fine. It interacts with the background vacuum energy all around us. Particles popping in and out of existence all around us. The meta-space wave we generate interacts with those, and propagates by ... virtually ... magically ... popping in and out of existence right along with those pretend particles, which lets it somehow travels faster than light. Much, much faster."

"Ok. So how does that jive with what you're reading?"

She shook her head. "I don't know, exactly. But what we're reading back there is like … it's almost like a meta-space signal is caught in some kind of loop. Which is weird all by itself because meta-space signals are like regular old light signals, or radio signals—they travel in a straight line. You can't have a light wave that just circles around a common center. Light doesn't *orbit* anything. Neither do meta-space waves."

He considered this for a moment. "Well, they *can* orbit one thing." He looked up at her, shrugging. "Black holes. Light can orbit a black hole, right at the event horizon. Any farther away and the light particle thingie eventually shoots off. Any closer and it falls in towards the black hole. But right there at the event horizon, it's like an eternal orbit."

She eyed him skeptically. "Ethan. I hate to break it to you, but … we definitely don't have a black hole in our cargo hold."

"I know, I'm just saying, for argument's sake, it *is* possible. Just … unlikely, in our current situation."

A sigh, and she collapsed further onto the deck, leaning back on her elbows. "Orbits eternal and ascending…." she murmured.

"Huh?"

She shook her head. "Just Grangerite mumbo jumbo. I get it every Thanksgiving from my brother-in-law. You mentioning light eternally orbiting a black hole reminded me of a thing he's always saying."

He sat down in the pilot's seat and faced her. "Ok, so back up here," he said. "You're reading a meta-space signal that looks like it's coming from the cargo hold, but it's … circular?"

She shook her head. "No, it's not quite that simple. It's not so much a meta-space *signal* as it is a meta-space *signature*. And I only say circular because it looks like it has no origin. There's just this spot right in the center of that cargo hold, where it looks like the meta-space … background energy, you know, coupled with the background vacuum energy, it's just … swirling. Not creating a new signal, but just, rotating around that spot."

A few moments of silence.

"Creepy," he finally said.

The console beeped again. He struggled to his knees and peered up at the dashboard.

"Get ready for q-jump number three hundred and fifty-six." He paused, and glanced back down at her. "You don't suppose this funky ghost reading back there can interfere with the q-drive?"

She shrugged.

"Well," he pulled himself back into his chair. "Perfect. Let's hope we don't explode before we show up at San Martin."

"Or get sucked into meta-space," she offered.

"Yeah, that too. Thought at this point, I'd be surprised if something *doesn't* happen."

A smile tugged at her lips. "It don't rain, but it shitstorms."

CHAPTER TWENTY-SEVEN

Irigoyen Sector, San Martin System, San Martin
Danny Proctor's apartment, Ciudad Libertador

Admiral Shelby Proctor knocked on the door, just in case someone might actually answer. Just in case Danny had been hiding out at the pub this whole time, and would now answer the door, hung-over and half naked.

Nothing. The street outside was quiet, with hardly any pedestrians, or ground cars, for that matter. A bodega down the street murmured gently as a customer got her unruly kids under control as she placed her order for coffee.

After waiting for nearly a minute, she nodded to her marine guard. "Wait here."

"Ma'am? We'd prefer at least one of us go in with you," said the shorter one. The one she'd nicknamed *Stretch* in her head.

"No. I'll be fine. See that no one comes in." She reached

for the door controls and entered the bypass code Admiral Tigre had given her, and the door slid open. Clothes and old food boxes littered the floor.

"Looks like someone trashed the place looking for something. Burglary?" said Stretch, peering in through the door, hand resting on his sidearm.

"No, I doubt it. Danny was never the cleanest kid…." She stepped into the front room and the door slid shut behind her. The smell of old pizza boxes and rotten fruit wrinkled her nose, but beyond that she could smell her nephew—his scent was unmistakable to her, having kissed his little head all the time while growing up. His dirty clothes were tossed haphazardly across the sofa and floor. A pile of socks lay in the corner.

"Dammit, Danny, haven't you ever learned to pick up after yourself?"

She tiptoed carefully through the mess, nearly losing her balance at one point when she stepped on a fork with her bad leg. "Shit," she mumbled. "Danny, Auntie Shelby is going to kill you if you're not already dead."

The remark nearly made her cry, so she focused on the apartment. It was about what one would expect from a twenty-year-old young man's first place he lived away from the civilizing influence of parents, or basic cleaning supplies. There were large framed pictures of starships in orbit around various planets hanging on the wall—Danny was always fascinated with ships. He'd play with his toy spaceships for hours every day, setting them up in mock battles, blockade lines, chases, orbital rail gun fights. Sometimes she'd overhear him chattering away, dropping ship names like *Constitution*, *Warrior*, *Victory*,

Chesapeake—all the names of the old Legacy Fleet that Aunt Shelby had served aboard—and she'd catch snippets about the evil Swarm, and the backstabbing Dolmasi, and the enigmatic Skiohra, and even the other two known alien races that humanity had never met, the Findiri and Quiassi, and Danny would make up names for the alien ships and descriptions of what the aliens looked like and how their ships—

Dammit, stop daydreaming, Shelby. It won't bring him back.

She studied one of the ships on the wall. This one was not in space, but rather a photograph of a bulky old transport freighter sitting in dry-dock at some planetary station somewhere.

It was the *Magdalena Issachar*. She recognized it from the video Admiral Tigre had shown her. She stepped closer, examining some writing near the bottom, almost like a signature, except with an added message.

Danny, she's all yours. -Rex

"Looks like you were right, Miguel," she said to herself. *Dammit.* That meant that the odds her nephew was now a collection of subatomic particles just ticked up a few notches. *Keep it together, Shelby.*

Her hand comm pad chirped in her pocket. She pulled it out and tapped it on.

"Proctor."

The voice on the other end was Yarbrough's. "Admiral, we've just received a report of a sighting of the alien ship."

"Where?"

"Here, actually. In the San Martin system. It appeared near San Martin's moon, just momentarily. Stayed for about two minutes. Then it q-jumped away."

She rubbed her elbow, where the bone was bruised from the explosion the day before. It already seemed like forever ago. She stared at the photo of the *Magdalena Issachar*—she felt like she'd lost a child.

"That's damn peculiar, Commander. It did nothing? Just jumped in, and jumped away?"

She could almost hear him nod. "That's right, Admiral. Shall we set a course? We can be there in a few hours. Or in just a few minutes if we t-jump there."

"No. Ask Admiral Tigre for any sensor data he's got from whatever monitoring base he's got out at the moon—I assume he has one—and that should be sufficient. I've got unfinished business here."

A pause. "Yes, ma'am."

She sensed his unease at the fact she was down on the surface, and not in the captain's chair where she belonged. He was mostly right. But not right enough. There was a *connection*, dammit. That Golgothic ship just appeared out of nowhere, almost immediately after the worst disaster since the Second Swarm War. No, not just a disaster. Terrorist attack.

"I'll just be awhile longer, Commander. Prepare the ship to break orbit when I get back."

"Yes, ma'am. Where should I tell Ensign Riisa we'll be going?"

"Wherever your analysis says the mystery ship went. Get the data from Tigre, science the shit out of it—don't let Commander Mumford tell you he can't work miracles—and then we'll be on our way."

"And if the ship is not still at the coordinates we come up with?"

She rolled her eyes. "Then we look in the closet and under the bed—that's where monsters usually hide. Proctor out." She tapped the link closed before she said something she would regret.

Look in the closet and under the bed.

"If it were only that easy." She remembered little Danny, no older than four, being scared of the Swarm monster under the bed and its Dolmasi cousin in the closet. She grit her teeth against the memory, and tiptoed her way back through the mess. She paused at the closet. Just to be sure, so she wouldn't doubt later, she pulled it open.

Empty, except for, yes—there was a God of miracles—a vacuum cleaner. She smirked—it looked pristine and unused. Satisfied there was nothing else there, she closed the door and eyed the bed in the corner. May as well be *sure* sure. She picked her way through the clutter, and holding onto the bed for support, sunk to her knees. The bad knee popped and a twinge of searing pain shot up her leg. "Dammit, Danny!"

She looked under the bed. More clothes.

And a piece of paper. No, not paper. A card. Like an old-fashioned business card. She plucked it up and turned it over. It actually was a business card. The electronic holographic sort. Black text scrolled across, flickering somewhat as the nano-batteries were on the verge of failure, and the unmistakable holographic image of a spaceship seemed to leap off the paper and hover just centimeters above it. She read the text.

Rex Ramanujan, certified used ship dealer.

It listed his address. 550 Alabama Boulevard, Ciudad Liberator, San Martin.

In the hallway, the marine guard snapped to attention. She

tossed the card to Stretch. "Get on your hand pad and drive us to Alabama Avenue."

CHAPTER TWENTY-EIGHT

Irigoyen Sector, San Martin System, El Amin
Shuttle Fenway

"Last jump," he said. Peering out the front viewport he could see the bright star at the center of the field of view. San Martin's sun. At this distance it was as bright as Eire during a sunset on Britannia, or like Venus burning brightly on the western horizon at evening on Earth.

"And we didn't even explode," she added, a lop-sided smile tipped toward him. "Or get shot at. I think this is a record for us."

"Don't count your chickens before they hatch." He glanced at the instruments before he authorized the computer to make the final q-jump. "Hold on," he said.

Something was off.

"What is it?"

"We're, uh, well we're close to El Amin. That might

explain it."

"Explain what? Is that the farthest planet in the San Martin system?"

He nodded, but bit his lip. "Yeah. And we're getting some funky readings on the ... surprise surprise, the meta-space scan."

"Is it a signal?" she asked.

"No. Just noise. Static." An idea occurred to him. "Hey, go back into the hold and look at our magical meta-space loop, will you? Just in case they're connected."

She nodded and left. Moments later, she called back from the hold. "Yeah, it's doing something. Like, flickering. Or something."

"Is it stable?" he called back.

She reappeared in the cabin. "Stable? I don't even know what it is. I say we hightail it to San Martin before we find out."

"Don't twist my arm ... that's the best idea I've heard all day. Hold on." He reached out and pressed the initiator button. A second later, the view out the window changed in an instant, a giant blue cloud-dappled planet replacing the sterile field of stars. "Aaaand ... here we are."

She shrugged. "Now what?"

"Yeah, I've been thinking about that. The shuttle logs say that it came here. But, given our experience back at Bolivar I don't think showing up at Shovik-Orion's headquarters is the most prudent thing to do."

"Right." She shook her head. "Or CENTCOM San Martin, given what you saw your two IDF buddies do to Jerry Underwood."

"Agreed." He started fiddling with the computer, trying to

access the IDF network without logging in or revealing his computer's access ID. "And yet we still need to find out where exactly this shuttle docked, and what the cargo was, and who was involved in the transfer. And find pops."

"But his location is classified."

"Right. But I can send him a message on the civilian network and it should be routed to him." He shrugged. "Eventually."

"Ok, that gets us to your pops, but what about the shuttle?"

He scratched his growing stubble on his chin—it had been two days now since he'd been able to shower. And he was already tired of shuttle food. "So here's the plan. Let's ... go hang out above the North Pole and monitor system transmissions and traffic until we have a better handle on things."

She eyed him skeptically. "Ethan, your plans suck."

He swiveled to face her. "Fine. What's *your* brilliant idea?"

"Well," she leaned back in the seat, "we have to assume that whoever was shooting at us has managed to send a metaspace signal to alert their people here to keep a lookout for us. Surely they'll be on the lookout for this shuttle. So the answer is obvious."

"Change the transponder?" he offered.

"No. You can't change a transponder without physically switching out the hardware, and doing some pretty fancy shit with the electronics to fool the shuttle's computer into thinking that the new hardware is legit. No. We need to ditch the shuttle."

"Come again?" He eyed her like she was crazy. "Are you

crazy?"

"As long as we're in this thing, we're a target."

"As long as we're *us* we're targets."

She smiled. "*Now* you're catching on."

It took him a moment to understand. "Wait, are you suggesting we not be *us*?"

"I am."

"Disguises? Sara, this isn't a movie. I can't just go put on a dress and think I'm going to fool anyone."

She eyed him skeptically. "You in a dress? Naw, you wouldn't be fooling anyone." He tried to unpack her retort, sensing an insult in there somewhere, but she continued. "No, we need to change our biometrics. Or at least mask them. Fool the facial recognition cameras and other other biometric signatures we have. You know. Fingerprints, heartbeat signature, heat signature, retina pattern, speech recognition, etc., etc."

"Woah. Yeah, no, we're not changing all that. It would take … months and money we don't have, and we don't have the time or—"

"Calm down, I'm not suggesting we change all that. Just the basics, to at least fool the facial recognition cameras. At least to give us some time to find a new ship, and figure out who we can trust. Maybe by then your dad will come through."

"Fine." He nodded, and looked around the shuttle's cabin. "Any ideas? I'm fresh out of wigs."

She stood up and walked over to the printer. "This thing can print basic tools and parts, and even food—"

"Shitty food," he interjected.

She shrugged. "*Shitty* is being generous. But all the same, it can print basically anything, within reasonable size restraints and basic material restraints. I mean, we're not printing out plutonium rods or anything," she said, fiddling with the printer controls.

"I fail to see how plutonium rods would make a good costume."

She ignored him. "But cellulose, adhesive. Pigment. Easy." She fiddled with the output selection screen at the printer for another minute before finally tapping the screen. "Yep, here we go."

He peered over her shoulder at the screen. "Prosthetic face masks? You've got to be kidding."

"I used to be on the theatre tech crew back in high school. Believe me, these are a cinch. I say we print two each, that way we can exit the shuttle wearing one—the cameras will surely be watching us as we leave and they'll eventually trace the shuttle to us, so after we find shelter somewhere we swap out our masks. Maybe shave your head. I'll dye my hair—you know the drill."

"I—" he was about to protest.

"Look," she interrupted in a huff. "You got a better idea? Because believe me, hanging out over the north pole is not the answer. That's liable to get us captured very quick-like once they figure out it's us, and they won't leave anything to chance this time—it'll be shoot first, pick up the pieces later. I don't know about you, but I want to live out the week."

She had a point. There was only so much they'd be able to tell just by tapping into IDF and Shovik-Orion broadcasts. The unencrypted ones, at least. And he just wasn't keen on getting shot at again—maybe going incognito would give them a brief respite from the bullets. Worth a shot, at least, until he could find his old man.

"Fine. Give me a facial."

She smirked, and clicked *print* on the output screen. "That's what she said."

He couldn't help but chuckle while he turned back to the navigational controls to bring them down to the planet. *I like this girl.*

CHAPTER TWENTY-NINE

Irigoyen Sector, San Martin System, San Martin
550 Alabama Boulevard, Ciudad Libertador

The used ship dealer's showroom was just a nondescript store with ugly, inconsistent branding on the sign hanging above the front door. Even though it was regular business hours, the place looked absolutely deserted. Just a dozen knee-high holographic kiosks that projected the owner's wares up into the air: dozens of ships, mostly smaller yachts, a few tiny cargo carriers and mineral haulers, and even a few decommissioned commercial passenger liners, all in various states of disrepair.

Ground cars and public transportation pods hummed along on the street, and a few people strolled the sidewalk. It seemed to be a seedier part of town, and Proctor wondered if she shouldn't have brought more than her usual two marines along with her. Stretch seemed to read her mind.

"Ma'am, request permission to augment your security detail," he said, as his eyes scanned over the broken windows of an abandoned building down the street.

"Fine. But I'll just be a few minutes. And if Rex isn't here, then Admiral Tigre will have to take over the investigation."

"Yes, ma'am," said Stretch. He muttered something into his shoulder comm set while he and the other, taller marine took positions on either side of the doors, scanning the cars, sidewalks, and windows across the street for potential threats.

As soon as she opened the door, a chime sounded, and a man emerged from the back office. He was short—shorter than Stretch. A smart business suit and slickly-parted hair told her this was Rex, the used-ship salesman.

"Good afternoon—" he glanced at the bars near her left shoulder, "Admiral? I'm sorry, I don't often get IDF folks in here."

"Yes, Admiral Proctor."

He smiled. "Ah, I haven't forgotten the ranks, at least. My brother served in IDF for two years back in the day. Pilot."

She took a few steps forward into the showroom, studying the ships projected up into the air, wondering if the *Magdalena Issachar* had once been displayed above one of the kiosks. "Rex Ramanujan?"

"Pleased to meet you, Admiral," he said, extending a hand. "How can I help you?"

"I'm looking for a ship. Heard of the *Magdalena Issachar*?"

His face went white. Interesting. His mouth opened, then closed, then opened again. "I have. It went missing a few weeks ago, if I'm not mistaken."

She took a few more steps into the showroom, glancing at

a few more of the holographic ships projected up into the air. She wondered how much a used, broken-down ship went for, and how Danny had managed to come up with the money. "Did you sell it to Danny?"

"To Danny? Ah. Admiral *Proctor*." He nodded a few times. "I understand. You're his aunt?"

She turned to him, surprised. "He mentioned me?"

"Of course! Danny's a good friend."

"So you *did* sell the *Issachar* to him."

"No. No I didn't. But … here, come, sit down with me. Coffee?" He motioned to the sitting area off to the side of the kiosks and began pouring two cups. "You know, Danny practically worships you."

She allowed herself to be led to the firm, low, commercial-grade couch, and silently groaned as her knee protested the deep bend required to sit. "He's a good kid. Always dreamed of piloting his own ship, but unfortunately never had any interest in IDF."

Rex nodded. "Sounds like Danny."

Proctor accepted the steaming cup, but frowned. "It sounds like you know him more than a typical used ship salesman knows his clients."

The man sat down across from her in a swiveling chair. "It's true. I know him very well. You see, long before I ever helped him get his ship, I was also his pastor."

Proctor did a double take. "Pastor?"

He nodded, solemnly.

"Danny was never religious."

"He wasn't. He is now. He said he'd felt a huge void in his life, and by the grace of God and his messenger, I helped him find his path."

So, Danny let himself be swayed by the god-folks. Interesting. Proctor had been raised by nominally Methodist parents, but went to meetings so rarely that she felt she grew up attending the holy church of jazz, as her parents took her to live combos almost every Sunday evening. She'd always meant to explore that side of her life more, perhaps find god, perhaps find some deeper meaning, but she'd always been too damn busy saving Earth and shit.

She only nodded, and waved for him to continue.

"Danny started coming to my meetings about a year ago. He'd just moved into his apartment here in Ciudad Libertador, and seemed to be struggling making friends and finding work. He was walking by on that very sidewalk outside while I was leading a prayer meeting here, and he pressed his face up to the window, staring at the holographic ships," he waved to the slowly rotating merchant freighters and yachts hovering over the kiosks, "and I motioned for him to come in. Well, he did, and sat through the whole prayer meeting, never taking his eyes off the ships. I finished the final prayer, and he said 'amen', still staring at the freighter next to him." Rex started to chuckle.

"Sounds like he converted to the church of the holy starliner, Mr. Ramanujan."

"He was truly taken, just smitten, by the idea of flying his own someday. *But* he started paying attention. And we became friends—he found a lot of friends among my small flock. And he eventually came to feel called to his Lord, and the Lord's messenger."

A cold feeling went up Proctor's spine at the words. He'd said something similar before, but the word had passed her by.

Messenger.

"And who is that messenger, Mr. Ramanujan? Christ? Mohammed? A Boddhisatva?"

Rex looked surprised. "Of course not. I worship God and his Christ, of course, but their messenger in these times is the Hero of Earth. Granger."

Oh, God. She lowered her face into a hand.

Her voice dropped to icy steel. "Mr. Ramanujan, I served with Tim Granger. He was my captain for four months. We went through hell and back together, and he did some amazing things, saving Earth and fifty billion people and humanity and all. But he was human. *Human.* He was no angel, no saint, and certainly no savior."

He smiled rapturously. "Your part in his ascension is well known to us, Admiral Proctor. You have an honored place in our theology."

"Theology?" She let out an exasperated puff of air. "Theology? How do you build a theology around someone I once saw sprawled on his couch, half drunk in his underwear picking at his toenails with a blunt kitchen knife and telling me it was all over and we should just go have one-night stands because tomorrow we were going to die?"

He waited several moments before answering. "The fact that he was able to overcome the flesh only makes his ascension that much more—"

"He's Tim! He's not your damn savior! He—" she broke off and brought her fist to her mouth to cut off the insults she was about to hurl.

Rex looked flustered, and set his cup down, still mostly full. "I'm sorry, Admiral Proctor, I didn't mean to upset you.

You're here to find Danny, and I want you to find him."

Her eyes narrowed. "How did you find out he was missing?"

"Well, for one, you're here looking for him. You don't search for something that is not lost. And second, he hasn't come to a meeting in weeks. He never misses a Sunday, and when he does, he always drops me a quick line telling me where he is, and when he forgets I'll send him a message and he always responds right back, wherever he is." He picked his coffee back up. "I should have never helped him get that ship."

"So you did sell it to him?"

"No, I didn't. But I did connect him with the folks that did. I know most of the other ship dealers in Ciudad Libertador. And Danny, well, he was persistent. He wanted a ship. Something to call his own. To get out and, well, to be free. Unfettered."

Damn. That *did* sound like Danny.

"Who?"

Rex finished his coffee and set the cup back down. "As we both know, Danny was quite the idealist. He believes in causes. He wanted to think that he was involved in something greater than—"

"Who?" she repeated, interrupting. The pastor liked to hear himself talk far too much.

"A company called Emigrant Metrics. But that's just a front. It's a GPC firm. I know the guy that runs it—GPC through and through. But Danny didn't care. He just wanted his own ship, and this was a cheap and easy way to get one. Sign up for the GPC, run a few missions for them in exchange for the freighter, and on the side he could take his own transport jobs and make enough to pay off the ship. He and two other friends went in on it together, though Danny was majority owner, I think. The other two were just in it for the easy money."

She nodded. His story checked out—at least the part about Emigrant Metrics. Miguel's information confirmed that much. "I want an introduction."

He nodded. Before he could say anything, Stretch opened the door and leaned in. "Ma'am, backup should be here shortly."

"Thank you, corporal—" but even as the words were half out of her mouth, she heard a crack. A fine red mist blew out from Stretch's forehead, and his confused face bloomed with an eruption of blood.

CHAPTER THIRTY

Irigoyen Sector, San Martin System, San Martin
Shuttle Fenway, High orbit

Zivic could hardly believe how fast she managed to get the mask adhered to his face and blended into his natural skin tone with a little—

"Wait, is that *make-up*?" He pulled away from the applicator in her hands.

"Oh don't be a big baby. Come'ere."

He grudgingly submitted, letting her apply the *disguise pigment*—he refused to even think of it as make-up in his head. "My dad would disown me, *again*, if he knew I was putting on makeup."

"Seriously? Stop being such as dick." She wrenched his head to the left and continued her work. "So … he actually disowned you? Like, literal disowning, with paperwork and all that?"

He started to shake his head no when she grabbed him again to keep him still. "Naw. I … I'm just a huge disappointment to him. When I was grounded—my fighter credentials revoked—that was like the final straw for him. We'd butted heads for years. And after mom and my stepdad died, well, he got kinda weird after that, and his disappointing son just pushed him over the edge, I guess."

"Oh. Sorry," she said. "About your mom. I lost my uncles and grandparents during the Swarm War. I wasn't born yet, of course. But one of my aunts was pretty maimed in a factory explosion—she was working on President Avery's secret antimatter project. Basically melted her skin off. Should've died."

"Oh god…" he said, trying to keep still for her to finish her work. "She ok now? I mean, it is thirty years on…."

"Yeah, she's fine. Face looks like shit after five operations to make her look normal, though I suppose she looks better than if they'd left it all melty. There!"

"Done?" He reached up to touch his cheek, which now lacked all feeling as it was covered in cellulose and adhesive.

She slapped his hand away. "Don't touch it! Still has to dry and set."

"Uh, we're kind of on a time crunch here. We can't just hang out in orbit while my … makeup dries."

She rolled her eyes at him. "Of course not. You're going to pilot us down to the commercial spaceport in Ciudad Libertador while I get my own mask on. And then find us a good place to stay while we switch masks and fiddle with our hair and plan the next step."

He swiveled back to the flight controls and plotted in a course to the spaceport down in the capital city. "We've got an

IDF transponder. They'll probably want us to divert to IDF CENTCOM's port, but I'm going to claim salvage, which, uh, isn't that far from the truth. That should at least get us on the landing platform and into customs. From there, we've got to find a way to give the authorities the slip while we can duck into a hotel and … uh, reapply our makeup."

The shuttle bumped a little bit as it descended through the atmosphere. He noticed Batak tense up, and reminded himself that not everyone found atmospheric flight as thrilling as he did. "So. What were your plans after…."

"After what?"

"You know. After you … do your time at Shovik-Orion, I guess."

"Do my *time*?"

The shuttle hit a patch of turbulence and nearly knocked them out of their chairs. "Buckle up," he said, pointing to the restraints. "Sorry, I didn't mean to make it sound like a prison sentence…."

She shrugged. "Well, you're right. It *is* like a prison sentence. Gotta eat somehow, you know? All social programs were cut after the war, right? That's old history. If your daddy ain't rich, if you don't feel like being a boot in IDF, and if you don't feel like rotting in a classroom at university, then this is it, honey. Hard, dirty work. No chance of promotion. Hardly any benefits. Long hours. Space jocks like you looking down their noses at me. Middle managers over-managing me, justifying their jobs by meddling in mine. And just being at the whim of administrators and bureaucrats who care more about dotting the 'I's on their contracts with IDF than actually, you know, taking care of its own people."

He fell silent. How do you reply to that?

"You seem like a smart woman—why not go into IDF?"

She fiddled with her face prosthetic and smeared some more adhesive underneath the forehead flap. "Because I don't *want* to. Never was cut out for the military."

"Then why not go to university? Be a scientist or senior engineer or something. You got the brains for it."

She shrugged. "Because I don't *want* to. I want to do my work. Get paid for it. Then go relax at home with my dogs, my brew, and my tunes."

Silence as she pressed the rest of the mask firmly to her cheeks and chin. "It's a wonder the GPC doesn't control half the UE by now."

"Huh?"

"Just sayin'. I'm a natural candidate for GPC recruitment. They're for the common man and woman. The worker. The ignored and left-behind. I'm right up their alley. Most of the GPC is staffed by people like me."

"Why aren't you?"

She started swiping cream onto the seams of the mask. "Because. You'd think that we learned our lesson thirty years ago. The Swarm struck right at our weakest moment, when we were most divided. The Russian Confederation and the UE government were almost in a state of open war—in fact, it *did* go to open war there for awhile, in the middle of the Swarm War. And the Caliphate? Relations sucked with them at the time. And the Chinese? They might not have fought us, but they weren't exactly our allies. They sure sucked up our money, though, even while IDF helped defend their worlds. So this time around, I'm not going to be one to contribute to our division. Divided we fall, and all that shit."

He nodded slowly. "That was … very philosophical of you."

"You sound surprised. Didn't think a mechanic had it in her?"

"No, not at all. I just—it's just hard to parse through your *that's what she said*'s with your lofty ideals there. Sorry, it's me, not you."

"Truer words…" she mumbled. The atmospheric turbulence had died down, and they were now soaring down towards the capital city, coming in high over the ocean. "How'd your mom die?"

He grit his teeth. No one had asked him that in two years. And he wasn't sure he was ready to start talking about it.

"I'd … rather talk about something else."

She shrugged. "Ok." It looked like she was finally done with her makeup—a strange face stared back at him, a little pudgier, whiter, and older. "Like what?"

He glanced back down at his instruments. And did a double-take, looking back and forth between the console and the viewport. "Like that squadron of IDF fighters heading straight towards us."

CHAPTER THIRTY-ONE

Irigoyen Sector, San Martin System, San Martin
550 Alabama Boulevard, Ciudad Libertador

Both Proctor and Rex bolted to their feet and retreated farther back into the store. The other marine standing outside dove through the door, which was now propped open by Stretch's bloody corpse, and brought his sidearm to bear on the street as he found cover behind a kiosk. A second later, the glass windows exploded in a hail of gunfire.

Rex grabbed Proctor's arm. "Into the office!"

She let him pull her through the door of the office, even as a constant pounding of assault rifle fire ripped the showroom to shreds.

"Corporal, get in here!" she yelled at the marine crouched behind the kiosk. He was peering around it, squeezing off a few rounds as he found targets.

"Multiple hostiles incoming!" he yelled, firing off three

more shots through the broken windows. A hail of gunfire answered him.

Rex yelled in her ear. "Come with me!"

She shrugged him off. He pushed the desk to one side and ripped up the shag rug from the floor, revealing the outline of a trapdoor. "Come!" he repeated, pulling the door up by an exposed hook.

More gunfire.

"I'm not getting in there," she yelled, scanning the room for anything she could use as a weapon, even as she scoffed at herself for the thought. What was she going to do, throw an employee of the month plaque at someone holding an assault rifle?

"It's not a room, it's a tunnel. Grangerites have been persecuted for years, and I've always kept an escape route just in case." He held out a hand. His face looked terrified. But honest. *Dammit.*

"Corporal, get in here. That's an order!" she yelled out into the showroom before grabbing Rex's hand. She let him lower her into the passage under the floor. Another barrage of gunfire rang out from the showroom, and moments later, the marine jumped down into the dark, dank space, followed by Rex himself. He pulled the door closed and locked it. Then, grabbing two iron bars on the floor, he shoved them through two other latches. No one was getting through that door without explosives. Which she assumed their attackers had.

"We can't stay here," said the marine, panting. Blood oozed out of his shoulder. Proctor swore, and reached for it. He shook her off. "Just cut by glass."

"We're *not* staying here. Follow me. Quickly." Rex shoved

past them to where the tunnel's roof narrowed down to just a meter off the ground. He stooped down and started crawling. Proctor followed, groaning as her bad knee struggled to support her weight without betraying her to searing pain. If the marine behind her felt any pain from the gash in his shoulder, he didn't say as he crawled steadily behind her.

Proctor was surprised at how fast she could move when she knew there were bullets trying to find her. They crawled at a steady clip for over two minutes, and the gunfire seemed to fade away before ending completely. She wondered if was just because they had crawled out of hearing range or if the unknown assailants had finally figured out that no one was firing back. Or if the police had finally arrived, though any regular police force would be overwhelmed with the firepower these people had. Those sounded like military-grade weapons. Either way, she crawled, trying to put as much distance in between them and the people with big guns.

"Here. The passage opens up a bit," said Rex. He was standing now, and offered a hand to Proctor to help her rise as well. They were now in a dim utility access corridor, lit only by glowing LED strips along the floor, half of which were unpowered.

"Do you know who those people are?" she asked.

"No. I thought you did."

She shrugged. "No. Lead on. I don't want to be stuck in this hole when they catch up to us." She turned back to the marine. "Have you gotten through yet?"

He shook his head. "No, ma'am. My comm set seems to be blocked. They might be interfering with the signal, whoever they are."

Damn. Whoever this was, their ambush was well executed, coordinated, and had tech support. This was no street gang, or even some GPC thugs. She waved them ahead. "Lead on."

Rex led them along the corridor, passing several access hatches, and finally, after what must have been three more minutes of walking, he pointed to a nondescript hatch to the left. "This one. It's our safe house."

"Our?"

"The local Grangerite Synod." He tapped a specific pattern on the metal of the hatch, and waited. Moments later, an answering tap came, with a complicated pattern. Rex replied with yet another series of thumps, some quick, some more spaced.

"Is that morse code?" she asked.

Rex raised an eyebrow. "You know it?"

"A little. Learned a little as a kid when I played Fleets and Swarm." His slight squint told her he had no idea what that was. "A board game you play, and you have to send secret messages to your teammates any way you can. I learned a few things I could tap to my friends."

"Did it help you win?"

She smiled at the memory, in spite of the urgent danger they were still in. "Every time."

Rex tapped a final code, which Proctor managed to translate as *Victory*—she assumed was a password, since the *ISS Victory* figured heavily into Grangerite mythology. *Her history*. Either way, the hatch creaked open. "Hurry," said Rex again, offering a hand to help her through.

The hatch closed with a clang, and firm, metallic thuds confirmed the locks fell into place, finally allowing Proctor to breathe. She'd faced death any number of times at the helm of a starship, staring down a Swarm carrier, or as was often the case, ten Swarm carriers. But facing such visceral, immediate danger as a gunman aiming for your head was an entirely different feeling. A faceless, nameless, inhuman enemy wanting her dead was one thing. It was another entirely to be targeted by another human with a name, face, and actual ideologies, however warped they were.

She found it terrifying.

"Anything yet?" she asked the marine, wishing now she'd remembered his name. It seemed like the least she could do for a young man who was putting his life on the line for hers.

"No, ma'am. All channels still blocked." He pulled his comm device out of one of his many pockets and fiddled with the screen. "With the kind of interference we're getting, I wouldn't be surprised if they've managed to hack into our terminals, Admiral. I don't see how they could block *every* channel otherwise."

She nodded. "Very well. Keep at it." And, turning to Rex, "Now what? Do you have a way out of here?"

"Of course. Follow us, please."

She just then noticed the kid standing next to the hatch. Tall, lanky, pimpled. Maybe fifteen or sixteen. Both Rex and the kid went down a narrow hallway leading from the small room the hatch was in, and emerged into a larger room full of boxes and crates, and past that, an even larger one, complete with couches, chairs, a refrigerator and sink, bunk beds lining the walls, and in the center, a small group of waiting people.

At the center of that group, a face. An incredibly charming face. One that was vaguely familiar. He stood up quickly and extended a hand. "Admiral Proctor, it is an incredible honor to meet you, companion of the Hero of Earth. Welcome."

She accepted the hand and shook. "Pleased to meet you, Mr. …?"

"Curiel."

The name jogged her memory. That face. She finally placed it. "Secretary General Curiel? Of the GPC?"

He bowed. "The one and only. I've been expecting you for several weeks now."

"Expecting me?" She glanced around the room, half expecting a dozen gunmen to spring out of the closets. What the hell was going on?

"It was prophesied. When the Hero made his final ascension and passed the event horizon, it was foretold that you'd be on the move again, preparing the way for his return. According to observations from the Penumbra Prime observatory, Granger officially passed the event horizon two weeks ago." Curiel smiled broadly at her. "And here you are."

CHAPTER THIRTY-TWO

Irigoyen Sector, San Martin System, San Martin
Galactic People's Congress safehouse, Ciudad Libertador

Proctor tried not to grimace at the religious mumbo jumbo mingled with tech jargon. She forced a thin smile. "So, you're a Grangerite? I had no idea the leader of the Galactic People's Congress was so … uh, pious."

Secretary General Curiel held both his hands up, as if in a signal of surrender. "I agree, Admiral. This looks and sounds like lunacy. Ten years ago I would have said the same. I don't blame you for having your doubts—"

She smiled again, this time more genuine. "*Doubts* doesn't really quite cover it, Mr. Secretary. More like, one hundred percent absolute surety that you folks are crazier than the local Pastafarian congregation that eagerly awaits the second coming of the flying spaghetti monster. I'm sorry, but I don't have time to waste on your delusions. Please show me out of here, preferably to a place where people aren't shooting at me, and where I can get a ride back up to my ship. You know, civilizations to save, planets to protect. The usual."

She didn't mean to let so much sarcasm seep into her words, but the absurdity, the lunacy of it all threatened to make her grab her marine's sidearm and start shooting people in the face. But, given how they currently had her at their mercy, she delayed the impulse to violence.

Secretary General Curiel nodded. "Again, I don't blame you, and I'm sorry we're meeting under these circumstances. I had hoped that we could eventually sit down and map out a course of peace—"

"Peace? You have your goons shoot up a store and kill my man back there, and you expect to sit down and discuss *peace*? What kind of deluded piece of shit are you?"

He shook his head. "Those were not my men. Admiral, you may find this hard to believe, but the Galactic People's Congress is an organization devoted to peace. Yet, as with any large organization dedicated to freedom for all people, it inevitably attracts, well, all kinds. There are several factions in the GPC that are out of my control, and frankly, a little extreme. And worse, several corporations that are pulling some of the strings of a few of those extremist groups."

Proctor stared him in the eye. "Mr. Secretary, I've come for my nephew. That's all I want. Just tell me who sold him his ship, and why the hell it exploded over Sangre taking fifty thousand people with it." She almost didn't want to know the next part, at least, not yet. "And if Danny survived it."

"I sold him the ship. It was mine. I'm sure your people will eventually confirm that, and track the registry back to a corporation under GPC control."

She nodded. Finally, some answers. "And the nuke?"

His face tightened. "Also mine."

"So you confess then? To war crimes? You understand that you likely face the death penalty. Life in prison at the least."

He shook his head vigorously. "I do not confess to war crimes. It was never our intention to actually use that device. It was only meant as ... political leverage."

She rolled her eyes. "Oh, please. Don't insult me, Mr. Secretary. You don't steal a thermonuclear device, and launch it at a defenseless colony, and then claim it was all just an innocent mistake and that you really only meant to thump your chest a little bit. Wave your dick around like one of the big boys."

Curiel's eyes flashed in anger, but he managed to smile tightly. "I tell you again, I did not order that launch. We meant to store the device in a secure bunker somewhere. Never to be used. Period. The fact of its ownership was meant to solidify support from some of our worlds that had been wavering. They needed to know that we were taking their defense seriously."

"Whatever." She blew him off. "Play your political games. Just tell me. If it wasn't you, then who was it?"

He closed his mouth. It seemed she'd thrown him off guard. "I don't know."

"Please," she scoffed again.

"I'm telling you, I don't know. It could be the Russian Confederation...."

She waved a dismissing hand. "Unlikely. After the Swarm War they retreated into themselves. They don't get into galactic politics anymore. They care about their own worlds, and that's it."

"Yes, but some of their worlds have rather large populations of GPC loyalists."

"What, you think they bombed Sangre and tried to make it look like you, so that the rest of the GPC worlds would be scared off from supporting you? Like a false-false-flag operation? Sounds a little absurd. Beyond far-fetched."

He shrugged. "It's not like they've ever hesitated to engage in such tactics before in their history. But like I said, I don't know. That's just a hunch. But I'll allow that it might be bad hunch."

"Clearly." She glared at him, then looked around the room at the others. A collection of men and women, some of whom seemed to be his aides, others she guessed were just there for the spectacle of seeing *the Hero's companion*, and several looked like security. Good—at least that might mean they'd be safe from whoever was aiming for her head.

"Admiral Proctor, when I heard you were here, I had to meet you. Not only for the, uh, faith aspect of it all. But for the very reason you have mentioned. Danny Proctor went silent shortly before the *Magdalena Issachar* plunged down into the atmosphere of Sangre de Cristo. I want to know why as much as you do. I suspect he was intercepted by … someone. Someone who not only wanted that nuke, but someone aboard a ship … with stealth technology."

"Stealth?"

"Yes. Honest-to-god photon-bending stealth. I know IDF is working on it, and has a few early beta trials running."

"How did you know that?"

He smiled. "I have my sources. But what I don't know is who intercepted Danny, or why, or what their motives are. For that, I need your help."

She rubbed her eyes. The shock of everything that had happened over the last half hour was starting to set in, and she felt a slight shiver, and recognized the signs of her core temperature falling from the shock. "How can I trust you? Tell me why I *should* trust you. Convince me."

He swallowed. "I can't. But if I was going to kill you, I'd have already done it."

Out of the corner of her eye, she saw her marine go tense. She held up a hand to steady him. "I need more than that. You're telling me I should trust you because you haven't killed me? Fuck you."

He stroked the stubble on his chin. He was not especially tall, but actually quite striking, with a natural charisma that Proctor was not surprised at, given his position. It would take someone of remarkable charisma to convince so many people to devote themselves to such a deluded cause.

"All right. I'll give you our other nukes."

She tried not to shiver. "*Other* nukes? How many do you have?"

"Nine. We stole ten, and with the loss of the one over Sangre, I'm starting to doubt their security, and the wisdom of even having them. As a show of good faith, I'll give them to you. All of them. But what I want in exchange is, well, *trust*, for one. And cooperation—we need to figure out who is behind Sangre. Otherwise, both your goals and mine will … go unrealized."

"You don't know what my goals are."

"I do." He stared at her, and for the first time, his smile was genuine. "You're the companion of the Hero. Your goal is the same as mine. To save humanity. Our means are different of course, as are—I suspect—our definitions of the word *save*, but I don't doubt your goal, nor should you doubt mine."

He paused, pointing upward toward the ceiling, as if to indicate an unseen enemy out in the deep of space. "But if we don't figure out who is working against both of us, then humanity falls."

She slowly nodded. It was a distraction, of course. She was in this to save her nephew, and for extra credit, to save Earth. Getting involved in galactic politics? She was done with that.

"Fine. Nine nukes for my cooperation in the investigation."

"Excellent," he said with a broad smile, which faltered slightly. "Except, I should clarify. I can give you eight nukes now, and the ninth to come soon."

Dammit. She knew there was a catch.

"When?"

He sighed. It sounded like defeat. "When we can figure out who stole it."

CHAPTER THIRTY-THREE

Irigoyen Sector, San Martin System, San Martin
Shuttle Fenway

"You're not actually thinking about outrunning them, are you?"

It was giving Zivic the creeps looking at Batak speak at him through the uncanny-valley face mask. He couldn't believe that they had actually thought it would be a good idea to go out in public like that.

"Of course I am. Hold on."

The shuttle lurched, and he could see her simultaneously grab her seat and her mouth as they shot straight down into the lower atmosphere, accelerated, steepening the angle of descent to a full-on dive, before leveling out just a few hundred meters above the ocean in a gut-churning arc.

Even though her face prosthetic was white, he could tell that even without it the blood would be gone from her face.

"Never … do … that … again," she managed to say through gritted teeth.

The comm buzzed to life. "Unidentified shuttle, you are advised to follow us to a landing site immediately, or we will take you down."

Dammit. "Sorry, I thought we could get out from under their sensors by skirting the water." He glanced at his sensors. "But look, we already lost six of them. There's only one following us now. The rest went off back to the city."

"Why would they—"

"Hold on," he repeated, interrupting her question. Knowing he was about to get another stream of profanity-laden protests from her, he pushed the accelerator downward, and the distance between them and the ocean dropped to nothing.

"ETHAN!"

The collision was not as rough as he would have expected, and he credited the impact mode of the inertial cancelers with half of the luck, and his last-second deceleration with the rest. Still, if it weren't for their restraints, they'd both be smeared on the front viewport. As it was, he could tell that his shoulders would not come away from this without deep bruising.

They were underwater. When the maelstrom of bubbles subsided, he could just make out rods of blue sunlight shimmering down at them from the surface about a dozen meters up.

"What … the hell … are you doing!" she yelled through gritted teeth.

"We tried to fool them your way, with makeup. Now we're fooling them my way."

"BY DYING?" she yelled again.

"They're going to think that we died in the crash, yes. By the time they get a recovery ship out here, we'll be long gone."

She couldn't seem to stop swearing under her breath. "And in the meantime, what do we do about the whole *not dying* thing?"

"Working on it…." He glanced at the instrument panel. Structural integrity was holding—ship hulls were designed to keep exactly one atmosphere of pressure in, not two atmospheres of pressure *out*. But the hull plates were holding, as were the seams between hull and viewport, and the feedthroughs for the sensor packages and propulsions units.

"Those propulsion units are never going to start up again," she said, as if reading his mind.

"I beg to differ. At the last second I shut them off and closed the exhaust panels. Our stabilizing thrusters are shot, of course, but main propulsion? No problemo."

He held his breath, waiting for the sensors to give him the all-clear. Their reach was severely attenuated by the shielding from the salt water above them, which acted like a huge grounding plate.

As if in answer, several white streaks shot through the water right across the view out the window. A second later, the comm crackled. "Unidentified shuttle, you will surface, and proceed to the coordinates I'm beaming you, or else I'll open fire. Be advised: this time, I won't miss."

He hung his head into a palm. They'd lost—they were caught. There was no escaping this time. "Fine. Bastards." He initiated the main engines with a flip of a finger, and released the containment panels that kept the water out. The shuttle lurched forward, and shot out of the water with what must have been an amazing splash for anyone lucky enough to have seen it, he supposed.

"Unidentified shuttle—"

"Don't get your panties in a bunch, I'm coming."

A pause on the other side of the comm as the pilot of the fighter considered his words. "You will accompany me up into the atmosphere. Any deviation from our course will result in several dozen red hot rounds coming up your ass. Got it?"

"If I didn't know any better, I'd say you were propositioning me, Lieutenant."

The pilot didn't sound amused. Batak glared at Zivic. Her eyes said *don't piss off the guy with the big guns pointed at us*.

"Unidentified shuttle—"

Zivic rolled his eyes. "Got it, Lieutenant. We're following you up. Any particular destination in mind?"

A pause. "Just follow me."

"Fine. Lead the way."

Much to Batak's chagrin the loss of the stabilizing thrusters meant the ascent was far rougher than the descent through the atmosphere, but it only lasted a few minutes as before long they were maneuvering into a gleaming-new IDF starship, that nevertheless looked like it had seen some intense action recently—there were several patched holes in its shining hull.

They landed in the shuttle bay. He flipped off the engines, and they stood up. "Well?" he started. "Masks on, or off?"

"Does it matter?" She asked.

"Touché. Let's go." He glanced out the viewport and saw a squad of marines surround the shuttle, assault rifles at the ready. *Well, shit.* "This doesn't end well," he grumbled. "Look, stay in here while I talk to them. Just in case."

"In case of what?"

"You know. Big guns." He flash a lopsided smile he didn't quite feel.

The ramp lowered, and he descended, with his hands in the air. A pair of marines sprang forward and slapped cuffs on his wrists and pushed him away from the ramp, towards the exit. "There's a civilian in the shuttle. She has nothing to do with this—just an innocent bystander—"

"Get them in the brig. Questions can wait," said a familiar voice over the comm speaker. Zivic glanced around for its source as it continued. "And get that shuttle out of the way. The Admiral will be here in a moment—I'm just on my way to go get her."

Zivic saw him. Up in the CIC, overlooking the fighter bay. "Dad?"

Captain Volz's eyes widened, and he stared at him for a moment, before rushing out of the CIC, down the stairs, and marched straight toward him, fire in his eyes. He looked Zivic over and reached out to tear the mask off. It hurt more than he thought it would.

His father glared at him, and cleared his throat. "Lieutenant Ethan *Zivic*, you are under arrest." He turned to the marines. "Get his ass in the brig."

"For what?" Zivic protested.

Volz reared on him—Zivic worried that he'd punch him, like last time. "For being an utter dipshit asshole. And breaking any number of IDF regulations, and possibly for murder."

"But I—"

Volz held up a hand to cut him off. "No more excuses, Ethan. Time to stop running from responsibility." He turned and marched back to the CIC. "Take them to the brig."

CHAPTER THIRTY-FOUR

Irigoyen Sector, San Martin System, San Martin
Galactic People's Congress safehouse, Ciudad Libertador

"You don't know where your damn stolen nukes are?" Proctor struggled to contain her anger. She was no longer half tempted to grab her marine's sidearm and blow Curiel's face off. She was full-on two-halves tempted.

Curiel held up his hands defensively. "Just one of them. And in my defense, it's the one that was least operational of the ten. Without some serious technical skill, that thing is staying inert." He trailed off, as if realizing how stupid he sounded. She raised an eyebrow at him. "Though, the bad news is, it's a MIRV. Fifteen actual warheads on it."

She swore. "I would think that if this shadowy organization you're pissing your panties about knows enough to be able to steal two nukes, hijack a freighter using a mysterious ship with supposed stealth technology, and is able to hack into and jam my state-of-the-art comm device," she held up her handset and shook it, "that they would have the technical know-how to be able to reassemble a bomb whose basic design and components have been around for seven hundred years!"

He gave another shrug—in a motion she'd come to call 'the penguin salute'—both arms stiff and semi-outstretched from his sides. "I'm sorry, Admiral. I know it's hard to recognize right now, but this is bigger than any single missing nuke—"

She waved him off. "Please tell me you've got the other eight secure. Please tell me you're not a complete ignoramus."

He nodded solemnly. "They're secure. My best, most trusted people are guarding them until we can offload them into your … capable hands."

"Well thank god for that." She glanced around at his entourage, most of whom were shifting uncomfortably on their feet, apparently unaccustomed to seeing their boss brow-beat like this. Except for the few that were obviously not there in a state capacity, but rather because they were highly ranked within the Grangerite … faith, if that was the right word. Those people were watching her with near-adulation. Apparently she'd met their expectations. Good. Maybe that would make them more pliable. "Are the nukes here? On San Martin?"

"Yes."

"Good. I'll take them off your hands within the day, if I can manage it. First I need to get to the *Independence*. Have the authorities responded yet? Is the street safe?" She turned to her marine. "Have you gotten through yet?"

"Making progress, ma'am. Looks like whatever they're using to hack into our system is finally running up against active counter measures from the *Independence*. Our IT team must be fighting back."

She turned back to Curiel. "I want everything you have on Danny. Everything on his ship. Sensor data, ship logs, maintenance reports, comm traffic logs, dossiers on his shipmates, and I understand he had a girlfriend who you may know."

His eyes narrowed. "Had?"

"She's dead."

The tightening of his jaw told her he hadn't known, and the news was distressing. "What?" She continued. "Was she a plant? She worked for Admiral Mullins at CENTCOM Bolivar. Was she one of yours too?"

He nodded. "Not exactly loyal to the GPC, or to IDF, for that matter. She was … complicated. That's why Danny liked her, I suppose. But she'd feed us info occasionally, and I know she'd do the same for Mullins."

"So if she wasn't loyal to you, or to Mullins, who was she loyal to?"

He shrugged.

"There's an awful lot you don't know, Mr. Secretary, for someone who's at the head of a galactic conspiracy to take down the legitimate government of United Earth."

"That is *not* what we're trying to do. We want independence and self determination. Freedom." He glowered at her. "We've had enough of your wars. Dying for your nationalistic causes. You try to make us hate the Russian Confederation, the Chinese, the Caliphate. And their leaders get their people to hate us back. It's a circle of hate, Admiral, spurred on by those in power—those with the most to lose if it all comes crashing down and the truth exposed. And we want out. We want off the merry-go-round."

Oh, please. She had no idea what else to say to such paranoid lunacy.

"Oh please. I've been saving Earth from slimy shit aliens since you were a snot-nosed whiny kid wishing he were tall enough to play with the big boys." He was about to protest, but she cut him off before he even started. "No. I'm not getting into a political argument with you. You get me the nukes before the day is out, and you get me that data, and I'll *think* about cooperating with you to help track down these people aiming for my head."

He glanced at his people. The aide closest to him shrugged, as if they were silently continuing a conversation. "We honestly have no idea why they're targeting you, Admiral. Whoever *they* are. It's clear to everyone that you're only back in the game because of the mystery ship, and that your goal is to save Earth. Again. Why these people would be opposed to that, I can't say."

She wanted to say, *Well clearly someone doesn't want me to save Earth, dumbass.* But one of the other men chimed in. She assumed he was not one of the aides, but rather one of the Grangerites, from the worshipful expression on his old, wrinkled face. Short-cropped white hair thinly covered a mottled scalp—she guessed he was north of ninety years old.

"It's because you're the *Companion of the Hero*, ma'am. With all due respect to both you and Secretary General Curiel, you're a symbol of far more than United Earth's dominance, or IDF's aggression against GPC sympathizer worlds. You're a symbol of humanity's ascendence. Its survival. Its destiny. Along with the Hero, you're the symbol of hope for humanity. Someone wants to destroy that symbol, that hope. Someone wants to demoralize us, to cow us into submission and defeat. Ever since Granger's ascension two weeks ago, I knew something was coming, to tear us all apart. To divide us. It was foretold."

"Foretold?" She decided to play along, against her better judgement. "By whom?"

He smiled coyly. "Well, by me. Tobey Huntsman. I'm the Patriarch of the Grangerite faith. Fifteen years ago I had a dream. *More* than a dream. When I woke up, I knew that what I had seen was not just a nightmare, but was, somehow, reality. What would come to pass after Granger's ascension, if we were not vigilant."

"What was it?"

He paused, hesitated, as if reluctant to say a word more. "I saw death. Unthinkable destruction. On a scale far greater than the Swarm War. I saw … the end of humanity. And it all started with the ascension. I saw you return, and lead the fight. And … I saw you fail." His face was pained, as if he wanted to say any other words than the ones he was saying. And hearing them sent a shiver down her spine, in spite of the fact she thought he was a lunatic. "I saw you marshall the defense of humanity, and fail. Earth burned. San Martin burned. Britannia fell. One by one, world by world, we fell. But it wasn't set in stone. Granger appeared to me, and told me it didn't have to be that way. Well, he didn't so much speak to me, as he *looked* at me, and I understood." He gathered himself up. "It was made clear to me that in the days to come after the ascension, humanity would be put through its greatest test. And that you would either lead us to victory, or a loss so utterly complete that we would cease to exist."

She shrugged. "What's new? Same old same old. Nothing we didn't go through thirty years ago." But she had to know. The curiosity ate at her. "And? What did old Tim say would be the determining factor? How do we get the best odds out of this shit show?"

He stared at her. Earnestly. So earnestly. It almost took her aback. "You need to remain true to Granger. Trust him. He'll deliver us again. I know it. *I know it.*"

She returned his earnest stare. "Tim Granger ... *is dead*. He died thirty years ago. I swear to you that I will honor his memory, and fight for the things he believed in to my last breath. But Tim is not ... coming ... back. Life just doesn't work that way."

The Patriarch allowed himself a small smirk. "He came back once. He'll do so again."

"That was different, Patriarch Huntsman. He fell into a Swarm singularity. It was artificial, and entirely controlled by their technology. He reappeared, same old Tim, and our scientists now have a pretty good grasp of how it all happened. He did not die, and come back. He went through a frickin wormhole. Hell, if it weren't for the ban on singularity research, we could probably reproduce the whole event."

The Patriarch smiled warmly. "Admiral Proctor, you think I'm crazy. I know. It's ok. But I don't believe in magic. I do believe in a higher power. Before I became the Patriarch, I was a bishop. A Mormon bishop. I believed in God, and I still do. But I know that God uses what tools he has, and in that case, he used Swarm technology to save us. It wasn't magic. And in this case, He'll use *something* … something that will send Granger back to us. Not magic. Not hocus pocus. But He'll do *something* to send us our Hero again. You'll see. You'll believe me, in the end."

An explosion rocked the building, and everyone cowered. A few screamed. Dammit, she'd expected the authorities to get a handle on the situation outside by now.

Out of all the people cowering, glancing up nervously at the ceiling or towards the walls, she alone stood rigid, smiling down at Patriarch Huntsman and Secretary General Curiel. "The end? Well this could be it, gentlemen."

Then the far wall, lined with bunks, boxes, and supplies, exploded inward. Proctor fell behind an overturned table, shoved there by her marine, who aimed his sidearm towards the gaping hole in the wall.

CHAPTER THIRTY-FIVE

Irigoyen Sector, San Martin System, San Martin
Galactic People's Congress safehouse, Ciudad Libertador

Admiral Proctor squinted through the dusty darkness of the room and watched Rex crawl over to her and the marine behind the table. Everyone else had sought cover, and Secretary General Curiel's security detail had taken positions on either side of the gaping hole in the wall, shooting at targets outside the building she couldn't see. Nor did she try to see.

"We can get you out through the way we came," said Rex, wincing as a few rounds struck the ceiling nearby.

She shook her head. "I'll take my chances with these guys," she said, indicating the soldiers leaning out of the hole. Somehow, they'd produced a few military grade assault rifles, probably from the storage crates lining the walls. At least it wasn't just her marine with his sidearm, though what she wouldn't give for a hundred IDF marines right now….

One of the soldiers fell back through the hole, cursing, bleeding from his shoulder. An aide to Curiel scrambled over and pulled him back from the wall and into the cover of another overturned table. The door burst open and several more soldiers replaced the man who'd fallen. A hail of gunfire peppered the opening in the wall, and the GPC soldiers responded in kind. Proctor covered her ears.

Oh god, this could be it.

A powerful, pulsing whine managed to pierce though the tumult of the gunfire, even through her hands pressed against her ears. It grew louder and louder, until finally something blazed past the opening in the wall, and Proctor only caught of glimpse of it before it passed.

It looked like an IDF fighter.

Another darted past the building, and Proctor heard the unmistakable sound of high caliber gunfire coming from the fighters. She hadn't heard that sound in decades—usually fighters fired their guns out in the silence of space. But these two were having a field day out in the street, making pass after pass, and eventually the assault rifles fell silent, either because they couldn't be heard over the constant rumble of the fighter's guns and engines, or because the unknown assailants wielding them were being mercilessly mowed down by shells meant to take out other fighters and capital ships.

Something chirped nearby. Her marine looked up in triumph, holding the comm device. "Finally got through, Admiral. The jamming is gone, and IT up on *Independence* broke through the hack."

She nodded, grabbing the handset. "This is Proctor. What's the situation?"

"Good to hear your voice, Shelby. Hold on…."

It was Ballsy. And it sounded like he was in a fighter or a shuttle. She didn't know whether to thank him, or berate him, for putting his life at risk when he should be sending his lieutenants, not himself, a captain, into the fight. What the hell was he thinking?

One of the fighters outside shot past again, firing its guns, and she heard the unmistakable sounds of exploding buildings nearby. She glanced over at Curiel. "I thought this was your *safe* house."

He nodded angrily. "We've been compromised. More than I thought."

Clearly.

The gunfire had ceased completely. Ballsy's voice blared through the handset again. "I think we got the last of them. I've got half my squadron patrolling the streets for three blocks in either direction, and all our marines are down here now, with another five units Admiral Tigre sent over. I'm sending a shuttle in to pick you up. It's going to nudge up right against that hole. My boys and I will provide cover while you jump in, just in case we missed any hostiles."

"Wait, you're not only down here, but you're piloting a *fighter*? What's gotten into you?"

He grunted. "Protecting my admiral, and my friend, Shelby. Couldn't trust the job to anyone else."

"Who the hell are they, Ballsy? Who's shooting at me?"

Ballsy grunted as he swung around the building—he clearly wasn't used to the g-forces of a fighter, especially one flying in a gravity well. "Still working on that. They managed to hack into our network and basically used your comm device to track you. Took Mumford forever to break through and block them. And the municipal police force is just overwhelmed—apparently there were a dozen other disturbances around the city at the same time they ambushed you, so the city's force was stretched thin. Hold on, coming in now. Can you see it?"

She peered around the table and saw the shuttle descend down from the sky and hold station right next to the hole, hovering a dozen meters off the ground—she hadn't noticed until then that she was on the third floor of a building. She hadn't even remembered climbing stairs.

"Ok Shelby, go. Shuttle's in position. I'm circling overhead with four other birds, and fifty marines are in the street below. Nothing is getting by us for the next sixty seconds. Go!"

She eyed the gap between the building and the open shuttle door with apprehension. It was only a few centimeters, but it was a long way down. "Can't the shuttle just land and I'll go down the stairs like a normal person?"

"Negative. The situation is still fluid. I'm getting you out of there now, while we have them confused and on the run, whoever they are."

"Fine." She stood up, tapping her marine's shoulder and motioning her head towards the shuttle. He ran ahead and stood by the hole, as the shuttle's engine's whined from the effort of hovering against gravity. Before she stepped over the gap, she looked around the jumbled mess of a room.

"Where's Curiel? And the Patriarch?"

One of the Secretary General's marines answered. "Taken to safety, ma'am."

She rolled her eyes. *Such a gentleman.*

From behind the table she had been hiding behind, Rex

was watching her. She nodded a farewell to him, and an implied *thank you* for his help. He nodded back. "Tell him I'll be in contact shortly. And that if he renegs, there will be swift hell to pay."

    She jumped.

CHAPTER THIRTY-SIX

Irigoyen Sector, San Martin System, San Martin
Bridge, ISS Independence

Proctor could barely contain her anger during the bumpy ascent through the atmosphere up to the *Independence*, and was still seething when she descended the ramp in the fighter bay. Ballsy and his fighters had preceded her by just a few minutes, and he was waiting for her when she got out.

"I want answers," she said, storming past him, aiming for the doors and beyond, the bridge. She nearly steamrolled over a young yeoman who was bent low over a power receptacle on the deck. His floppy hair bounced as he pulled out of the way at the last second. Normally she'd stop to apologize, but she was too angry at getting almost killed to remember social niceties.

"S—Sorry, ma'am," he stammered, and gave a quick salute before returning to his work.

She nodded a quick acknowledgment to the young man

before continuing on towards the bridge. "Answers, Ballsy, I want them." He fell into step next to her.

"Me too. What the hell happened? Who were you talking to to ruffle so many feathers? And guns?" He fell into step next to her, tossing his helmet to one of the flight crew.

"Curiel."

Ballsy did a double-take. "You're kidding."

She glared at him. "Does this look like a face that kids?"

His eyes darted up to her forehead. "Shelby, you're injured. Again. We're stopping by sickbay—"

She felt her head, and the hand came away with a small spot of blood. "Like hell we are. It's nothing. Bumped my head. Before I go anywhere near a doctor I want to know who the hell that was, and I want them neutralized. How the hell can I save civilization as we know it when we've got a bunch of thugs taking pot shots at me?"

The elevator doors barely opened in time to keep her from bumping into them. As the lift carried them to the bridge she filled him in on everything Rex had told her about Danny and the *Magdalena Issachar*, and everything she'd learned from Curiel and the Patriarch Huntsman and his Grangerite devotees.

Volz puffed air incredulously. "Unbelievable. I just can't fathom anyone worshiping an old fart like that, even if it *is* Tim. And the ambush? What did Curiel have to say about it? Those people were way too well equipped to just be some street thugs."

"I think Secretary General Curiel is not entirely in control of his own insurgency. The wheels are coming off the GPC, and I think he's not even in the driver's seat." The doors opened to the bridge, and she eyed Volz before stepping out.

"But *someone* is, Ballsy."

"Hold on," he said, reaching out to her arm before she entered the bridge. "Just so you know, we picked up … my son, Ethan, down on San Martin. Don't worry, it wasn't related to what happened to you," he added, when he saw her reaction. "But he was on a stolen shuttle from Bolivar. Was apparently on *Watchdog* when it blew. Thought you ought to know."

"What the hell is he doing here? By shuttle that's far."

"No idea. Haven't had time to ask him. We're still not … close."

She sighed, and touched her forehead to make sure the wound had stopped bleeding. "Ballsy, you're going to have to let go of that. He's your damn *son*."

"I know," he grunted. "He's a reckless jackass, but yes. I know."

Proctor shrugged, and started moving towards the open doors of the bridge. "Apple doesn't fall far from the tree, I guess." She turned back to smile. "Thanks for the rescue, Ballsy. Now get to the CIC, and get me some answers."

The bridge was in disarray with half the teams on their feet, darting back and forth between coordinating the marines' return from the surface, the IT team still cracking the code of the hackers, and who knew what else. "Admiral on the bridge!" said the marine standing at attention.

"Admiral," said Commander Yarbrough, relief spreading across his face. "Good to see you're safe."

"What's our status?" she strode to her seat—she didn't know if it was still the adrenaline rushing through her veins or what, but she didn't even have a hint of a limp. No—the pain was still there. Except rather than wince from it, she was letting it fuel her anger.

Rayna Scott was at the ops station, coordinating auxiliary systems repair efforts. Grime and scorch marks covered her uniform, but she otherwise looked like she was finally back in her element—repairing starships after battle. Her face lit up into a wrinkled smile when she saw Proctor. "Good to see you in one piece, Shelby. Engines and power plant back up to green. Patched our holes and we're ready to rumble."

Proctor sat down and nodded at the chief. "Thank you, Rayna." She turned to Commander Yarbrough. "What news from the surface?"

"I've been in contact with Admiral Tigre and the municipal authorities. They've collected bodies from the scene, and it looks like the perpetrators are a mix. Some IDF, some GPC, some street thugs that look like they were used for cannon fodder. We're trying to track down how they hacked into our system."

"The fact that there were some IDF people on the ground on *their* side tells me we've probably got some IT people on their side too. All our systems could be at risk." She sat down, and her knee exploded in pain. *Good. Let it piss you off, Shelby.*

"Admiral," began Qwerty, "transmission from CENTCOM San Martin. It's Admiral Tigre."

"Put him through."

Tigre's worried face filled the screen. "Dear god, Shelby, I'm so glad you're all right."

"So am I, Miguel. What can you tell me?"

He grunted. "Not much. We're still in the middle of sifting through the rubble and apprehending folks, but I think it's pretty clear this was a fringe element of the GPC. But the coordination and level of tech here was staggering. They must have some big-name backers."

"I want those names, Miguel. This is all connected—Danny, the *Magdalena Issachar* and Sangre de Cristo, the missing nuke—"

He did a double take. "Come again?"

She sighed. "You need to have a little talk with *Secretary General* Curiel. He's got eight more nukes of the same variety that hit Sangre, and one more that's missing, presumably taken by the same people taking potshots at me."

"Good god…."

"God has nothing to do with it, in spite of what the Grangerites think. And if he does, he's certainly not good. Let me know when you have more, Miguel, I've got a lot going on here."

He nodded. "Very well. I'll get in touch with Curiel. Tigre out."

She let out a deep breath. It was as if she hadn't had a chance to breathe since stepping into that used ship showroom just a few hours earlier. Who in the world would want to nuke millions of colonists? Who the hell would want it to look like Danny who'd done it?

Did Danny do it on purpose, thinking he'd ingratiate himself with someone? Or thinking that if he attacked a GPC-loyal world like Sangre that he'd influence popular opinion and sympathy for the GPC, and help it win independence and legitimacy? *Impossible.* She banished the thought.

"Admiral." Qwerty looked up, his face pale. "Receiving a wide-beam meta-space signal from the IDF station orbiting El

Amin. It's the farthest planet out in the San Martin system, about two light-hours away. The mystery ship is here."

Dammit.

She glanced over at Ballsy, who was huddled with Commander Mumford. "Are we ready?"

Ballsy shrugged. "We've been working on the new tactics. I guess we'll find out. Welterweight here sure thinks we're ready though."

Mumford looked like he wanted to contest the nickname, but only cleared his throat. "I've been working on the … uh, emotional projection issue, ma'am. I think I've figured it out. Well, enough to attenuate the signal. I've set up a regular EM grid across the hull, basically creating a thin meta-material shield. Like a Faraday cage, except this picks out the meta-space accompanied EM signal coming off the alien ship, and automatically adjusts the effective molecular orbital spacing of the meta-material shield to compensate."

"Good man. How sure are you that it works?"

Mumford cocked his head, as if calculating risk factors in his head. "The first few minutes might be rocky, but it'll automatically learn and adjust. And I've uploaded the program into all the fighters, too. Their EM field generators should be able to handle it."

So this was it. She paused, before making the decision. "Are we ready?" she repeated to the two men.

"As ready as we'll ever be, Shelby." Ballsy looked grim, but determined. That was enough for her.

"Ensign Riisa. Set a t-jump course to El Amin. It's time we go on offense."

CHAPTER THIRTY-SEVEN

Irigoyen Sector, San Martin System, El Amin
Bridge, ISS Independence

The t-jump made her less queasy this time, and Proctor wondered if it was just because she was acclimating to the process, or if doing such a short jump meant less spatial and temporal distortion. Either way, when they arrived, the viewscreen shifted from a video feed of the tranquil blue San Martin to the icy gray El Amin. The camera zoomed in, and the Golgothic ship bloomed across the screen.

She felt a wave of irrational fear and consternation, which just as quickly dissipated. Commander Mumford called out from the rear of the bridge. "The meta-material shield is working, Admiral. The other ship's EM field isn't penetrating the hull."

"For now." She watched the screen, studying the alien, abrupt curves of the other ship. "How are we doing on scanning that thing? Are the sensors able to penetrate it yet?"

"Working on it, Admiral," said Mumford. "I have a few ideas on that front. Just get me some time...."

"I'll stall for as long as we can afford it."

Yarbrough had sidled up behind her. "Is stalling wise?"

"I want to know what we're shooting at before we shoot at it."

He frowned. "For reasons of conscience?" The implication was clear. She was the reluctant annihilator of the remnants of the Swarm, and the *Mother Killer* of the Skiohra.

"For tactical reasons, Commander. Before we start firing, I want to make sure our shots count, because we might only have a few shots to begin with." She turned to him. "Unless you prefer we start firing blindly and willy nilly? Just take our chances and hope for the best?"

He backed off. "Of course, Admiral. I'll prep the emergency crews for damage response."

"Good."

They spent a tense half hour watching the ship, which slowly orbited the tiny gray planet. Each time they passed the IDF station it reflected the weak light of San Martin's sun back at them, which at this distance only looked like a very bright star.

"So it's ignoring the orbital station this time, and us." She tapped her armrests impatiently. "Tell me about El Amin. What's down there?"

Lieutenant Whitehorse worked her console and brought up the data. "Basically just a giant ball of water ice and rock. Molten iron-nickel core. About the size of Pluto, if that helps. There is a small research station down on the surface."

"IDF?"

"No, ma'am. A research outpost run by one of the private universities on San Martin."

"Population?"

"A few hundred."

She went through the grim moral calculus involved with balancing the needs of a few hundred civilians on the ground, the few dozen IDF officers on the station, and the crew of the *Independence*, along with the billions who were depending on her, in this moment. It was ghoulish to think about, but those unfortunate people down on the planet were not the highest priority.

Qwerty looked up from the comm station. "They're asking for assistance, Admiral. And they're suffering the full effect of the Golgothic broadcast, so they're ... a little agitated."

"Tell them we're occupied, but that they should evacuate immediately."

Lieutenant Whitehorse shouted. "Alien ship is firing!"

On the screen they all watched as the same purple-white beam lanced out from the strange ship, not towards the *Independence*, but down at the icy planet below.

"Are they hitting the research station?"

Whitehorse shook her head. "No, ma'am. It's just drilling into the surface like it did at Ido."

Yarbrough stiffened. "Are we going to respond? It's still a direct attack on a UE world, with UE civilians on it. Those people are in immediate danger."

"I agree, they're in immediate danger," said Proctor, "but I want to be sure of what we're doing before we rush in with all guns firing—" she held up a hand as he started to interrupt her. "There are bigger stakes here than a research station, Commander. If we get this wrong, billions die, instead of hundreds."

His expression was cold. "Small comfort for the families of those students and researchers down there."

She turned back to the screen. "I didn't say we were doing nothing. Ballsy, you there?" She tapped on the comm.

Moments later, from the comm speaker, "Shelby?"

"I want an evacuation of El Amin. Now. Every available shuttle. Even the fighters—we can fit up to three people in those if they get cozy. And hurry."

"Aye, Admiral," he said, and started barking orders at his staff in the background.

"And Tyler," she added. Using his given name caught his attention, like she wanted.

"Shelby?"

"I mean *all* shuttles. And *all* pilots. Got it?"

A long pause.

"Understood."

She turned back to Lieutenant Whitehorse. "Progress of the beam?"

"It's drilled down about ten percent into El Amin's crust. Will hit the mantle soon."

Commander Mumford called from the science station. "Ma'am, El Amin is fundamentally different than Ido. Ido was essentially a giant rock. Never even attained hydrostatic equilibrium or planetary differentiation—you know, its core was essentially the same as its outer regions, with no mantle or —"

Proctor sighed. "Commander, I *am* a scientist. No need for

the science lesson. Please get to the point."

"Yes, ma'am. So El Amin is different. There's a crust, a mantle, a core—you know, like a regular old planet. And with that beam drilling into it...."

She filled in the blanks. "Ok. So we're looking at a magma eruption." She glanced at the sensor readout on her command console. The science station's data stream scrolled down, and she only caught snippets of the readings. "What's the pressure? How much magma, how far will it blast out, and, more importantly, what's the risk to the research station?"

Mumford shook his head. "This is a PhD dissertation here, ma'am. We could study the geo-dynamics problem for years. But, best guess, we're looking at a ... large ... eruption. Soon." He looked up, his face somber. "The drilling site is only a hundred kilometers from the research station. Even a minor eruption, given the lack of atmosphere and low gravity, is going to wreak havoc on the station—possibly completely destroy it."

She nodded. "Proctor to Captain Volz."

"Yeah, Admiral?"

"Ballsy, you know how I said *hurry*?"

"Yeah, Admiral?"

She watched the seismic readings on her science data feed begin to stir, immediately reaching up to the top of the scale. "What I meant was, *hurry ... the hell ... up.*"

CHAPTER THIRTY-EIGHT

Irigoyen Sector, San Martin System, El Amin
Brig, ISS Independence

The door to his cell slid open, and there he was. *Oh god, just turn me over to CENTCOM, already.*

Zivic forced a smile. "So soon? I wasn't expecting you for another ... oh, ten years. Like last time."

Volz glared at him icily. "Shut up and listen. We're engaging the alien ship again." He hesitated. "The Admiral ordered that *every* available pilot assist in the effort."

Zivic did a double take. "You want *me* to fly a fighter out there against that thing?"

"Don't be silly. I wouldn't let you near a fighter if my life depended on it." Volz's scowl deepened. "There's a research station down there on El Amin. Just a few hundred people. You're going to take the shuttle you came in on, get in, grab people, and get out. Simple. Can you handle that?"

Zivic shrugged. He desperately wanted to reach down into his boot for his metal flask, but remembered it was long since empty. "Sounds easy enough."

His father cocked his head at him, his eyes still hard as ice. "*Without* getting anyone killed. Nothing fancy. Just in, and out."

Zivic glared back. *How dare he?* He bit off a curse, and forced a painfully thin smile. "Of course."

It looked like Volz was expecting more verbal fireworks than that and almost looked disappointed, but after a brief awkward moment he held out an arm indicating the door.

They walked quickly, in silence, the two decks it took to get to the fighter bay. The shuttle he'd arrived in was sitting off to the side, its ramp descended, just waiting for a pilot. At the top, he stopped and turned to look at his father.

"Remember. In, and out. Nothing fancy. Nothing heroic. You're there to save as many students as you can."

"Got it," he turned back towards the cockpit.

"And Ethan," Volz added, making Zivic pause at the hatch, "that EM field that brings out the crazies in people is active. We've figured out how to shield the *Independence* from it, and we've modified the shuttle. But the people down there are going to be … agitated. And you will be too. Be careful."

Be careful? He tried to smile again. "Thanks for the concern. I'll be fine."

The hatch closed, and he flipped the engines on before he could even sit down. Ten seconds later he was soaring out of the fighter bay, still half dazed at the sudden turn of events. He'd spent the past hour in his cell wondering if his father had suddenly turned revolutionary, leading the GPC cause at the helm of a new warship. But his mentioning of the *Admiral*—

there was only one *Admiral* to his father—told Zivic that maybe he'd gotten lucky after all. There was no way in hell that Shelby Proctor was at the head of a multi-organizational galactic conspiracy.

The giant gray orb of El Amin filled his viewport, and given how small the planet actually was the visual told him they must be pretty damn close to it. In the distance, maybe a hundred kilometers away, he could just make out the dot of the mystery ship, and the shimmering purple-white beam that was boring into the surface. He aimed the shuttle down at the research station just a handful of kilometers away from the impact zone and punched the accelerator.

"Here goes nothing," he breathed. The craft shot forward, and the planet started growing even larger in the viewport, filling the entire area. Down below, several dozen kilometers away, he gulped as he saw bright red magma leap up out of the widening hole being dug by the alien's beam, and he knew that time was not on his side.

"Is that thing going to blow anytime soon?" he asked.

The comm cracked. "Yes," came his father's reply.

"Ok…." He pushed down on the accelerator, maxing it out. "Uh, any advice?"

"Hurry," was all his father said. The comm fell silent.

"Got it," he replied to no one. "Ok, no atmosphere, so no brakes. Time to reverse thrust in," he glanced at the surface range-finder, "three … two … one…." He cut off the main thrusters and switched to the forward thrusters. The inertial cancelers took a moment to adjust, making his stomach churn a bit as the g forces thrust him forward against the restraints, far more than the collision into San Martin's ocean had just an hour earlier. *Good thing Sara isn't here….*

The research station loomed ahead. A small armada of fighters and shuttles from the *Independence* was in the process of either landing or taking off from the station's lone shuttle bay, the protective energy field holding in the air pressure shimmering each time a ship passed through. In the distance, kilometers away, the purple-white beam illuminated the entire landscape, casting long, alien shadows over the ice rocks and craggy peaks the rippled away into the distance.

He passed through the field and found an unoccupied spot to land on the deck. As soon as the engines were idling, he popped the hatch and started dashing down the still-descending ramp….

And was immediately assaulted by a wave of fear, excitement, anger, rage, sadness, all at once. Just like he'd felt back on *Watchdog*. *Oh shit*, he thought. *This is going to get intense*.

Barely able to suppress his mix of anger and fear he ran towards the doors at the end of the bay—where was the anger coming from? His father, of course. The fear? Obvious—he was about to die. The sadness? Who the hell knew? All he knew, all he focused on, all he could force himself to think about was, *rescue. Find the students. Find as many as I can, and cram them into the shuttle, and get the hell out.*

He rushed into the hallway where another fighter pilot was ushering a group of frightened-looking college students back towards the bay. The other pilot, obviously trying to suppress his own mix of fear and emotion, waved towards a door at the end of the corridor. "They've all assembled in the mess. Just a few left. Grayson should be able to fit most of them in his shuttle, but the rest will need to go in yours."

"Got it," he said in a rush, and ran down the hallway. In the mess hall, the pilot he assumed was Grayson was arguing with one of the women he assumed was a professor or senior researcher. Everyone—the dozen or so students, the researcher, Grayson—looked terrified. The alien's field was taking its toll on all of them. "What's the problem?" he yelled.

The researcher pointed at another door in the mess hall. "There's more. They've barricaded themselves in a lab. I can't convince them to leave. It's ... it's...." She balled her fists and actually *shrieked*. This was getting out of control, he thought. *Should I smack her?* He batted the irrational thought aside and pointed at the exit, yelling at Grayson.

"Get them all in your shuttle. I'll handle the stubborn ones."

"You sure?"

"Yeah. GO!" He grabbed one of the students sitting on a cafeteria bench fidgeting uncontrollably with his hands, and shoved him towards the door. "GO! All of you, go!"

Luckily, they all ran for the door, and he didn't have to resort to violence. *Unfortunately.* He was kind of hoping for an outlet. Maybe as consolation he could have a little.... He reached down to his boot, and caught himself halfway when he realized, again, that it was empty. *Dammit.*

He ran towards the door the researcher had indicated, and nearly fell over as the entire room shifted, sloping down to his right. "Holy shit," he mumbled. The walls and floor were shaking violently, and all the tables slid down towards the far wall to his right as he stumbled towards the door.

He wrenched it open—luckily it didn't jamb with the shifting orientation of the entire building—and ran down the hallway lined with laboratories, struggling to keep his footing against the rightward slope, as well as the glass that was falling out of the laboratories' windows. Which was a blessing and a curse, he supposed, as looking through all the shattering windows let him know that none of the labs were occupied.

Except for the door at the very end of the hall. It was shut, and through the tiny still-unbroken window next to it he could see a fear-filled face looking out.

Using the leaning wall as leverage to occasionally redirect his course, he launched himself down the hallway, and pushed on the door's handle.

It didn't budge.

"Oh, *hell* no."

Supporting himself on the slanting wall, he kicked the door. The dull thud of his boot told him the door was not exactly made to be kicked in. In fact, it probably served as an emergency airlock, by the looks of it.

The wide eyes staring out the tiny window watched him in terror. Zivic cupped his hands around his mouth and yelled into the glass. "We've got to get out of here! This place is going to blow!"

Wide-eyes retreated from the window further into the lab, and Zivic peered in. Three other students huddled in the corner, while a fourth lay sprawled out near the other corner.

A pool of blood surrounded his head.

"Aw, shit," he said. The building started to tremble again as another earthquake struck. His comm device crackled from his pocket.

"Ethan, you're out of time," said the father. "The alien's hole is full-on erupting now. Magma is jetting out into the sky like a fountain. You've got a billion tons of a hot lava rain incoming within minutes."

"Double shit." He peered back into the room. *Ok, new plan, Ethan.* One of the pair of students in the corner had thick glasses, and his eyes were flitting back and forth nervously. His mouth moved as if he was mumbling under his breath— though for all Zivic knew the kid could be shouting since he could hear hardly a thing through that window. The other kid in the corner only held his head in his hands, sobbing, while Wide-eyes paced back and forth.

An idea struck him. *Ethan, you're a horrible, horrible man.* He pounded on the window, and wide-eyes looked up, his eyes somehow getting even wider. Zivic pointed to the corner. "Hey! That one! Four eyes! He's a fucking alien! He's going to fucking kill you both!"

Part of him—the juvenile, evil half—wanted to laugh out loud as Wide-eyes and Cry-baby both snapped their heads to look at Four-eyes, and before he could even smile the pair of them bolted towards the door.

Zivic was waiting for them. He reached down and picked up a piece of railing that had fallen onto the floor and brandished it behind his back, just in case. The door opened and Wide-eyes burst out, followed by Cry-baby.

He concentrated, trying to keep all snark, all anger, all fear out of his voice. Anything more could set them off—the whole situation could go downhill very fast. He thought of the sloped floor beneath him. *Well, further downhill.* "I'm an IDF pilot. I'm here to rescue you. Go to the bay and wait right next to the shuttle. Move!"

They both blinked wildly. Wide-eyes dashed off, making

Zivic relax his arm a little—looked like he wouldn't be needing the piece of railing he was holding. But Crying-baby just retreated to the corner in the hallway by the door and whimpered. Zivic dropped the railing, grit his teeth against the raging emotions jumbling his thoughts, and took a step forward. He reached out and touched the kid's shoulder. Couldn't be more than eighteen.

"Hey. What's your name? My name's Ethan."

The whimpering paused. "N—N—Nicky. Nicky Epstein."

"Listen, Nicky," he squeezed the kid's shoulder. This one needed a softer touch than Wide-eyes, apparently. Good God, where the hell was that flask? "We've got to go. Time to run. Can you run?"

He nodded quickly.

"Good." He smiled, and squeezed again. "Then run." He pointed down the hallway. "Run!"

The kid swallowed visibly, and ran.

One more.

The building rocked, as if something had slammed into it. "Shit." He dashed into the room and knelt down to check on the kid laying in his blood. The building shook again. He reached for the neck, feeling for a pulse.

Nothing.

His comm cracked again. "Ethan, NOW!"

Four-eyes was still sitting in the corner, crying now. He ran up the slope of the floor, grabbed the kid by the wrist, and started pulling. Luckily, the kid let himself be led through the door, and even managed to keep up through the hallway and into the cafeteria.

But as he tried running past one of the cafeteria tables, the kid tripped on debris, slipped, and hit his head on the bench on the way down.

Knocked out. Cold.

The building shook again as something else hit it. "Dammit!" he yelled, and bent over to lift the kid up. Four-eyes was rail-thin and light as a ten-year-old, despite the post-pubescent stubble on his chin. Zivic, adrenaline-fueled, lifted the kid over his shoulders and resumed his sprint towards the bay.

A voice blared out from his pocket. "Ethan, if you're pretending to be a hero when you should be getting people out, I'm going to—"

Zivic slapped his pocket and the comm flipped off. He ran towards the bay, where, in the space beyond the shimmering force field holding in the atmosphere, he saw the unmistakable sight of giant balls of lava crashing down on the landscape all around them.

"Well, kid, this is going to be a close one," he murmured.

And he ran.

CHAPTER THIRTY-NINE

Irigoyen Sector, San Martin System, El Amin
Bridge, ISS Independence

Admiral Proctor nervously tapped her armrest. The Golgothic's purple-white beam continued drilling down into El Amin's crust, and magma was spewing out into the skies of the tiny planet, hundreds of kilometers out in all directions, splashing down in great red globs all across the surface. Where they struck, ice explosively sublimed and steamed out into the non-existent atmosphere like great roiling white oceans that dissipated as they boiled off into the vacuum.

"Any word from him?"

The comm speaker nearby answered. "Haven't heard from him in a few minutes," said Volz.

He sounded pissed.

The magma eruption intensified. Vast showers of lava rained down, with several large globes slamming into one of the wings of the research station. Proctor stared at the screen.

Something moved against the backdrop of the station and the rain of fire. Fast. "Is that him?"

Lieutenant Whitehorse nodded. "Yeah. It's the shuttle."

"Zoom in." She breathed a little easier.

But not for long. The screen zoomed in to the shuttle as it streaked away from the station, just as a giant globe of lava crashed into the landing pad of the shuttle bay.

The entire station exploded. With gut-churning weaves and barrel-rolls, the shuttle dodged another hail of falling lava, with maneuvers that Proctor was sure would have resulted in the contents of her stomach being smeared all over the shuttle's window had she been aboard.

"That's…" began Ensign Riisa at the helm. "That's … incredible. I've never seen anyone fly like that."

Proctor nodded in agreement. It was true—out of any fighter pilot she'd ever met, Ballsy's kid outshone them all. Even Ballsy. She supposed that was half of why he hated the kid, in spite of what Ballsy claimed.

But the fiery hell he was flying through was worse than any fighter battle with the Swarm she'd ever seen. Thousands of globules were falling down through the black sky all around the shuttle….

And yet it still weaved, looped, darted, rolled, and banked its way through. She found herself gripping the armrests so tight that her knuckles turned white.

"No!" Lieutenant Whitehorse yelled from behind her. Proctor stared in horror. One of the globs of lava had struck the shuttle. Red-hot streams of the stuff fell away as the shuttle accelerated upwards, and Proctor realized what he was doing—since there was no atmosphere to blast the lava off the shuttle, he had to rely on the shuttle's acceleration to shed the boiling rock.

Another glob struck the shuttle. And another....

And it was free. Clear of the maelstrom of lava rain, it accelerated even faster, and the rest of the lava coating the ravaged surface of the shuttle streamed away as it made a beeline for the *Independence*.

Proctor breathed a sigh of relief. She tapped her comm on. "Lieutenant Zivic, this is Admiral Proctor. Well done, Ethan. You guys okay in there?"

"Yeah..." came the hesitant reply. "I guess."

"You guess?"

"Well ... just covered in the vomit from three other people, each of whom have also soiled themselves. We might have to just hose out the entire shuttle."

Proctor smirked at that. "Well if that's the worst that happened, we can thank our lucky stars."

A pause. "I ... uh ... I did lose someone. Couldn't carry two people at once. I left the injured one. At least, I think he was injured, but he might have been dead. I ... guess I could have tried to carry both—"

"It's not your fault, Ethan," she said, "you saved three lives. If it weren't for you, they'd be dead. Remember that. We can't save *everyone*."

"But—"

"End of conversation. Report to the fighter bay, and for reassignment to the fighter squadron."

Zivic protested. "But, ma'am, I don't think I'm ready for that."

"Bullshit. After that fancy flying? No. You've got your wings back, I don't care what your father says. Proctor out."

She glanced at the timer on her console, then back up at the screen where the alien mystery ship was still drilling into the planet. *Plenty of time*, she thought. and turned back at Whitehorse. "You think he can handle it?"

Whitehorse shrugged. "Honestly? Don't know, ma'am."

"You two were pretty serious for awhile, from what Ballsy tells me. No one here knows him better than you. Even Ballsy—parents' perceptions of their kids can get … colored, over time."

Parents, and aunts, she thought, her mind drifting momentarily to the news about Danny that Curiel and Rex had given her.

"He's good," Whitehorse said, reaching back to re-tie her hair into a tight regulation bun. "The best. But his mental state? Ever since his mom and stepdad?" She shook her head. "That changed him. Almost killed him. It was soon after that when I ended it between us—I just couldn't handle it anymore. There's … there are some things you just don't come back from, accident or no."

Proctor nodded. It reminded her of her little speech to Curiel about Granger. There are some things you just don't come back from. *Black holes chief among them,* she thought wryly.

"He'll get over it. He has to. And the way I figure it, he just saved three kids. That evens the score." Proctor glanced at the timer again. *Almost there….*

"With all due respect, ma'am … I don't think it works that way," said Whitehorse, somberly.

She was right, of course. But she'd made her own share of

mistakes—innocent, honest mistakes, made in the heat of battle, the spur of the moment, that led to deaths. Some of those mistakes led to untold numbers of deaths. But in the rush to save humanity, what the hell else could she have done? "No, it doesn't. But whether redemption or a lighter conscience comes or not, we need him." She glanced at the ship again, still drilling away. "And given current events, we're going to need thousands more like him."

The timer approached zero, and she finally turned to Commander Mumford. "Status?"

He nodded. "The progress of the drilling is proceeding just like at Ido. Identical to a T."

"You ready with the scans? As soon as we start this thing, I want to be ready. I want to know everything about that ship, and we don't get a second shot at this."

"Yes, ma'am. We're ready."

She tapped the comm on. "Ballsy, your boys ready?"

A few seconds later he answered. "Yeah. Last of them just offloaded the passengers, and we're ready to launch."

Commander Yarbrough looked up from his XO's station, and nodded once. "All systems reporting ready, Admiral."

She gripped her armrests. "Good. All hands, prepare for Operation Proctor One."

A deep breath. *Here goes nothing.*

"Now."

CHAPTER FORTY

Irigoyen Sector, San Martin System, El Amin Bridge, ISS Independence

Commander Yarbrough nodded his acknowledgement. "Launch fighters. Ensign Riisa, move the *Independence* to flank the Golgothics at z plus five kilometers. All mag-rail crews prepare to fire. Laser crews, standby."

"Aye, aye, sir," said Riisa at the helm. The other ship grew large on the viewscreen as they closed in, and several dozen fighters flitted out into the shrinking gap between them.

"Emergency response crews report ready," said Yarbrough, looking up from his station.

Proctor nodded. "Good. Let's get this show on the road. Ballsy?" She leaned toward the comm speaker on her armrest.

"Admiral?"

"You have authorization to begin firing when they're in position. And remember, we only get one shot at this." She glanced over at Commander Mumford at the science station. "Status?"

"The drilling beam has reached the core." He shook his head. "Still not detecting any change on the ship's surface, and sensors still can't penetrate the hull."

Yarbrough stood up and paced nervously. Everyone was staring at the screen. "It could be different this time. We only have one data point we're going off."

He had a point, Proctor thought. Still, it was their best bet. The last time that port opened they'd been able to reach inside with their sensors, but only barely. And best bet or no, they didn't have time to—

"Now!" yelled Commander Mumford. "A port is opening on the underside."

"Open fire," said Proctor.

Through the deck plates she could feel the stutter and pulse of the mag-rail guns as they opened up a barrage of high-velocity slugs at the alien ship. "Concentrate on one location," she said, indicating one section of the ship on her tactical readout and sending the coordinates over to the tactical crew. "See if you can't punch through in one spot. Didn't work last time, but you never know."

"All fighters are engaging the hatch," said Ballsy through the comm. "They've opened fire. No opening mechanisms in sight, but we're raining hell on it all the same."

"Good. No return fire yet?" She turned to Lieutenant Whitehorse at tactical and her crew. The sensor officer shook his head.

"No, ma'am."

Proctor turned back to the viewscreen. "Well that's damn

peculiar. They're still drilling into the planet. Mumford, I thought you said it had reached the core?"

"It has." Mumford scratched his head. "They've decreased the intensity of the beam down to less than one percent power. I should amend my previous statement—they've reached the core, but the pressures down there are so intense that most of the hole immediately fills with liquid nickel-iron from the outer core."

"So what's the beam doing right now?"

Mumford shook his head. "Maybe just maintaining part of the hole open until it can launch its doohickey. No sign of that either, though."

"But the port on the ship is still open? Maybe the fighters are having an effect. Ballsy?" Proctor gripped the chair and leaned towards the comm.

Ballsy's booming voice filled the room. "We're spraying that hole with everything we've got, Shelby. Whatever armor they've got, it's damn thick, and probably juiced up with something like the old smart-steel armor our ships used to have back in the day, but, you know, a billion times stronger, since we can't seem to make a dent in this thing."

She nodded, and watched the Golgothic's purple-white beam as it started flickering, puttering towards the end of its life. "Whatever you're doing, it looks like it might be working. The beam is shutting down, and the ship hasn't launched its cargo yet like last time at Ido." She turned to tactical. "Are the mag-rails having any effect?"

Whitehorse shook her head. "Minimal. We're hitting the same spot we were with the whole fleet last time. Finally gouging out a decent-sized hole, but that armor is …

formidable."

Proctor stroked her chin. "At least we've shown it's mortal." She eyed the alien ship on the screen as its beam ramped down, pulsing, flickering. "This is unnerving. Why isn't it fighting back like last time?"

Commander Yarbrough studied his data readout. "It could be that it no longer even views us as a threat. When a few ants attack the treads of your boot, do you stop what you're doing to stomp on them?"

"Depends on the ant," she murmured, trying to put the pieces together. Something was off. She turned back to Mumford. "Are we getting what we came for?"

"Making progress … but I'm still running into heavy interference just inside that hatch. It would sure help if—"

"Captain! Something's coming out!" Whitehorse pointed up at the screen. Sure enough, the same small metallic sphere emerged from the ship's hatch, and in a flicker of near instantaneous acceleration, launched itself down to the surface, following the remains of the purple-white beam, which still flickering and pulsing as it decayed.

"Ballsy, target that thing and destroy it," she said into the comm.

On the viewscreen they all watched as several of the fighters looped around the ship and shot down towards the metallic sphere as it sped towards the hole on the planet's surface.

One of the fighters exploded.

"The ship is firing!" yelled Whitehorse, even as they watched a second fighter explode.

"Tactical, take that thing out." Proctor said, standing up

suddenly. "All available mag-rails. Fire."

Whitehorse shook her head. "It's moving too fast for the mag-rail targeting computers."

Another fighter exploded as the Golgothic ship launched a massive rail gun slug of its own. There were three fighters left trailing the sphere, unloading their guns into it, to no avail. Proctor shook her head. "Call them off, Ballsy."

The three fighters pulled off. Only a few dozen kilometers remained between the sphere and the hole, and the distance shrunk quickly. Before long, the sphere plunged into the fiery storm of lava rain that was erupting from the hole, and completely disappeared from view.

"It's moving," said Whitehorse. They all watched as the Golgothics started pulling away, the beam now completely shut off. "The hatch is closing."

Proctor paced back to the science station. "Commander, what's the word? Did we get anything?"

Mumford shook his head slowly. "I'll need more time to break through that interference."

"How much time?"

He shrugged. "Five minutes? Maybe? This thing is like nothing I've ever seen. It's almost like a meta-space shielding going on in there, since I can't even probe it with virtual particle scans."

"Ensign Riisa," she called down to the lower bridge. "Flank it. Get in its way. Match its course if it turns. If it wants to leave, it's got to go through us."

The general murmur of battle operations on the bridge fell quieter as they all understood the implications of that order. "Aye, aye, Admiral."

Yarbrough came up behind her and murmured in her ear. "This had better be worth it. We're sacrificing a lot just for some data."

Proctor nodded. "Without data, we're shooting blanks, Commander."

The *Independence* darted forward into the path of the alien ship. Proctor could feel the strain of the inertial cancelers pulse against the deck plates. "Is it slowing?"

Riisa shook her head. "No, ma'am."

"Three kilometers," said Whitehorse.

Proctor had returned to stand behind her chair, and gripped the headrest tightly.

"Two kilometers."

Whitehorse was shaking her head. "Still not slowing down." She looked up, her face ashen white. "One kilometer."

Something darted out from the bottom of the viewscreen towards the alien ship, moving fast.

A shuttle.

Proctor's grip on the headrest tightened. "Who the hell is that?!"

CHAPTER FORTY-ONE

Irigoyen Sector, San Martin System, El Amin
Fighter bay, ISS Independence

Zivic had no sooner touched the shuttle down onto the deckplate of the fighter bay when the three students ripped their seat restraints away and raced towards the exit hatch.

All three of them were covered in vomit. One of them had a wet crotch. Zivic rolled his eyes, but part of him couldn't blame the kid—he'd put them through the wringer with those maneuvers. It was like nothing he'd ever done before. Not even since—

As soon as the memory surfaced he shoved it aside. Seeing his father had finally brought it to the surface, and he'd been working hard to suppress it. But now was not the time. There were bigger fish to fry.

He followed them out the hatch and bounded down the ramp. A deck hand was already examining the exterior of the ship. The nameplate, with the word *Fenway* printed on it, had nearly half melted off. "She going to live?" asked Zivic.

The deck hand shrugged, his floppy blonde hair swishing as he shook his head. "I suppose it was either her skin, or yours, sir."

Not knowing where to go, the three students had grouped up at the bottom of the ramp, so Zivic pointed to the exit. "Your people are assembling in the flight deck mess hall. Out the door, to the right. You can't miss it. There are bathrooms there so you can ... uh, clean up." His eyes darted down towards their stained clothing.

One of the kids—Four-Eyes, the one who'd been cowering in the corner—looked like he was finally coming out of his daze. "Did you ... did anyone get Chen?"

Zivic paused. "I'm sorry, who?"

"He was injured. I think. It's hard to remember. But I remember him hitting his head, and he fell. I remember blood, but I was too freaked out at the time to ... well ... to check on him."

The other kid. The one laying on the floor in his own blood. His pulse had been undetectable. Though, in the heat of the escape, Zivic wasn't one hundred percent sure he'd been dead. Ninety-nine percent sure, but ... could he have saved him, too?

Zivic shook his head. But he couldn't bring himself to say the words. *He's dead, kid.* "Let's ... just go to the mess hall. Get you guys cleaned up."

He ushered them to the door and pointed down the hall. When they'd gone, he glanced up at the window to the CIC. *He'd* be up there. Zivic half wanted to just go back to his cell.

Go lay down. Commiserate with Sara, who he supposed was still locked up in a cell of her own.

But he climbed the stairs.

"What's the situation?"

Volz glanced up, a shadow of a scowl clouding his face. "Nice flying."

"Thanks."

Volz turned back to the situational screens. "Just figuring out how to get this hatch on the mystery ship to stay open." Zivic followed his father's eyes to the video feed, where he watched the alien ship start to move.

Through the comm, Admiral Proctor's voice boomed. "Ballsy, target that thing and destroy it!"

Volz tapped the comm open to the group of fighters closest to the alien ship. "Raptor squad, pursue and engage the hatch. Unload everything you have. We've got to keep that thing open."

The six fighters of the Raptor squad looped around the alien ship and darted down underneath it, positioning themselves for shots at the hatch.

"Can't you target its opening mechanism?"

Volz didn't even look at him. "Thanks, Sherlock. Already tried it."

"Can't we—"

Volz's head snapped towards him. "Get the hell out! Kinda busy here." His thumb jabbed towards the door.

On the tactical screen, one of the glowing icons indicating the fighters blipped out. The other screen confirmed it—a brief fireball marked where one of the fighters had been.

One of the assistant CAGs swore. "Cliffhanger's gone."

Another icon blipped out. Another fireball. "And Highside, too."

Zivic shook his head and left. He took the stairs three at a time and landed painfully on the flight deck. Before he could even see what the deck hand was doing, he was already flying up the ramp to the shuttle *Fenway*. He paused to yell down at him. "Detach that refueling line or there's going to be some serious whiplash."

To his credit, the deck hand took it in stride, dropped what he was doing with some cylinders in the corner and rushed to snap the fuel line off the shuttle, his blonde hair flopping almost like a breeze was blowing it. "Good to go, sir."

Moments later the shuttle was arcing quickly out the bay doors, passing the atmospheric containment field. He clicked over to autopilot and set a destination: the alien ship. With the shuttle flying itself he sprung over to the flight suit locker near the hatch. *Please don't be empty*, he thought.

It wasn't. He pulled the suit on without removing his vomit-stained clothes, and jammed the helmet into place. The seals engaged. He'd no sooner sat back down at the controls when the comm erupted in an explosion of yelling and cursing.

"Ethan get your ass back here NOW!"

His father did not sound pleased.

Rather than waste time on a response, he angled the shuttle straight towards the hatch. The autopilot had gotten him close, but of course it had maintained a safe following distance.

Safety was the last thing on his mind. The hatch was closing, and he doubted his effort would make a difference. But according to pops, and Admiral Proctor, that hatch had to stay open. So he'd keep it open, dammit.

The distance closed rapidly, and at the last second he applied lateral thrust, rotating the shuttle such that the hatch was pointing away from the alien ship.

The collision threw him out of his chair—he'd forgotten to secure the seat restraint. He flew out sideways and into the wall. A pop told him his shoulder dislocated, but the pain was absent, replaced by an adrenaline-fueled sense of GET THE HELL OUT.

One glance out the front viewport told him he'd succeeded. The shuttle was firmly wedged into the alien ship's hatch, whose door was now grinding down on the hull. If he was going to get out, now was the time.

He punched the opening mechanism on the shuttle's hatch with his good arm. It started to open, but ground to a halt. Jammed. "Well, shit," he murmured. A quick glance out the hatch's tiny window told him there was no chance it would open any further.

The roof of the shuttle buckled as the alien ship's hatch door closed down upon it, clenching the shuttle like a powerful jaw. All the air was evacuated by that point, but he could almost imagine the shrieking twisting steel of the shuttle protest the crushing force.

"Think, Zivic. Think," he murmured to himself, scanning the inside of the shuttle for something, anything, that would help him get out. He opened the armory locker. Empty. *Of course*, he thought wryly. *It don't rain but it shitstorms*. That's what Sara would have said.

What would Sara *do*? She seemed to have an uncanny knack for surviving, during the two days that he'd gotten to know her. An image of her popped into his mind, standing above him in the bay of the *Miguel Urquiza*, brandishing the plasma welding torch she'd used to knock the Bolivaran Intelligence officer cold.

Plasma welder. He yanked the utility locker open and sure enough there it was, right where she'd left it. He primed it, and cranked it on, crying out when the bright spot of plasma seared itself into his vision. His helmet should have automatically darkened, but it seemed to be malfunctioning.

He felt the steel of the shuttle grind and shriek through his feet. His malfunctioning helmet was the least of his worries. Luckily, the welder was rated at vacuum: the sharp plasma flame was bright despite the lack of air in the compartment. He brought it to bear on the bottom edge of the hatch, where there was the most space already open to the the outside.

Please cut, please cut, please cut, please cut.... The thing was a welder, not a ... cutter? Is that a thing? He didn't have time to think about it. He cranked the power up to maximum and, with a thrill of relief, sliced clean through the metal like it was butter.

Very hard, cold butter. It was slow work, but a minute later he pulled the plasma torch away, anchored himself against the opposing wall, and kicked the section of the hatch away with a grunt.

It flew out into space. He grabbed the edges of the hole he'd cut, his dislocated shoulder burning with fiery pain, and moments later he was sailing through the vacuum, tumbling end over end from the slight torque he'd applied to himself as he'd left the shuttle. Each time he spun around he saw the alien ship brooding large above him, with its hatch now jammed half open.

He heard a hiss. An alarm sounded in his helmet. The heads-up display showed the oxygen status of the suit—the pressure was dropping. Fast.

But he'd done it. He watched the alien ship's hatch reopen, then close, catching again on the shuttle.

"Suck it, bitch," he said, before passing out.

CHAPTER FORTY-TWO

Irigoyen Sector, San Martin System, El Amin
Bridge, ISS Independence

Proctor watched in disbelief as the shuttle banked hard and careened sideways into the alien ship's hatch. She slapped the comm. "Ballsy, who the hell is that?"

The comm microphone picked up his sigh. "Who the hell do you think?"

"Admiral," began Commander Mumford, "I'm nearly there. The meta-space shielding has a modulation pattern that … well, long story short, just a few more minutes and sensors will be able to penetrate."

Lieutenant Whitehorse pointed up at the viewscreen. "It stopped." Proctor looked up and confirmed: the Golgothics had indeed stopped accelerating away. "Shall we fire, Admiral? They might be vulnerable."

They could finally be gaining the upper hand against this

thing. She shifted from one foot to the other, about to give the confirmation to fire. A flash on the screen caught her eye.

"What is that?"

They all stared at the screen at the alien ship. The camera zoomed in on the hatch as Lieutenant Whitehorse adjusted the image. A bright, flickering light was pulsing through the metal of the shuttle's hatch.

"He's cutting through," she murmured to herself. She pointed back at Whitehorse. "Hold fire." They all watched with bated breath as the flickering light moved in a wide arc around the bottom part of the shuttle's hatch. The Golgothic vessel appeared to be trying to disgorge the shuttle, its own hatch door opening then shutting against the shuttle repeatedly. Several pieces of the shuttle exterior instrumentation flew out as debris.

An idea struck her. She paced over to the comm station. "Lieutenant Qwerty, can you tap into the shuttle's systems?"

A nod. "Yes'm," he drawled.

"Lieutenant Whitehorse, is the shuttle's reactor still active?" she said, watching as Qwerty established a link to the shuttle's computer.

A moment later she replied. "Yes, Admiral, it is." Whitehorse cocked her head. "Are you going to…?"

"Of course I am. Qwerty?" she leaned down to peer at the Lieutenant's work.

He nodded. "I'm in control of the shuttle's systems. I assume you're gonna order a cascade failure of the drive?"

"Please," she said.

"One quantum cascade failure coming right up. Might take a moment. They build these things to *not* overload, you know."

They all watched the screen—it seemed they all knew, without speaking, that if the pilot was going to escape, it had to be *now*.

"I'm ready, ma'am," said Qwerty.

Proctor nodded. "Mumford?"

The science chief was tapping his foot nervously. "I think I've got it. Sensors piercing up into the ship now. Trying to interpret—"

"Scan now, interpret later. Get all the data you can—"

A flash on the screen, and tenth of a second later, the deckplate under her feet rumbled. "It's firing!" yelled Whitehorse.

Commander Yarbrough called out from the XO's station. "It punched a hole down on decks seven through ten. Clean through the hull." He pointed nervously up at the screen. "Admiral, it's now or never."

She swore, and cast a glance at Mumford. "Commander?"

He shook his head. "Scanning. But could use another few minutes for a more complete—"

"We don't have a few minutes, Admiral!" yelled Yarbrough.

The deck rumbled again with another impact of the alien ship's devastating rail gun slug. And again a third time.

The fourth struck much closer, and the lights momentarily went out. She studied the viewscreen, finally seeing a telltale movement close to the Golgothics.

"Lieutenant, is that what I think it is?"

Whitehorse furrowed her brow, studying her sensor display. "It's Zivic."

The camera zoomed in even further, and showed the pilot tumbling end over end, away from the hole he'd cut in the shuttle door.

"Admiral!" said Yarbrough impatiently. "We've got eleven dead on deck seven alone. How much longer are we going to wait?"

She grit her teeth as she watched Zivic tumble away. He was still too close to the shuttle, and a core explosion would mean instant death for him at that distance.

"Almost," she murmured.

The deck rumbled again. And again.

"Two more impacts, deck fifteen, sections one and four," said Yarbrough. He shook his head. "Complete decompression. At least five dead."

She turned to Mumford, eyeing him questioningly. He shrugged. "The more time, the better on this sensor feed. But we've already gotten quite a package of data."

Fine. It was time. "Lieutenant Qwerty, initiate feedback."

Zivic continued his slow tumble, now nearly a kilometer away.

It would have to do.

A moment later, the screen oversaturated with the piercing light of the shuttle's explosion.

When the screen cleared, Proctor gasped.

"Was it that easy?" she murmured.

The alien ship was gone.

CHAPTER FORTY-THREE

Irigoyen Sector, San Martin System, El Amin
Captain's ready room, ISS Independence

An hour later, confident that Commander Yarbrough had a handle on the recovery and repair operations, Proctor took a moment to retreat to the ready room. Just to breathe. The door slid shut behind her, and all she could think about was the epithet: *Mother-killer.*

Years ago, just before the final battle of the Second Swarm War, she'd earned that title. She'd killed a Skiohra matriarch by whacking her head with a steel pipe. She'd only meant to incapacitate the alien, but Skiohra physiology was still unknown to her, and the impact resulted in the Matriarch's death. And with her, over fifty-thousand embryo Skiohra who, as far as she understood, were all completely developed individuals living inside the matriarch, just waiting for their bodies. Most never live long enough to get a body. In the case of the Matriarch Proctor killed, none of them did.

Fifty thousand dead. With one blow from Proctor. Such a small, insignificant action that had unthinkable consequences.

They'd won the war. The Swarm was destroyed, and the Skiohra liberated from the Swarm's influence. Not to mention humanity saved. The upper Skiohra leadership officially forgave her for her actions, but the anger simmered under the surface. And in the few dealings she'd had with the Skiohra since then, the name followed her: *Mother-killer*.

She felt it even more acutely now, in the aftermath of the battle with the Golgothics, and she collapsed on the couch by the wall. In the final analysis, forty-two crew members had died that day. Eight of them while she was waiting for Zivic to float far enough away from the shuttle to survive the explosion. Waiting for Mumford to take his data.

Eight. Including Ensign Flay. Pregnant Ensign Flay. *Mother-killer*.

The door chimed. She didn't answer.

It opened anyway, and Captain Volz stepped through. "Ballsy," she whispered, not even moving from her prone position.

He sat down next to her, still silent.

"I messed up. It's all my fault."

A moment's silence.

"That doesn't sound like the Shelby I know."

She stared at him. She wanted to glare, but didn't even have *that* in her. All she wanted to do was escape. Disappear. Run from the ever-growing pile of bodies left in her wake. "How can I keep going? Keep doing this? Letting people die. *Making* people die, through my actions. Or inactions. If I breathe, someone dies. If I give a command, someone dies. If I don't give a command, someone dies. I just … can't. Not anymore. Not again. It's all my fault."

"Bullshit," he said.

She sat up and faced him, hoping against hope that the tear on her cheek was just sweat. She was *not* a crier. "I killed eight people today, Ballsy."

"And you saved my son," he said, his lips tightening. "For as much as I hate the bastard, I'm … I'm glad he's alive. Thank you, Shelby."

"But I killed eight people doing it," she said. A pit had formed in her stomach. The same pit she'd felt decades ago when she'd realized what she'd done to the Skiohra.

"Again, if you'll permit me to repeat myself …" he leaned in close to her, face to face. "Bull. Shit."

She pushed him away. "Just … stop. Let me wallow in self-pity in peace. It's part of the magic of command, you know. I've got to be the Iron Lady out there. But I pay for it every now and then in here with a good pansy-ass cry."

He chuckled. Grimly. "Shelby, do I need to say it? Again? Bullshit. Seriously, you're what, seventy years old? You've commanded more ships and men and women into battle than any officer *alive*. You of all people should know that you don't bear responsibility for those deaths."

"Of course I do!" She swiveled on the couch to face him. "Of course I do! I'm the commanding officer of this ship, and anyone that dies here is *my* responsibility."

He waved a hand, as if batting aside her argument. "Yeah, yeah, whatever. Shelby, we both know that the responsibility for those deaths lies in one place, and only one place." He pointed over to the bulkhead. "That ship. Those aliens. The Golgothics, or whatever we're calling them. *They're* responsible for those deaths. No one else. You? You're responsible for the rest of us being *alive*. Never forget that."

She wiped her eye with a sleeve. "Ballsy, I … look. You remember the Skiohra? My history with them? Mother-killer? I just … it just all came back to me today. Between getting shot at down there on San Martin, then leading us through that battle, and making decisions that lead to deaths, after over a decade of not having to make a decision more monumental than where to go out to lunch, it's just … a little jarring. Plus, Ensign Flay…."

He nodded. "Yeah. I heard. That's why I'm here, because I knew you'd take that hard."

A long silence.

She turned away and leaned back to the wall behind the couch. "You know I miscarried once?" She watched his face. Studying his reaction. He flinched slightly. There was something there.

"I'm sorry. I didn't know," he said. "When was that?"

"Oh, long, *long* time ago. I was like twenty. Had a fling with a guy. He was … fantastic, but lied about his protection. Before I knew it I was two months along and … well, I was two years into my *first* science degree—"

He snorted, then flushed. "Sorry. Bad time to call you a nerd?"

She shook her head in mock disgust. Ballsy was always ballsy. "—Two years along, and I decided, well, I decided I'd keep it, of course. And then, a month later, he was gone."

He. At that moment she realized she'd never even told

anyone besides her brother and his wife, never mind revealing the sex.

"I'm sorry," he repeated. "I know it must be hard for you. With Ensign Flay. I've lost people too, Shelby. Lots of people. Hundreds. It never got easy. Even when it seemed routine, it was never easy. I just … you know this better than anyone alive … I just got numb to it. Like a strange combination of searing pain and guilt every time it happened, and a dull numbness at the ghoulish routine of it all."

She nodded in agreement. "You paused there. A moment ago, when I mentioned the miscarriage." She phrased it as a statement, but the question was implied.

He shook his head. "Not my place to say. I'll let her tell you, if she wants to."

"Who?"

He shook his head. "Not my place. But I'll say this. Ethan was grounded from flying for very good reason. He was reckless. Unbelievably reckless. Like he was trying to one-up me and his mom."

"Spacechamp," she said, remembering the pilot from the *ISS Warrior*.

"Yeah. I mean, Ethan and I had a huge falling out after the divorce. Accused me of … well, doesn't matter. He was only fifteen. His mom married a guy right away. Zivic. And Ethan changed his last name just to spite me. He was young. And I was…."

"You. You were you."

"Yeah." He breathed deep. "Anyway, he had this chip on his shoulder. Had something to prove, you know? Parents were two of the most legendary fighter pilots of the war. He had to be his own man. Be better than us. So he was … reckless. Around the time of the accident, he'd hitched up with Jerusha—"

"*Hitched up?* I didn't know they were *that* serious."

He chuckled. "Heh, yeah, at the time, neither did I. Anyway, they were an item. Had plans to get married. Start a family. She was going to retire early and he was going to keep flying and … well. Then the accident."

"Tell me about it. All of it. I only heard snippets and rumors. I was fleet admiral at the time, but stuff like that didn't always trickle up to me. I only read the final report."

He shrugged. "Nothing much to tell, really, beyond what was probably in that report. He was flying his mom and stepdad around in a shuttle over France during leave, and he was trying to impress them, and … crashed. Like I said. Reckless. He was a wreck. So was I. We … fought. More. At the funeral, no less—your stereotypical family brawl right over the grave."

"Oh—" she said.

"Yeah." He nodded. "And things got really rough between him and Jerusha. Really rough. She was a wreck. And she, well … between the trauma and the fighting and the grief…."

"Oh my god," she said, putting two and two together. "She was pregnant."

"You didn't hear it from me. Not my place. But I just tell you all this so you know the history there, before you decide to put Ethan back into the cockpit of another bird. Before you decide to put more lives in his hands."

She held her head in her own hands. But after a moment, she stood up and unsecured two cups from the cupboard. "He was amazing today, Ballsy. He may have singlehandedly destroyed that ship, helped us extract vital intel from the inside of it by giving us enough time to complete the scan—you know, in case they come back in greater numbers I'd sure as hell like to be prepared."

He nodded. "And he saved those three kids from the research station."

She poured tea into the two cups and handed one to him. "That too. All the more reason that we need to consider using him again, assuming this situation isn't over yet. If these aliens come back, I want all the weapons and tools at my disposal that we have. And your son is one of them."

The door chimed, and Proctor waved the door open. Lieutenant Qwerty took a step inside. "Ma'am, meta-space message from Admiral Mullins at CENTCOM Bolivar. He's demanding you deliver Lieutenant Zivic to his custody immediately. Uh, and the shuttle that he stole. *Fenway*. And the mechanic that came with him. Sara Batak."

Proctor raised an eyebrow. "Speak of the devil." She turned to Ballsy. "Has Ethan said anything about what happened back at *Watchdog*?"

He shrugged. "Haven't had time to talk to him yet. He's still in sickbay. Got a bad radiation dose from that explosion."

She stood back up, setting her tea aside. "Thank you, Commander. Please tell Admiral Mullins that we'll be there as soon as the situation permits. Dismissed."

Qwerty retreated, and the door closed. Ballsy stood up and handed the empty cup back to her. "Sounds like we need to have a long heart to heart with my son."

She nodded, and walked to the door. "Yes. But not yet. I

think it's time we go talk to his companion."

CHAPTER FORTY-FOUR

Irigoyen Sector, Bolivar System, Bolivar
CENTCOM Bolivar, Command center

"Admiral Mullins?"

The aide poked his head into the office, and Mullins waved him in. "Any word?"

A curt nod. The lieutenant handed him a datapad. "The *Independence* is damaged from its engagement with the Golgothics, sir. They're going to continue repair operations, and get to us when they can."

"And they confirmed they have Zivic and the mechanic in their custody?" He leaned forward in his seat, studying the message from the *Independence*'s comm officer.

"Yes, sir."

Mullins scanned through the data file on the *Independence*, her status, damage from the battle—everything that the comm officer had attached to the meta-space message he'd sent in reply to Mullins's own.

Something popped out at him. A name in the list of officers.

Volz. Commander Air Group.

Mullins stood up abruptly. "Alert the captains. We need to accelerate the schedule."

"Sir?"

Mullins urgently paced out into the hallway and back to the operations center. "You heard me."

"Aye, sir. But, shouldn't we wait until—"

Mullins cut him off with a brisk shake of his head. "No. No time. There's something we all missed."

"What?"

The door to the operations center slid open at the last second. "That Lieutenant Zivic's old man is on the *Independence*. We can't afford a lapse of operational security right now. Tell the captains."

The aide nodded and saluted. "Aye, aye, sir." He turned away to go to the comm center.

"And Lieutenant?"

"Yes, sir?"

Mullins dropped his voice. "I don't need to remind you to keep this off any channel that Curiel can monitor."

The aide nodded again. "Of course, sir. Non-IDF channels are harder to encrypt, but we have a workaround."

"Good. Dismissed."

CHAPTER FORTY-FIVE

Irigoyen Sector, San Martin System, El Amin
Brig, ISS Independence

They don't make brigs like they used to, thought Proctor. The shiny plastic door slid open to reveal the cell beyond, whose walls were made of the same smooth material, looking more like a sterile, plastic psych ward room than a jail cell. She supposed the flimsiness of it was a purposeful deception. The door could probably withstand several rpg blasts and a plasma torch. Lure would-be escapees into revealing their hand, only to be stopped by progress in materials science. The irreverent slogan of her favorite college professor rang in her ears. *Science, bitches!*

"Sara Batak?" said Proctor, stepping into the cell. Captain Volz followed.

"Ma'am," protested the marine on duty. "It's against regulation for flag officers to go into detainee's cells without

—"

She spun around to face him and held up a hand to quiet him. "*That* will be all, corporal. Dismissed. Please guard the doors and see that we're not disturbed."

Chagrined, the marine took a step back, and looked from Batak to Proctor to Volz. Apparently deciding the mechanic didn't pose a threat to either of them, he saluted and retreated past the doors to the brig and shut them inside. She turned back to Batak.

"You were on *Watchdog* Station when it blew?"

The mechanic nodded.

"Going through your records it appears you're an employee of something called Snell Staffing Corporation? I presume you've been contracted out to one of the major defense conglomerates?"

"That's right." Batak nodded. "Snell hired us out to Shovik-Orion as temp workers about a year ago. I figure Shovik-Orion don't want to pay benefits, so they rely on places like Snell to get them through the loopholes."

"Is that legal?" Ballsy turned to Proctor. "Can they do that?"

Proctor nodded. Unfortunately, during her stint as fleet admiral she'd witnessed the grift, waste, fraud, and abuse firsthand. But as the corporations were private entities and she was military, her hands were tied. She could steer contracts to the certain reputable contractors, but in her opinion, it was always simply to the least bad of all the available options.

She continued. "And when the alien ship arrived at Bolivar, what happened? I know the official report, but I want your perspective. What was going on on the station?"

Batak shrugged. "Look, Admiral, I'd love to talk, but seeing how I'm in a jail cell, I think it might be best to have a lawyer around."

She folded her arms. She was done talking already, and Proctor could tell by the defiant look on her face that she meant it.

"Look, Ms. Batak, you're in this cell now for two reasons. One, is that this is a military vessel at red alert in wartime. We don't have room for civilians and this just happens to be the easiest non-classified area to keep you in. Two, someone well-placed wants you back at Bolivar. Very badly. Enough that one of my admirals asked for you by name."

She supposed a white lie was permissible, given the circumstances. Mullins hadn't, in fact, used her name. But he didn't have to. The fact that he was demanding her return, and Zivic's, was just a little … off. Normal procedure would have been to drop them off at the nearest IDF CENTCOM base, which in this case would be with Admiral Tigre right there in the San Martin system. Not all the way back at Bolivar.

Batak smirked. "Good reason for me to keep my damn mouth shut then, ma'am." The lopsided smile disappeared, replaced by ice. "I'd like a lawyer, please."

Ballsy leaned in to whisper in Proctor's ear. "I don't think we're going to get anywhere. Let's go talk to Ethan. Doc will revive him if I ask."

Batak cocked her head at him, a look of … recognition spreading over her face. At least, it looked like recognition— Proctor wondered where Batak would recognize him from. Though there *was* that whole celebrity thing from being a hero of the Swarm War. For that matter, why didn't Proctor warrant the same look of recognition? She *was* the companion of the Hero of Earth, after all. Proctor laughed inwardly. At least the girl wasn't a Grangerite. Her attitude would have been much more deferential if she had been.

"You're him, aren't you?" said the mechanic. "You're his dad? Zivic's."

Ballsy eyed her. "I am. Why? Has he talked about me?"

She nodded. "Yeah. Quite a bit, actually."

Proctor's heart sank a little. Any chance that the girl might talk seemed to have left the room, and get torpedoed by one of the alien ship's super-rail-gun slugs.

Ballsy stayed quiet, as if hoping she'd continue unprompted. Luckily, she did.

"He said you two had a major falling out. Detests you, actually. That much was clear."

"Well, let's just say we've had our … issues," Ballsy said, his lips tight.

Batak regarded him, as if weighing her choices. "He … well … he also said … that he could trust you. That's why we're here. He was looking for you. Said you were the only one he trusted to tell it to. He was desperate to get you some information."

Proctor's ears perked up. "Information?"

Batak sighed, as if she was committing to an action she wasn't sure about, but was going to do nonetheless, consequences and regrets be damned. "Ok, I'll tell you what I know. What we came here to tell you," she said, looking straight at Ballsy. "Ethan said he could trust you, so I'll trust you. I just hope that after all is said and done, I can go home. You know … alive, and all."

Proctor turned back to fully face the girl. *Girl*, she thought. She kept on thinking about the mechanic as a girl when she must have been at least twenty-five or so. *Have I gotten that old?* "Sara. I promise, I'll do everything in my power to protect you. But the truth is, *something* is going on. Something deeper than just a deadly alien invasion—and heaven help us, *that's* bad enough. But between Sangre de Cristo, the multiple attempts on my life, my missing nephew, a simmering resistance movement that seems like its about to break out into open revolt and revolution, and a host of other details that I don't have time to go into right now, I think we're looking at something far bigger, far deeper than that. I'll be honest: *we need you*." She breathed. Why the hell was she opening up to a mechanic? Oh well—she supposed it might make the girl feel more inclined to hold nothing back. *Good Psych-ops, Shelby*, she could hear Granger telling her.

"Ok." Batak nodded. "Everything. Look, Ethan and I have been thinking the same thing. There's something big going on." She proceeded to lay it all out. From when she'd been assigned to *Watchdog* Station and started seeing odd sudden changes in personnel, to the alien-induced hysteria when the mystery ship attacked, to the assassination of the Shovik-Orion contractor, Jerry Underwood, that Ethan witnessed. Their subsequent escape from both *Watchdog* Station and the *Miguel Urquiza*, then from San Martin, and their theories about Shovik-Orion and the GPC being in bed together. And the meta-space echo on board their shuttle.

"Excuse me? Did you say meta-space echo?" said Proctor. Before she knew it, she was on her feet, though she didn't quite understand why.

"Yeah, that's right. I mean, that's the best way I could describe it. I'm no scientist. Just a grunt mechanic, ma'am. But those readings—it was like the ghost of a meta-space reading, coming in and out, almost ... circular, around a point in that shuttle. I mean, I know that's crazy, there's no such thing as a *circular* meta-space signal, but—"

"Holy shit," breathed Proctor. She turned to Volz. "Ballsy, we've got to talk. Excuse us please, Sara—"

Batak stood up too, looking quite angry. "Wait, I tell you all that, and you just leave to go—"

Proctor touched her shoulder. "We'll get you some quarters. And I'll have guards posted. *Discreetly*," she added, noting the sudden look of panic on the girl's face. "They'll keep you safe. But I need to go. You've reminded me of something critically important." She motioned them all to door. "Come on."

Before they even approached the door to the brig, the comm crackled to life. "Admiral Proctor?"

It was Commander Yarbrough.

"Yes, Commander?"

"Sir, we have ... a situation here."

Another one?

"I'll be right there." She pointed them all through the door, and glancing at Ballsy, she thumbed towards Batak, indicating he arrange accommodations and guard for her. "What's the situation, Commander?"

"We've been holding station in orbit around El Amin as ordered, ma'am. Except we have a guest. A very ... *large* guest."

Proctor's blood ran cold. That meta-space *ghost* of a signal on that shuttle couldn't have.... No, it couldn't have....

The Swarm couldn't be back. They couldn't. They were dead. She killed their last ship, years ago.

She cleared her throat. "Swarm?"

"No, ma'am. Skiohra. One of their six main generation ships. And their leader is asking for you. By name."

CHAPTER FORTY-SIX

Irigoyen Sector, San Martin System, El Amin Bridge, ISS Independence

Proctor wasn't sure what she'd find on the bridge. Would the appearance of a one hundred kilometer long alien generation ship would provoke an eerie calm among her bridge crew, or would they be running around with their heads cut off at the sight of a ship that could destroy the *Independence* a thousand times over? The massive ship packed a punch greater than a hundred of the old Swarm carriers, using the same antimatter beam turrets as their old enemy, a weapon so powerful it could slice through even the old Legacy Fleet carriers like the *Constitution* and the *Warrior*.

And for that matter, the *Chesapeake*. The thought of Captain Diaz's boat, *her* old boat—the last of the Legacy Fleet—succumbing to the mysterious alien ship just a few days ago filled her with ... what was that feeling? Anger?

Sadness? As angry as she was, it sure felt a lot more like mourning. Nostalgia, more like it. It was like the end of an era had come. The Legacy Fleet was no more. A simpler time had passed. Straightforward enemies of old had been replaced with mysterious shadows that threatened to destroy them all from within.

You're being melodramatic, Shelby. She smiled—maybe so. But all the same, what she wouldn't give to have Granger, Prucha, Diaz, and Spacechamp back. And the *Warrior* and *Chesapeake*. All the old crew. Her friends. Her family. Too many had passed on, and in the meantime it seemed their problems only multiplied and grew more complex.

The bridge doors opened, and to their credit, the bridge crew was calm and confident, working steadily, even as the unimaginably massive Skiohra vessel filled the screen. A super dreadnought, that's what they called them back in the closing days of the Swarm War. It stretched off into the distance, its surface details getting lost in the blackness of space. The light from San Martin's sun was too weak at this distance to illuminate it further.

"Status." Proctor approached her chair, but didn't sit down. Rather, she stood behind and gripped the headrest. It seemed to be her preferred position these days. Face death standing up—that's what she supposed her subconscious was trying to do.

Commander Yarbrough looked up from the XO's station. "They're waiting to talk to you, ma'am."

Proctor eyed the ship. She'd studied the Skiohra for years after the war, in her spare time as captain of the *Chesapeake*, and even during her tenure as fleet admiral. It was a scientific interest, certainly, but there was something else about the aliens that called to her. "Which ship is it?"

"Ma'am?"

"The name. Which one is it? There's only six of them. *Benevolence*?"

Yarbrough scanned through the data on his console. "I ... one moment, Admiral. I'm sure it's here in their transponder data—"

Her eyes found the telltale damage on the ship, now decades old. And one spot in particular—a giant, gaping hole that the Skiohra had apparently not filled in, but rather just patched around the edges. "It's the *Benevolence*."

"Are you sure?"

She pointed at the damage on the ship. "That's where the *Constitution* hit. General Norton—God bless his cankered soul—brought the damaged Old Bird with him during operation Battleaxe and flew it straight through *Benevolence*'s heart." She was murmuring, mostly to herself. The memories seemed fresh, like they happened yesterday. She could almost see the great gouts of debris and fire erupt from the *Benevolence* as the *Constitution* flew through at horrific speed. The Old Bird had been close to being repaired and recommissioned, and then Norton flushed it away like a turd. Tossed it like a disposable brick.

"They're standing by, Admiral," said Lieutenant Qwerty. "Shall I put them onscreen?"

She nodded, and came around to stand in front of her chair. She assumed the Skiohra position of greeting, trying to remember the correct pose. Arms raised in front of her, palms up. Or was it down? *Shit*.

The viewscreen shifted from displaying the ship to the image of an alien. A Skiohra matriarch. Unimaginably old—thousands of years—though due to the Swarm Matter that had coursed through her veins for centuries, she'd been preserved, her lifespan stretching far past the already-long length of a typical Skiohra.

The Matriarch had her arms extended in front of her, palms up. Good, she'd gotten it right.

"I am Vice Imperator Pulrum Krull. Do you remember me, Mother-killer?"

The name cut her to her core. *Mother-killer.* They hadn't forgotten, apparently. "I do, Krull. And I see you still call me by that ... odious epithet."

Krull lowered her arms. "It is not meant as an insult, Mother-killer. Merely as a statement of fact. It is only a descriptive term. Like you would call someone Captain, or Admiral, or President, or even ... mother."

"Still, I think I'd prefer it if you called me Admiral Proctor. Or just Admiral, thank you very much."

Krull nodded once. "Very well, Admiral. You've summoned us here. My question to you is, *why?*"

"Excuse me?" *Summoned?* She glanced over at Commander Yarbrough, who shrugged.

The matriarch continued. "Through the Ligature. The meta-space link. You remember it, do you not? You must, for you've used it to summon us. In a rather ... crude manner."

Proctor shook her head. "I'm sorry, Vice Imperator Krull. I have no idea what you're talking about."

"The Ligature," Krull repeated, insistently. "All races subjugated by the Swarm used it. The mental link. You call it *meta-space*, but that is such a crude, sterile term. The Ligature is alive." Krull paused, as if waiting for an answer, but Proctor had none to give. The alien sighed, and continued. "It started with us, you know. Our people developed it, over hundreds of thousands of years. Then the Swarm stole it, and used it as part of their campaign of subjugation and domination. Even Granger had it placed within him. And now you've used it to summon us. Why?"

"Lieutenant Qwerty," Proctor began, without looking over at him, her eyes still resting on the alien on the screen, "have we sent any meta-space messages in the past few hours?"

"Just a few ma'am," he replied. "Two to Admiral Mullins on Bolivar, one to CENTCOM on Earth, one to Admiral Tigre on San Martin." He shook his head. "That's it."

Krull shook her head. "No, Admiral. You don't understand. This was not a meta-space message. This was a *summons*. A clear, unmistakable sign to all beings connected by the Ligature for millions of parsecs around, saying quite clearly, *here ... we ... are.*"

Another chill went up Proctor's spine. A summons. *Here we are*. Perhaps the most dangerous message any race could say to the unfathomably expansive black depths of the universe.

"And it wasn't the first. It wasn't even the most powerful. The one sent two weeks ago nearly incapacitated all of us."

The chill deepened. "Two weeks ago?" *No. It couldn't be.* "Vice Imperator, where did that other signal originate from?"

Proctor knew the answer before the alien could reply. There was only one place it could have come from. *Oh, Danny, what the hell were you up to?*

"From the world you call Sangre de Cristo."

CHAPTER FORTY-SEVEN

Irigoyen Sector, San Martin System, El Amin
Bridge, ISS Independence

"How? What could cause something like that?" Proctor took a few steps towards the screen as she spoke. "Do you have any idea?"

Vice Imperator Krull regarded her solemnly. "I thought you could tell me. Because it has caused an uproar among my people. For days, my ship was filled with mayhem. Discord. It disrupted the Ligature. If it had been any stronger, it would have damaged us. How it has affected the Dolmasi, and the other client races of the Swarm, I can't even fathom."

"But how is that possible?"

Krull shook her head. "Like I said, Admiral, it was as if a large amount of energy was channeled into meta-space somehow. It was unmistakable, unorganized, and utterly powerful."

Proctor turned away and paced back to her chair, but still didn't sit. "Krull, two weeks ago, Sangre de Cristo was attacked by terrorists. They detonated a nuclear weapon in the atmosphere above one of the cities, completely destroying it. Are you saying that a nuclear explosion can cause a release of energy into meta-space?"

"No," said Krull. "Nuclear technology is familiar to us. And archaic. Our people haven't used it for millennia, beyond simple fusion power devices, and even those are outdated by thousands of years. But either way, nuclear reactions do not have an effect on meta-space."

"Then what happened on Sangre de Cristo to cause such a meta-space disruption?" Proctor turned back to the screen. It felt like they were close, so close to figuring out the mystery. The conspiracy. Or multiple conspiracies. Or multiple coincidences.

There were no coincidences. Not like this.

Krull gave a most decidedly human expression—a shrug. Apparently she'd studied human communication over the decades. Proctor remembered that the matriarch had tens of thousands of primordial, bodiless children living inside her, all with fully developed minds, each with personalities and passions. Some of them probably devoted themselves to understanding human communication, and Krull was most likely drawing upon their knowledge right now.

"What do your children say, Krull? Surely you have some within you, living the Interior Life, that have devoted their lives to understanding meta-space physics and technology."

She nodded. "I do. Hundreds, in fact. They form quite the vocal faction within me."

"And?" Proctor said, trying not to let exasperation creep into her voice. "What do they think?"

"They only have theories. Hypotheses. But the dominant opinion is that there was, somehow, a meta-space shunt attached to that nuclear weapon. Some sort of device that could channel raw energy into meta-space."

Proctor nodded. "A meta-space shunt. And, theoretically, what would such a device look like? Would it have some sort of meta-space signature by which we could detect it?"

"*Theoretically*," began Krull, "it would utilize one of the artificial singularities that you humans provided to the Swarm years ago. It would be altered, and kept as a microscopic virtual particle, no larger than the space between sub-atomic particles in quantum condensate—a Planck Length, I believe your science would call it. And it would be manipulated to attract all energy in its environs. Catch it in a circular orbit, and while the energy is orbiting the singularity, shunt it into meta-space."

Shit.

"Krull, artificial singularity technology was banned right after the war, thirty years ago. All singularity devices were destroyed. Every Swarm ship was destroyed. I made sure that there were none left."

Krull shrugged again. "All the same, Admiral, that is the leading theory among my children. It may be that a few singularities ... slipped through the cracks, as you might say."

The implications were disturbing. Frightening. That meant that whatever individuals caused the explosion over Sangre, their reach extended up into the highest echelons of IDF leadership, and had for years. Possibly decades.

It meant that they'd been planning this for years.

It meant that there could be more singularities out there. Weapons that caused unthinkable destruction in the hands of the Swarm.

It meant that ... *oh hell*. The shuttle. The circular *ghost* meta-space readings that Batak and Zivic detected.

"Krull, you say we summoned you here. Was the signal the same? Did it match the one from Sangre?"

"It was ... *similar*. But far less powerful, by many, many orders of magnitude. It was just a shadow of the same effect. A human might call it, a ghost of a signal."

A ghost of a signal. She made a mental note to track the origins of that shuttle, and find out every stop that it ever made. It might not have had the meta-space shunt on board when it exploded, but it might have held one at one point. And the meta-space signature might have imprinted itself on the shuttle, somehow.

"One more thing, Vice Imperator." She hesitated to even ask the question. She almost didn't want to know. "Is the Swarm back? That ship we destroyed—surely you've seen it by now. Is it the Swarm? Are they back?"

Her answer was surprisingly confident. "No. It is not the Swarm. We would have known, through the Ligature, if they had returned. That ship, whatever it is, is not Swarm. It is ... new. Something ... some alien we have never seen before."

Proctor breathed a little easier, and at the same time the knot in her stomach tightened even further. So it wasn't the Swarm. That was good. But the enemy you knew was often far preferable to the enemy you didn't. "We call them the Golgothics. They project a field that interferes with our ... emotional control."

Krull raised two hands. "As good a name as any. And yes, we have felt it, though, thankfully, it does not affect us as it does you. But I warn you Admiral, be careful. It's ... strange, how this projection field feels to us. Familiar, and not. Deadly, and not. It is tied into meta-space, like the Ligature, and yet, not. We do not understand it. I am sorry I can't be of more help. I will contact you if we discover more about it."

"Thank you, Krull. I will investigate this meta-space shunt, as you call it. If it's caused as much damage among your people as you say, then ... well, that's an act of war, no?"

Krull nodded slowly. "I was not going to suggest as much, Admiral. I am trying to give you the benefit of the doubt. But given your history, your reputation, among my people, many were prone to believe the worst."

Mother-killer. The term was implied.

"And Admiral, I believe you are mistaken."

"Oh? Mistaken? About what?"

Krull eyed her, with what looked like sadness. "You speak of the ship in the past tense. You say you destroyed it."

No.

Krull continued. "It is not destroyed. It travels, even now, into the very heart of your space."

CHAPTER FORTY-EIGHT

Irigoyen Sector, San Martin System, El Amin
Bridge, ISS Independence

The screen had no sooner gone dark and replaced by the view of the still-erupting El Amin, than Proctor spun around and strode over to the tactical station. "Lieutenant Whitehorse, can we confirm that? We clearly saw no debris, but we also clearly did not pick up any q-jump signatures from that ship when the shuttle exploded."

Whitehorse furrowed her brow, bringing up all the recorded data from the battle. "Correct on both counts, Admiral."

"Then where the hell did it go?"

"Working on it, Admiral," she said.

"Admiral," said Commander Mumford from the science station. "It could be that the explosion from the shuttle's core going critical may have masked a q-jump signal."

Proctor drummed her fingers impatiently on the tactical console. "And? Can you verify that, Commander? If what Krull says is true, then the next target might not just be a dead moon, but something a little more substantial. Like, for example, Britannia. Or Earth."

Mumford dashed over to the tactical station and sat next to Whitehorse. "Bring up a standard signature from a criticality event and overlay over our data. Then we run a Fourier transfer, subtract, reverse the transform, and what's left should be the signal."

Whitehorse nodded. "Got it."

Proctor pointed down at the data. "Don't forget to de-correlate the residuals from the data."

They both looked up at her in surprise.

"What? Oh come on, you knew I was a scientist … *am* a scientist."

Whitehorse returned to her data, but still smirked. "Yes, ma'am, but I thought you were a biologist."

Oh, for the love…. "Biology's science! Data is data!"

Whitehorse kept smiling, but also, thankfully, kept working. *Data is data.* It wasn't only true, it was crucial, Proctor thought. You can manipulate conclusions, but you can't escape data. Her college advisor, besides occasionally yelling out *Science, bitches!* would also from time to time dispense helpful advice and catchphrases, one of which was *Trust your data, and it will trust you.* "Trust the data, Shelby," she murmured.

"Ma'am?" Mumford looked sidelong at her.

"Nothing. Anything yet?"

"Almost there, ma'am."

Proctor began to pace impatiently. Time was running out,

she knew, and they'd wasted precious hours at El Amin making repairs and assessing the situation. She supposed making repairs wasn't a complete waste of time, but all the same, the Golgothic ship had given them the slip, and had an hour head start. That was unacceptable.

Trust your data. She glanced up at Yarbrough, who was still engaged with repair efforts. "Commander, a word."

"Admiral?" He paused his conversation with an assistant and looked up at her.

She approached and lowered her voice. "I need you to look into something for me."

He nodded discreetly. "Ma'am?"

"We need to know more about this shunt. Every ship, every shuttle, every fighter, and every cargo container that comes aboard a capital ship like the *Independence* is still subjected to a rigorous battery of sensor screens, correct?"

"Yes, ma'am."

"Good. I want you to go into the database, and pull the records of every single scan of everything that has come aboard this ship in the past … three months."

His eyebrows shot up. "Three?"

"That's when the *Independence* was commissioned, yes. I want it all. I want to know if we can see a meta-space shunt just from the previous sensor logs, and if anything else has some aboard the ship without us knowing, like with Zivic's shuttle. These lapses in operational security are unacceptable, and they end now. Understood?"

Her tone was no-nonsense, and he snapped to attention. "Yes, ma'am."

She leaned in closer. "Go. Pull the logs immediately. Send

them to both Volz and me."

With that, he retreated to the XO's station and got to work, pulling in his two assistants to help parse the volumes of data that were to be pulled.

"Ok, I think we're close." Whitehorse tapped a few more buttons, and finally nodded. "Got it. It's pretty garbled—no chance we'll be able to derive a heading from this—but yes, it made a q-jump."

Proctor's skin prickled. *Straight into the heart of your territory*, Krull had said.

She couldn't take any chances. "Ensign Riisa, plot a course for Earth."

"How do we know it went to Earth, ma'am?" said Whitehorse. Proctor regarded the young woman, remembering what Ballsy had said about her, about the trauma she'd been through at the hands of his own son. She hid it well—Proctor noted that even during the height of the Golgothic's emotional control-crippling broadcast, she'd kept her cool. The lieutenant's control was admirable.

"We don't, Lieutenant. But in this case I'd rather be safe than sorry."

"But don't you worry that it might show up at Britannia, or another heavily populated system?"

Do I worry? Yes, but like you, Lieutenant, I'm not going to show it. "That's a risk we'll have to take. Ensign Riisa, are the jumps calculated?"

"Yes, ma'am."

"Initiate." She stood back up and headed for the door. "Get us most of the way there, but pause for the last t-jump until I get back."

INDEPENDENCE

Time to run through the data with Ballsy.

CHAPTER FORTY-NINE

Irigoyen Sector, Interstellar space
Sickbay, ISS Independence

When he woke up, Sara was staring down at him. That was the first thing he noticed.

The second thing was the terrible raging fire all up and down his right side and back. It wasn't so much pain as it was pure itch. Like the second day of the worst sunburn in his life, times a hundred.

"Ow," he mumbled. Zivic's jaw was slack and his tongue stiff. They probably still had him heavily medicated, he supposed.

"Well if it don't rain…," she said, breaking out into a smile. "Welcome back, Ethan."

He worked his jaw until it moved properly. "Did it work?"

"Huh? You mean, whatever you did that landed you the best seat in the house?" she said, waving an arm around her, indicating the main floor of sickbay, which looked unnervingly occupied by wounded.

"Yeah."

She shrugged. "No idea. I'm just a mechanic, remember? And I only just broke out of jail—they don't tell me too many things around here yet."

"Hey, look at us! Both out of jail. We've made incredible progress today." He chuckled, which he immediately regretted. The bandages all down his side seared with pain.

Her smile disappeared, and she leaned in close to him. "I … I thought I'd lost you there. When they wheeled you in … shit. You looked dead."

"Sorry to disappoint," he said, with a wink. Winking was okay—it didn't hurt like laughing did.

She kissed his cheek. He looked side-long at her—to flirt, or not to flirt, that was the question. "You missed."

"Funny." She smirked at him, but leaned in close to his ear. "But seriously, don't ever do that again. I mean, we just met a few days ago and everything, but…." She grunted, and pulled away, leaning back in the chair next to the bed. "Just don't do that again, okay?"

"Agreed." He nodded, and started taking stock of himself. Wiggling his toes he realized his boots were still on. Moving his legs around told him his pants were still on, thank god, and all his bones seemed to be intact. He flexed his shoulder, which was sore, but which also seemed to be back in its socket. Convinced he was just fine after all, except for the sunburn of a lifetime, he lifted himself up to a sitting position, wincing at the burning pain under the bandages. He waved the doctor over, whose eyes bulged when he saw Zivic sitting upright.

"Lieutenant Zivic, lay back down. Now. You've got three days minimum recovery time in that bed while the reconstructive gels do their work." The doctor pointed down to the pillow authoritatively.

"Doc, I've got work to do. The alien ship is still out there, right?"

The doctor shook his head. "None of your concern anymore. Your job right now is to heal. You're of no use to anyone in your condition."

His frustration was oddly gratifying. To finally feel *useful*, after two years of sitting at dead-end assignments. To finally feel important. To finally, well, *help* people. And now he had to sit again. Sit and wait.

Frustrating. Yes, it felt frustrating. But also damn good. It had been too long. He was born to fly—he had it in his blood, in his heart, and he'd let his mistakes get into his head too much. He'd let them linger there too long. The past was the past, dammit. Time to move on.

"Fine. I'll be good." He slowly leaned back, and the doctor nodded approvingly. "Is there at least *something* I can be doing while I wait this out?"

"Your bandages could use changing. The nurses are pretty damn busy with all the casualties. It's something your friend could help with, if she's comfortable." He showed them the tubes of reconstructive gels that would need to be reapplied, then left in a hurry to go attend to a groaning patient on the other end of the room.

He flexed his feet again, feeling his calves slide against the interior of the boots. Something was missing.

The flasks. Both of them. He normally kept them tucked

right in at the tops right below his knees. They must have fallen out during one of the mad dashes he'd had to make over the last day or so.

And he smiled—he didn't miss them in the slightest.

"Hey, want to do something really gross?" he said, pointing to his bandages, waggling his eyebrows.

Batak made a face, but then grinned. "That's what she said." She leaned forward and started unwrapping.

CHAPTER FIFTY

Terran Sector, Terran System
Combat Operations Center, Fighter bay, ISS Independence

"Wait here, please," Proctor said to her marine escort as they passed the doors to the fighter bay. They saluted, and she walked into the bay, which was bustling with activity. Deck hands scurried around wheeling fuel containers, ordnance loaders, and giant wrenches—like the one she'd used to club that Matriarch.

Mother-killer!

A group of fighter pilots bunched up near the door parted for her, greeting her with nods and salutes. Before she could ascend the stairs to the CIC she nearly ran into the young man she'd seen earlier, with the flopping blonde barely-regulation hair and the youthful nervous face.

"Admiral! Sorry, let me get this out of your way...." He grunted, struggling to push the heavy cylinder away from the stairs. "Just needed a place to put it during the tooling rotation of the last shift's shuttle and fighter inspection and I—"

She smiled, trying to set the young man at ease. "It's all right, yeoman. You're doing a fine job."

"Yeoman Sanders, ma'am," he added, nervously. *Good god, kid, get a grip. Haven't you seen an admiral bef—*

Oh. She saw the look of nervous adoration on his face. She'd seen it before. *Grangerite.*

"Thank you, Yeoman Sanders," she said when he'd cleared the path. "Excellent work. Keep it up."

He saluted, and kept pushing the cylinder out of the way. She climbed the stairs to the CIC, grunting against the lingering pain of her injuries. When this was all over, she told herself, she needed about two months laying on the beach.

"Welcome to the jock-cave," said Captain Volz from his computer terminal in the corner. "This is where the magic happens. Don't worry, I've got all the fighter jocks runnings sims, and my assistants are out mopping floors."

Good. He was alone. "Have you uncovered anything about Shovik-Orion?" she said, closing the door to the CIC behind her.

"Just a little bit, Shelby. Without connecting to IDF's network I'm only going off what we have on the ship's database."

"And?" She sat down next to him, glancing over his terminal.

"Just the standard stuff. They're one of the largest military contractors, we knew that. Their contracts total over fifty trillion per year."

"Shit," she murmured. "That's gone up since I left. They

used to be a minor player. Like, two, three trillion, tops."

"Yeah. Hell, I'm thinking about retiring and taking a consulting position with them for a year. Then buy myself a tropical island on Britannia."

She leaned in to read the company profile. "Who's their CEO?"

He frowned. "I ... don't know. The last one resigned suddenly about six months ago, and for all I know they haven't replaced him. At least, the *Independence*'s computer doesn't know."

Strange. "How does a major company like that go six months without a CEO?"

He shrugged. "Board of directors? Maybe there's company infighting. With that much in contracts coming in, politics get ... serious. In the past five years they've gone through three CEOs, four presidents, and half their corporate board has turned over."

She nodded. "Makes interdepartmental politics at my university seem like a toddler splashy pool."

"The more money, the higher the stakes."

It didn't seem right, though. "I think we're dealing with more here than just standard posturing within a company. This is one of the most powerful organizations in existence right now, outside of UE's government and the other players. Russian Confederation. Chinese Intersolar Republic. Hell, just this one company has a higher cash flow than the entire Caliphate. They renamed the capital city on Bolivar *Shovik-Orion City*, remember?"

"Yeah. They officially moved their headquarters there two years ago. The mayor's on the corporate board, of course?"

Proctor frowned. "Now *that's* not legal."

"Technically, it is. There was a little-noticed amendment to a funding bill in the senate two years ago that exempted Bolivar and several other worlds out in the Irigoyen and Veracruz sectors from certain corporate regulations."

"Figures. Let me guess: the *other* party?"

"It always is," Ballsy said with a smirk. "We're talking about the same party, right?"

It was a running joke between them—they'd long been members of opposing political parties—and it was something that finally made her smile. She realized that that hadn't happened all day. "It's always the other party." She wracked her brain, struggling to think, to remember ... anything. Any missed detail or loose thread she'd forgotten.

It all came back to Danny. *Where the hell are you?*

"The girlfriend. Danny's girlfriend. The one that was killed in the bombing at CENTCOM Bolivar. Bring up everything we've got on her."

Volz tapped a few keys. "Do we know her name?"

After a pause, she remembered. "Fiona Liu."

He pulled up her data file, which was thin. "Born on San Martin, twenty-two years old ... well that's interesting."

"What?"

"She attended the IDF intel academy on Britannia for two years, then dropped out."

"Intel? She was training to be an intelligence agent for IDF?"

He nodded. "Looks like it. But she abruptly left. Took a job with ... you guessed it. Shovik-Orion."

She shook her head. "So, Danny's girlfriend gets some

intel training. Quits, and takes a job with Shovik-Orion. Falls in love with my nephew, somehow ends up as an informant for both Admiral Mullins and Secretary General Curiel, and then pays for it with her life. Did I miss anything?"

"That about sums it up. Look, Shelby, I know it's hard to think about, but maybe your nephew was up to something no good. Maybe Liu finds out about it, the GPC gets wind, and they blow her up to cover their tracks, just ... just like they probably did with Danny."

She couldn't accept that. Danny wouldn't, he just *wouldn't* do something like this. But Ballsy was right. Or, at least, he was getting very, very close to the truth. The pieces were starting to come together. She stood up and started to pace. "Ok, let's fit your son into this. And Batak. *Watchdog* Station gets slagged by the alien ship. In the confusion, Ethan escapes, but not before seeing two IDF officers execute a contractor—a *Shovik-Orion* contractor, remember."

He stroked his stubble. "Ok, so those two IDF guys might actually be either GPC, or Shovik-Orion themselves. They're heavily involved in the meta-space shunt, possibly the nuke. And they see the station is about to blow up anyway, so they know there's little risk in covering their tracks by killing their own guy. He's going to be dust in a few minutes anyway."

"Right. The contractor has loaded this meta-space shunt into the shuttle. He gets shot. The two IDF guys take the shuttle and the shunt, not thinking anyone saw them. But then Ethan zooms out of the station at the last moment, and *someone* is watching and they realize that your boy might have seen something he shouldn't have. So they pretend they're with the *Bolivaran Intelligence Agency*—"

"—a completely made-up organization," he added,

"—and try to kill the two potential witnesses. Ethan and Batak escape, and then the *entire ship*, the *Miguel Urquiza* changes course to chase them."

Volz shook his head in what she supposed what disbelief. "Whoever these people are, they've got influence."

She went on, piecing the puzzle together. "But by the time Ethan and Batak take the shuttle, the shunt has already been offloaded onto the *Urquiza*, leaving behind that ghost meta-space signature in the shuttle's hold."

"So where did it go?"

Proctor shrugged. "From the *Urquiza*? No idea. Could be anywhere by now. So, we've got another meta-space shunt out there somewhere, and according to Curiel, there's a missing nuke."

"Do you believe him?"

"Well, he *did* give up all the other nukes the GPC had. Admiral Tigre confirmed that an hour ago. Why would Curiel give those up if he was planning on using them?"

"To give him cover to use the one he *kept*." Ballsy looked at her. "If I was a terrorist that was trying to confuse the shit out of everyone, keep everyone off balance? Might be something I'd do."

She nodded, and rubbed the bridge of her nose. Nested conspiracies, people willing to murder to cover their tracks, corporate overreach and abuse beyond any criminal enterprise she'd ever seen. If Shovik-Orion was truly involved in the Sangre incident, and the meta-space shunt business, then the consequences were … frightening. What was their end game? What did they want?

Volz pointed at his screen. "Data packet from Commander Yarbrough just showed up."

"I'd asked him to collect all the scans of every shuttle, every container that has come aboard *Independence*. To see if there was something in the data that we missed. If the sensors were sensitive enough to pick up the meta-space ghost signal on Zivic's shuttle, then maybe we could see if anything else suspicious had passed through the holds."

"Expecting to see something else there?" He started sifting through the data files Yarbrough had sent.

"At this point? I've gotten to the point where if the unexpected doesn't happen, then I'm pleasantly surprised."

He shrugged. "I'll look it over. I just don't think we're going to find anything here. We need to get into the classified files at CENTCOM Earth or Britannia, and dig up the real dirt on Shovik-Orion's IDF contacts. I bet we'll find some real gems in there."

"Perhaps."

He cocked his head at the screen. "You're right. When the shuttle first came aboard, the routine sensor scan picked up a minuscule variation in the q-band radiation signature. Wasn't high enough to trip any automatic warnings, but it was definitely there."

She smiled. Good. They finally had real data. "Trust the data, and it'll trust us," she said, absentmindedly.

"Hm?" Volz scanned more files.

"Just something my thesis advisor always said." She began pacing the CIC. "Don't forget timestamps, cross-tabs, origination files, authorship credentials … everything. Dot the 'I's on this, Ballsy. We can't afford anything less."

"You got it."

She crossed her arms and stopped pacing. "Also, given that IDF at the highest levels seems to be compromised, I think we should keep an eye out for—"

"Admiral Proctor to the bridge!" Commander Yarbrough's voice boomed through the CIC out of the speaker.

Her eyes widened. "Commander? Status?"

"We're one jump away from Earth, Admiral. And based on meta-space chatter, it looks like we're seconds behind Curiel's fleet."

"His *fleet*? He has a fleet?"

"Looks like it, ma'am. And he's broadcasting some sort of ultimatum. I think you'd better get up here."

"Jump us the rest of the way in. I'll be right there."

CHAPTER FIFTY-ONE

Terran Sector, Earth
Bridge, ISS Independence

Proctor made it to the bridge in record time, and it still felt too slow. By the time she got there, the bridge was dead silent, except for the comm speakers which were broadcasting Curiel's voice.

"... suffered indignation after indignation. Outrage after outrage. And Sangre de Cristo was just the tip of the iceberg, my fellow citizens. For decades, those of us on the periphery have suffered in silence while the rich get richer, those in power accumulate more power, and the small portion of society that is at the top grinds their heels down on the rest of us. The evidence that I've broadcast today is indisputable, and the conclusion obvious. And let me be clear. I come in peace. The Galactic People's Congress is a peaceful, democratic organization devoted to the just and peaceful and fair government of all humanity, whatever world or moon or station they live on. If weapons are fired now or hereafter, it will never start with us. For we are—"

Proctor glanced at Lieutenant Qwerty and motioned her hand across her throat. Curiel's voice dropped down to a background murmur. "How long has he been going on like that? And what is this evidence he referred to?"

"About five minutes so far of his political garbage," said Yarbrough, with what Proctor interpreted as pure derision. "And the evidence is flimsy, at best. He claims to have a video of the Sangre incident. Contends that one of his ships was transporting a recovered nuke to CENTCOM San Martin to turn over to UE authorities when it was hijacked by an alleged shadow organization within IDF who then launched the nuke at the planet."

"A video? Heavily edited, no doubt. Let's see it." Proctor sat down in the captain's chair.

Qwerty nodded and brought the video up on the front viewscreen. The familiar view of Earth was replaced by a now equally familiar view of the *Magdalena Issachar*—familiar at least to Proctor, who had spent enough time looking at a rendering of the ship, wondering if it had been her nephew's coffin.

Except the *Magdalena Issachar* wasn't alone. A larger, sleeker vessel approached rapidly. Its lines and angles along with the subtle bristling weapons dotting the hull, made it clear that it was a state-of-the-art military ship. "Commander Yarbrough, you've been involved in our shipbuilding program. Is that one of ours?"

He hesitated. "Yes, ma'am. But, according to the video, there are no hull markings. No nameplate. Nothing to identify it."

A pit formed in her stomach as she watched the ship dock with the *Magdalena Issachar*. Nothing happened for a minute, so she motioned for Qwerty to advance the video until there was more movement.

A figure emerged from one of the smaller airlocks, clad in a vacuum suit. The distance was too great to see a face, but somehow, from the posture and the way it carried itself, the way it moved, she *knew*.

"Danny," she breathed.

The tiny figure crawled along the hull, away from the military vessel attached to the docking port. Before long, the other ship detached, and left, and moments later the *Magdalena Issachar's* engines came to life, propelling it towards the surface of Sangre de Cristo. The figure crouched on the hull, and then *jumped*. Both the ship and the tiny figure grew small in the video feed as they plummeted down, until finally the feed washed out with the explosion of the ship just kilometers above one of the habitat domes on the surface.

So Danny was dead, then. She had, somehow, known deep down that was the case, and yet all along she had to be sure. Now she was sure.

And now it was time for payback.

"Admiral, the broadcast stopped. Secretary General Curiel is hailing us," said Qwerty.

She nodded. "Put him on." The screen had returned to a view of Earth, with a smattering of ships in the foreground—Curiel's fleet. A collection of what looked like second-hand frigates, freighters, cruise-liners, and colonial ships. Proctor suddenly understood where the fleet had come from. "Rex," she said. The man was more than a used ship salesman. He must also have been the GPC's lead ship procurer.

Curiel appeared on the screen. His attractive face lined but resolute. He knew a million cameras were recording him, so he was putting on his best show. "Admiral. I'm glad you're here."

"Me too, Curiel. Though I wonder why you are."

"Redress of grievances, Admiral. A basic right guaranteed by our government."

She shrugged. "Backed up by a fleet? Looks more like a threat to me."

"Honor guard. And please. These ships are no match for you or any IDF battleship."

Lieutenant Qwerty caught her attention. "Admiral, it's President Quimby. He wants to talk to both you and Curiel."

Perfect. Just like the old days, caught up in a galactic diplomatic incident while there's a war for survival going on. "Put him on." *Join the party*.

Now there were two men looking down at her from the screen. One telegenic and determined, leading a burgeoning resistance movement and knowing he had to come across as plausible and presidential, the other old but just as telegenic as all presidents must be, the leader of all of United Earth. "Mr. President," she said.

"Aren't you supposed to be out saving civilization, Admiral?" he said. "Where's the alien ship? Have you destroyed it yet?"

She understood what was going on, at least on President Quimby's end. The cameras were running, after all. Setting himself up as above politics, concerned only for the safety and security of all humanity.

"President Quimby, you are intentionally avoiding the important issues and people I am here representing," began Curiel. "I demand an immediate—"

"Really, Mr. Curiel? Earth and all its worlds face an existential threat, and all you care about is politics?" Quimby tutted, and turned back to Proctor. "Admiral? I asked you a question."

She nodded. Dammit—getting thrust into politics was as far down her to-do list as it was possible to be. Right after scrubbing the mold off the grout in her shower. "That's why I'm here, Mr. President. I have reason to believe that Earth itself is in immediate danger."

"And why would you think that, Admiral? The alien ship is not here. Do you have intel suggesting it's on its way?"

"I do, yes." She didn't know how much to tell him, at least about the cryptic warning given to her by the Skiohra matriarch, and especially over a channel that was being broadcast all over Earth.

"And what are you here to do about it?"

Lieutenant Whitehorse cut in. "Admiral!"

She spun around. "What?"

"The fighter bay. Something just came out of it. A large container. It's—the readings are … odd."

"Odd?" The pit in her stomach grew deeper. "Put it onscreen."

The faces of the president and secretary general were replaced by a backdrop of Earth, with a storage container tumbling on its axis.

"Get me Captain Volz," she said.

Qwerty shook his head. "Comm to the CIC is down. But

there is an audio broadcast coming from the bay itself." He tapped a few buttons, and the speakers blared with a vaguely familiar voice. Young and nervous.

"Long live the Galactic People's Congress. I do this on the orders of Secretary General Curiel, Admiral Proctor, and on behalf of all freedom-loving people across the worlds of Earth." The voice paused, and Proctor finally recognized it. The deck hand. Floppy blonde hair kid. The one who was almost overcome with awe at the sight of her. Yeoman Sanders continued, voice rising in emotion: "We'll never forget … we'll never forget Sangre."

The voice cut out, overwhelmed by the sound of an explosion.

She felt it underneath her feet as it shook the whole ship.

CHAPTER FIFTY-TWO

Terran Sector, Earth
Bridge, ISS Independence

"Explosion in the fighter bay, Admiral!" Whitehorse yelled from tactical. "Reading massive damage down there."

Proctor's mouth hung open. "Ballsy," she whispered.

And on the screen, something happened, almost in slow motion it was so unthinkable. The walls of the storage container drifting down towards Earth fell away, revealing the contents.

A missile, topped by the unmistakable shape of a nuclear warhead. The rocket engine at the rear ignited, and it leaped away towards the surface.

"Commander," she rushed over the Qwerty, "hack into it. Disable it. Disarm it."

"Working on it, ma'am." His hands danced over the console like it was a piano and he was a maestro, but to her chagrin he shook his head. "I can't get into the warhead's control system, Admiral. It's … wait a second. Hold on—"

She gripped the edge of the comm station. Qwerty finally nodded. "I disabled the thrusters. It's just ballistic now."

She turned to the screen. Sure enough, the rocket engine had turned off, but it was still plummeting down towards the surface. Proctor recognized the European continent down below, clouds covering half of England and France. The Alps glistened with snow down towards the southeast in the distance. "Time to impact?"

"About twelve minutes, twenty seconds, ma'am," said Lieutenant Whitehorse, "depending on what elevation it's programmed to detonate at."

"Prepare rail-guns."

Whitehorse shook her head. "I don't recommend that, ma'am."

"Why not?" said Proctor. "That missile is big enough to hit with mag-rail slugs," she said, doing some quick mental calculations. The slug would hit atmosphere and encounter heavy turbulence and eddies, but it would stay on course long enough to hit the nuke. "If we miss, we'll take another shot. As many as it takes."

"It's a MIRV, ma'am. There are at least fifteen warheads on that thing. If we hit it just right, then maybe. But we hit it wrong, then we have fifteen ballistic nukes on our hands."

"Fine. Then we start targeting all fifteen—"

Whitehorse's brow furrowed. "Hang on, that's odd."

Now what? Before she could ask, Lieutenant Qwerty waved a hand to get her attention. "Admiral, an IDF fleet just q-jumped into the vicinity. I've got Admiral Mullins on the comm."

"*Mullins*? What the hell is he doing all the way out here?" She spun around to Commander Yarbrough, who was busy with coordinating damage control for the fighter bay, presumably. "Commander? Do you know anything about this? You've been in contact with him."

He didn't even look up. "Sorry, Admiral. I can't answer that. My hands are a little full at the moment."

Whitehorse finally looked up, her expression pale. "Admiral. Weapons systems are ... locked down. I can't get into the system."

Proctor's spine stiffened. *The conspiracy ran deeper than I thought*. She wanted to kick herself for being so careless. Attention to detail used to be *her thing*. When she was a captain, she'd have noticed all the little details and assembled a complete picture of the threat before anyone else even realized something was up.

Now she was caught with her pants down.

"Admiral Mullins coming onscreen, ma'am," said Qwerty.

She turned to the face on the screen. "Ted, thank god. We've had an ... *incident* over here and we've lost access to our —"

His face glowered at her. "How could you, Shelby? Fleet Admiral Oppenheimer trusted you to protect us against that ... *thing*. And here you are conspiring against the legitimate government of United Earth."

So. Her suspicions were correct. The explosion at CENTCOM Bolivar. The officers Zivic had seen murder the contractor. The *Miguel Urquiza* pausing rescue operations to chase after Zivic and Batak. Mullins's demand that Proctor return the two of them to him at Bolivar rather than to Admiral Tigre on San Martin. It all started to add up.

And the CEO vacancy at the top of Shovik-Orion. CENTCOM Bolivar was in the heart of Shovik-Orion city.

"Admiral Mullins. I'd expect no less from the CEO of Shovik-Orion. Tell me how that job is working out for you? Invested heavily into meta-space singularity research, I presume?"

He smiled, thinly, strained. It was clear the fact she was on to him had caught him off guard. But knowing he was on camera for all of Earth to see, he had to keep playing his part. "You are hereby under arrest. Your authority over this mission vacated. All security credentials revoked. You are ordered to—"

She turned to Qwerty and cut her hand across her throat. "Shut him the hell up." A moment later the admiral's angry face was replaced by the image of Earth. The camera had zoomed in to the missile which was still falling down to the vulnerable surface below. "Lieutenant Whitehorse. Are the lasers charged, at least?"

"Yes, ma'am."

"Give me a targeting option, and open fire when ready."

Whitehorse nodded and worked her controls, but then hesitated again. "Ma'am, I'm reading an odd sensor signature coming off the missile."

Odd? "How so?"

She knew before Whitehorse could reply. Somehow, Mullins had done it. If they'd smuggled a nuke onto the *Independence*, then surely they'd smuggled the other part too.

"A meta-space background signature." She shook her head.

"It's just … odd, is all. Shall I fire?"

The meta-space shunt. If that nuke blew, dumping not just one warhead's worth of energy into the meta-space shunt, but fifteen, who knew what the consequences would be? The Skiohra Matriarch, Krull, had claimed that the earlier explosion over Sangre had momentarily incapacitated every living Skiohra, and implied the Dolmasi fared far worse.

Was that Mullins's angle? Incapacitate the known alien races? Or start a war? Wars were profitable things, after all, and the new CEO of Shovik-Orion might have brought a new revenue stream with him.

"No. Do not fire."

"Ma'am?" Whitehorse looked up at her in surprise. As did the whole bridge crew.

"Do … not … fire," she said, slowly, urgently. "We need another option. There is a device on that thing that will—"

She noticed that everyone's heads were turned not towards her, but towards a point behind her. She turned. Commander Yarbrough stood there, a sidearm pointed at her chest. "Admiral Proctor, I'm sorry. You're under arrest."

CHAPTER FIFTY-THREE

Terran Sector, Earth
Bridge, ISS Independence

She stared down the barrel of the gun. What caliber was it, she wondered? Would it hurt? It was pointed straight at her heart—death would come quickly. Her blood pressure would plummet within a second, resulting in rapid loss of consciousness. She would stumble, probably grab for her chair, and fail as she blacked out. Would they try to take her to sickbay and attempt to revive her? She went through the odds: revival from a bullet through the heart? They'd have to quickly hook her up to the life-support machine to have even the remotest possibility of saving her, then they'd have to patch her heart, inject it with stimulants, and hope for the best.

It was strange what the mind thought of when confronted with existential danger, the thought occurred to her. She almost laughed. In the face of death, she'd slipped back into scientist mode, looking at her situation with the cold, clinical eye of someone studying an interesting problem.

It felt good.

"Commander Yarbrough. Trust me. You don't want to do this." She slowly put her hands up.

He flipped the safety off. "Oh? You've betrayed us all, Admiral. First you and your nephew colluded with Admiral Tigre to bomb Sangre, trying to make it look like a GPC false-flag attack on its own people. And now you're willing to write off tens of millions of people down in Europe. No, I think I really do want to do this."

So. Yarbrough was in on it too. Figures.

"Commander Yarbrough," she repeated, slower. "You *don't* want to do this. Lower your weapon, now."

He sneered. "Why?"

Two seconds later, a fine pink mist exploded out of the side of his forehead, and a hole bloomed blood. He instantly collapsed. Behind him, covered in soot, grime, and blood of his own, stood Ballsy.

"That's why," she said, considering the body on the floor in mild dismay. She'd prefer he didn't die, but given the circumstances, better him than her.

"You ok?" asked Ballsy.

"Fine. You?" She looked closer at his grimy face. His cheeks, temple, and forehead were scored with cuts and gashes, and one eye was swollen shut.

"Been better. You were right about that data file. I checked everything, and found something strange. The timestamps for the sensor logs of several supply shipments were dated to an hour ago. Someone overwrote them. And then the fighter bay exploded. I figured that and us launching that nuke, there had to be *someone* on board who was in on the whole thing. Someone on the bridge, no less. He must have been GPC all along," he said, indicating the body.

"Or Shovik-Orion."

Ballsy shrugged. "Does it matter?"

"It will eventually. But right now?" She glanced up at the screen, at the nuke still tumbling down towards northern Europe. "Ballsy we've got to disable that thing within the next ten minutes."

"Fine. Shoot it."

"Can't."

The realization on his face was easy to ready. "Oh. Metaspace shunt? If we hit it, the nuke explodes and the Skiohra get juiced."

"And the Dolmasi. Fifteen times as powerful as the one on Sangre. And Ballsy, the more I think about this, the more I'm of the opinion that the mystery ship did not show up at random. This was not a coincidence."

He was still gripping the gun, staring down at his gruesome handiwork. The entire bridge crew was still too shocked to say anything, and so they listened. "Right. So. Stop the nuke." A shadow passed over his face. "I know just the man to help us."

Proctor considered. She knew what he was suggesting, but it didn't seem likely, or possible. "The fighter bay is in ruins, isn't it?"

"It is." He turned back to the exit and before he left he called back, "but shuttle bay's ok."

Before she could reply or protest, he was gone, and she

was left staring at the corpse bleeding out on the deck.
Godspeed, Ethan.

CHAPTER FIFTY-FOUR

Terran Sector, Earth
Sickbay, ISS Independence

Zivic grunted. "Ow! Careful!"

"Sorry!"

He steeled his jaw while she tried again. After all the advances in medical technology, it seemed peeling away crusty wound dressings would always hurt. She worked slowly, gingerly, but with eyes that made clear she thought it was the coolest thing in the world. "You're like a machine, you know."

He mustered a chuckle. "Why, uh, thank you. I get that a lot."

She play-slapped him on the knee before returning her attention to his shoulder. "No, dumbass. I mean your body. My body. Like machines. I became a mechanic because I liked taking things apart, but, shit, this is fun." She peeled off another wrap, tearing away some crusty coagulated blood and fluid with it.

"Sh … *it*!" He bit down on a fist as another wrap came off. "You can take them apart, yes, but can you put them back together?"

"Oh, don't be a baby," she said, pulling another wrap away, a little too quickly. He grunted in pain.

"Can't we call a nurse over or something?" he said through gritted teeth. "How many are left?" He craned his neck to see, but half the bandages were on his back, where the direct rays from the shuttle's explosion had hit him.

"Just a few. And, no," her tone became grim. "They're all busy. With casualties."

"*I'm* a casualty."

She pulled the last one off. "You're alive. That's more than half of the people who came through those doors can say."

He glanced out the window of their little examination room, out onto the main floor of sickbay. Nearly every bed was full, and, to his chagrin, he saw she was right. Many of the beds held figures completely draped in a sheet. The doctor and nurses on staff were rushing between the dozen or so patients that were alive, but only just. "Guess I had it lucky."

The door to sickbay burst open. It was *him*. Volz scanned the room, then caught his eye through the window.

"We have company," he said, watching his father make his way through the maze of temporary beds laid out.

Volz wasted no time once he passed the threshold. He glanced once over his raw, exposed side and back, and nodded, as if he were saying, *it's not all that bad.* "Come on. We've got a mission." The tone of his voice said he wasn't there for an argument. That shit was serious.

"Can I get these replaced?" Zivic said, inclining his head towards his side.

"No. No time. Europe is going to get iced within eight minutes unless we move now. We've got a nuke to catch."

Batak whistled.

Zivic stood up and followed Volz out, without another word. Bandages could wait. As they jogged down the halls towards the shuttle bay, his shirt still off and the breeze soothing his raw skin, his father gave him the rundown.

"So we can't just blow it up because of the shunt, otherwise bad aliens show up. Got it."

"Can't we just remove the shunt?" said a voice behind him. He glanced back, surprised to see Batak running behind him.

"What the hell are you doing?" he said, as they passed the threshold of the shuttle bay's anteroom.

"Sounded like you guys needed a mechanic," she said, shrugging.

Volz waved them both towards a shuttle, which was already idling. "Join the party. You may be right, we could use an extra set of hands, especially ones that know what they're doing."

Zivic stopped halfway up the ramp. "Wait, *you're* not coming too, are you?"

"Of course I am. You're going to do some fancy flying while I suit up, jump out, and lasso us a nuke."

Zivic wanted to protest more, but he knew time was running out. "Sounds like as good a plan as any." He sat down in the pilot's seat and didn't even wait for them to sit before he punched the engines and pushed the shuttle out of the bay. Out of the corner of his eye he saw both his father and Batak shimmy into vacuum suits.

"Six minutes," he said, glancing at the timer displayed on the console—he'd noticed the tactical crew on the bridge had linked up to his computer and were sending him all the telemetry data he'd need to maneuver safely up to the missile. *Safely*, though, was a relative word.

Had the situation not been so dire, he might have enjoyed the breathtaking view. Coming down through Earth's atmosphere was always a treat. Other planets had continents and shining atmospheres and green landmasses and blue cloud-dappled oceans, but none of them looked like this.

And none of them were where he'd killed his own mother and step-father. He grimaced. He had promised himself he wouldn't think about it, but the memory was unavoidable, now that he was descending down through the exact same airspace where it had happened.

You'll love Paris, his mother had said. *You and Jerusha should come with us.* Jerusha had been busy with exams and couldn't come, but Zivic had gone, flying the shuttle himself from Westphalia station down through IDF's western European airspace. His buddies from the academy were stationed at EURWESCOM, and so he knew they'd be watching his descent. He thought he'd show off a little. Give them a little show. Give his step-father a little thrill—the man hated flying, after all….

"Ethan! Head in the game!" Volz yelled.

He'd been staring out the viewport, and now he snapped to. "Nearly there," he announced. He glanced back. Both his father and Batak had finished suiting up. "So, I suppose you have a plan?"

Volz shrugged. "It's in development." He pulled open a compartment and hefted out a tow of utility cable. "I suppose we could latch onto it somehow and arrest its descent. That'll at least buy us time."

"You're the boss, boss." He angled the shuttle up above the tumbling missile now that it showed up on his scopes. "It's spinning. You'll never be able to latch on. Not without clanging into it, and wouldn't it be just our luck if that initiated detonation."

Volz nodded. "Once it hits the upper atmosphere the tail fins will right it. We'll have to move fast before it gets any lower into the atmosphere, though."

His father fiddled with the cable and hooks while Zivic maneuvered the shuttle to just a few dozen meters away from the missile.

A familiar voice came over the comm. "Ethan, it's Jerusha."

Like ghost from his past. He shoved his complicated, conflicted feelings down deep and answered. "What is it?"

"The nuke. We've been scanning it, and it looks like the hair trigger is engaged."

"What does that mean for us?" Though he knew the answer already. It meant that their current plan was shit.

"Just one tap and that thing blows. It can handle atmospheric re-entry, and the stray particle of dust or sand flying at a thousand kph, but it's triggered to go off at the slightest touch of anything bigger than that."

No one said a word. Zivic could hear his father mutter a stream of profanities under his breath. Finally, Batak leaned over his seat and spoke into the comm. "What about just a person touching it? Enough to disengage the shunt?"

Whitehorse hesitated. "I … I suppose that might be ok. Honestly, I don't know. I just know that if your plan is to try and wrangle that thing into the shuttle's cargo hold while that trigger is engaged, you're toast. Not just toast. Vapor, is more like it."

Volz dropped the cable. "Ok. I'm going out there. Ride that thing like one of the horses of the apocalypse until I can pry the damn shunt off."

Batak was studying the sensor readout of the missile, tracing her finger along lines only she could see. "No. You can't pry it off without severe dislocation stress at the point of attachment. It's got to be disabled, not detached."

"Can you do that?" Zivic called back to his father.

Before he could respond, Batak nodded. "No, he can't." She yanked open a utility drawer and pulled out a repair kit and slung it over her shoulder. "But I can."

CHAPTER FIFTY-FIVE

Terran Sector, Earth
Bridge, ISS Independence

Proctor watched the scene unfold on the monitor as a small figure emerged from the hatch of the shuttle. She gripped her armrests tightly, holding her breath, silently willing the bomb not to explode. The background murmur of the bridge dropped away completely as everyone watched in silence.

The missile had righted itself as the upper atmosphere finally created enough drag on the tail, and the figure holding onto the shuttle's hatch crouched down.

And jumped.

Miraculously, she reached out and grabbed onto a small protrusion on the missile and pulled herself in, straddling the thing like she was riding a horse. Proctor almost couldn't believe her eyes, until she looked around at the rest of the bridge crew to confirm they were watching the same thing. The figure was clutching onto the missile with her thighs, a cable dangling off her ankle and flapping slightly in the thin atmosphere, leading back up to the shuttle where another figure—Ballsy, she supposed—stood at the hatch, one hand on the cable where it connected to the shuttle.

"Admiral, the *Vanguard* is maneuver to intercept," said Whitehorse.

She pointed to Qwerty. "Open a channel."

"Open, ma'am."

Proctor stood up. "Admiral Mullins, this is Proctor. Hold your distance, Ted, or things get messy."

A chuckle. "Was that a threat, Shelby?"

She knew the whole world was listening, including the top brass of IDF, the government of UE, and President Quimby himself. Most of what she was about to say was classified. Screw it.

"Mullins, back the hell off. That thing has a device on it that will shunt half the energy into meta-space. For all we know it will summon the Golgothic ship here."

Another laugh. "And how would you know that, Shelby, unless you had designed the thing? You're digging your own grave here, Admiral. Now get out of the way so I can take the shot. Lives are at stake, you know. I'm not going to stand by while you let Europe burn."

Bastard. If nothing else, that confirmed for her that he was the one who'd arranged for the meta-space shunts to be designed and built, and somehow smuggled onto the *Independence*. No other reason to pin the blame on her for all of humanity to hear.

"Ensign Riisa, keep us between the *Vanguard* and the shuttle. Match their every move." She turned to tactical. "Status?"

"From these readings, looks like the shunt is still active."

The comm crackled. It was Batak, breathing heavily. "Ok, guys, I'm about to cut into the shunt. I want you far away from this thing when I do."

"Bull," said Zivic, his voice answering her over the comm. "We're not going anywhere. We're pulling you out the second you get that thing off."

On the screen, the tiny figure of Batak reached down to her ankle, fiddled a moment, and pulled the utility cable off. It flapped away.

"Sara!" Zivic yelled.

"Get the hell out of here, Ethan. You can come back for me when I'm done. Go. Now!" She was breathing heavily.

The timer on the viewscreen was down to under a minute. After a moment, the shuttle wavered a bit, as if the pilot were going back and forth with a decision, before finally pulling off and shooting upward into the sky as the missile continued its descent. It was entering the stratosphere now, and the winds looked to be terrible, since Batak had hunched over and hugged the missile tightly, one hand still poking something into the protrusion on the warhead.

"Almost there," she breathed. "Cutting through the power source...."

Proctor could hardly breathe.

"Admiral!" Whitehorse yelled out from tactical. "The *Vanguard* is accelerating to port. They've got a clear shot."

"Riisa, match them!"

"Trying, ma'am," the ensign said, rattled.

The breathing over the comm grew rapid and heavy. "Main power off, thank god. Auxiliary still attached. One moment … Ethan, be ready to come get me—"

Whitehorse called across the bridge. "*Vanguard* is firing lasers."

With a crackle, the comm cut out. And on the screen the reason was clear. Complete saturation overwhelmed the viewscreen. When it cleared slightly, she could barely make out the shuttle shooting up out of the atmosphere. At the periphery of her hearing she could hear Zivic screaming profanities through the comm. She wanted to shout them at Mullins herself.

It was like the atmosphere below them was glowing incandescent. She'd remembered the old images from the First Swarm War, when the Swarm had bombed their cities with weaponry so powerful it sent giant mushroom clouds up nearly into orbit. Then, during the Second Swarm War, with her own eyes, she'd seen something similar repeated dozens of times over. Entire continents exploding upward as the crust and mantle below was sucked into a singularity, creating unthinkable pressures which then lifted the ground to the sky. Some planets' surfaces didn't see the sun again for years from all the dust.

This was different. It was still so high up that obviously there was no dust to kick up, and the air was so thin anyway that very little differentiation took place. Instead, they saw a glowing teardrop falling in slow motion upward towards space.

And in the center of it would be the gaseous remains—free floating atoms and molecules—of Sara Batak.

Her enemy now had a face. It was not the face of some mysterious alien ship that poked holes into sparsely inhabited moons. It was the face of Admiral Mullins. It was the face of betrayal.

"Lieutenant Qwerty," she said, as measured and calmly as possible. "What did we pick up on meta-space?"

The comm officer studied his console, before shaking his head. "Looks like with the main power cut to the shunt, the worst of it stayed there in the atmosphere. But some of it leaked into meta-space, probably because it was partially powered by the auxiliary batteries, I suppose."

Was it enough? Had Batak given her life for a reason?

"The President is ordering the fleet to intercept Curiel's ships and take him into custody," said Qwerty.

She shook her head. "That's just going to heighten tensions. There will be civil war before the week is over."

Admiral Mullins's fleet started to surround the small GPC force, flanking them, preventing them from going into a higher orbit, where they could make q-jumps.

More flickers on the screen announced the arrival of yet more ships. "Now what?" Proctor said.

"Admiral Mullins, this is Admiral Tigre. What the hell is going on? We were hanging back at Lunar Base and we just detected a nuclear explosion in the atmosphere over Europe!"

There was a lot of cross-chatter between the two admirals, CENTCOM, the president, and Proctor tried to keep up with the conversation, while simultaneously tracking the progress of the shuttle, and keeping an eye on the long-range meta-space comm, looking for what she hoped not to see.

It came anyway.

"Ma'am, picking up a meta-space broadcast from Saturn," said Lieutenant Qwerty. He looked up, his face turning white.

"The Golgothics are here."

CHAPTER FIFTY-SIX

Terran Sector, Earth
Bridge, ISS Independence

"What's it doing?" She was standing over the comm station, not even remembering how she got there. The arrival of the alien ship could only mean one thing. It was going for the prize. Earth. The auxiliary-powered shunt on that bomb was still enough to catch the attention of the Golgothics.

"The message from Brandenburg Station on Rhea says they've detected an unidentified vessel matching the description of our alien ship that just q-jumped into the Saturnian system. It's moving towards … Titan."

Titan?

"There's nothing on Titan," she murmured, before turning back to Mumford. "Am I right? Nothing on Titan?"

He shook his head. "Too inhospitable, ma'am. There used to be a research station there, but it's long since been abandoned. There is an orbital station, though. Just a supply and refuel depot. A few hundred people living there, tops."

She nodded. "Very well. Ensign Riisa, plot a t-jump to Titan."

"Ma'am?" said Lieutenant Whitehorse, "is it worth leaving the current … situation, to go save a few hundred station-folk?"

"It is, Lieutenant. It's our mission. Because after Titan? What's next for that thing? The Saturnian system alone has millions of people living on the moons. Rhea? Mimas? New Mongolia City on Iapetus? I'm not going to abandon them because a corporation wants to engage in a little petty war-profiteering and have bought off an admiral to do it. Riisa, are we ready?"

"Ready, Admiral."

"Initiate."

The background chatter on the comm dropped away, and the cooling nuclear teardrop cloud disappeared. In the place of a cloud-dappled blue Earth came a misty, rust-colored globe.

"Arrived at Titan and entering orbit, Admiral," said Ensign Riisa.

Proctor stalked back to her seat at the center of the bridge. "Lieutenant? Anything on sensors?"

"Yes, ma'am. Detecting the alien ship holding station at a northern latitude,"

She sat down. It was showtime. "Get the hell off my lawn," she murmured.

A familiar voice behind her. "You sound like a grumpy old man, Shelby." Captain Volz walked onto the bridge. "Sounds like something I would say. Hell, sounds like something *Tim* would have said."

Proctor nodded. "If only Granger were actually here. President Quimby might actually listen to him."

Volz shook his head. "Every time needs its own hero, Shelby. And this time, you're it." He thumbed up at the screen. "Let's get this done and go home."

"Let's go home," she repeated, still staring at the screen. The Golgothic ship was still a dot at the center, hovering over a spot on the northern hemisphere. "Is Ethan ok? And why are you up here, Ballsy?"

"He'll ... be fine, eventually. And have you seen the CIC? Fighter bay is gone. No reason for me to be down there. Figured I'd be more help up here."

"Fine. You're my new XO." She swiveled to face him. "Did you have to kill him, Ballsy?" It was still so raw. It had been years since she'd seen death and blood, and now between Captain Prucha and Commander Yarbrough, she'd seen too much of it. "Was that necessary? You could have shot his leg out, or something. He was a witness. He could have been interrogated. Implicated everyone else. I think Mullins and Shovik-Orion is up to something ... sinister. But I can't prove it yet. I needed Yarbrough to testify."

"And what if he refused to testify?"

She risked some dark humor. "Then I at least would have liked to break his leg trying to wring the information out of him."

A shadow passed over Volz's face and he gripped the hand rail. "The bastard killed a few good pilots down there, Shelby, and half a dozen deck hands. And he had a gun pointed straight at your chest. If I hadn't acted, you might be dead." He walked over to the XO's station, which had sat vacant for the past half hour. She hadn't even noticed when they'd removed Yarbrough's body.

That was the worst part of war. The trivialization of death. Ten thousand here. A million there. A body on the floor one moment, now it's gone. Where did it go? Didn't matter—there were more. There were always more.

If only the Grangerites knew what Granger, what Proctor, what all of them had to turn into to win a war. You had to be a killing machine, or else you died. You became a factory, whose input was weapons, hordes of willing heroic young men and women, and a shit-ton of coffee, and the output was bodies. Lots of them. And if you died, then humanity fell, simple as that. Be the last one standing, and humanity lives on.

Fuck war, she thought.

Language, Shelby! came her mother's voice. In her mind's eye, she flipped off her pearl-clutching mom. Proctor was old, and she felt it in her bones, in her body, in her soul. She was tired. All she wanted was sleep, a beach, and some good wine, and yet here she was as Earth's first defense. She wondered if Granger felt the same way during his last stand over Earth all those years ago. *Of course he did.* She was old enough, had seen enough, experienced enough—she knew the stakes if she failed. And the lifetime of regret and pain and momentary and fleeting triumphs gave her the tenacity, the energy, the will to say what needed saying.

"Get off my fucking lawn." She pointed up at the alien ship on the screen. "Whitehorse, rail-guns loaded? Lasers caps primed?"

"Yes, Admiral."

She waved back at Mumford. "Have you gone through that data yet? The price we paid was high enough—it had better have been worth it."

He nodded. "It was, ma'am. I've located several spots on their hull that might be vulnerable. And from these new scans it looks like Lieutenant Zivic's stunt actually did far more damage than anything we've hit it with so far. The hatch where those spheres came out of is stuck open and the structural integrity around the blast zone is greatly diminished."

She smiled grimly. "Good. Let's go finish the job."

CHAPTER FIFTY-SEVEN

Terran Sector, Saturn System, Titan
Bridge, ISS Independence

"The ship is opening fire, Admiral. Drilling beam is tunneling down into Titan," said Whitehorse.

"They're nothing if not predictable." Proctor stroked her chin. So far, there had been no word from the Bolivar system about any change on Ido, besides the minuscule but unmistakably persistent increase in mass. Same with El Amin. And she supposed there were any number of other moons that the Golgothics had targeted that they simply didn't know about, because United Earth only had worlds or outposts in perhaps five percent of all star systems. Only so many Earths and Britannias to go around. "Position us right under that hatch Mr. Zivic was kind enough to destroy for us."

A minute later, they were there. On the screen, with the golden mists of Titan forming a striking backdrop, the alien ship with its burrowing purple-white beam hung in space with its damaged section exposed to their view.

Proctor secured her seat restraint. "Open fire."

The distant thumps from the deck told her the rail-guns were firing, and the viewscreen confirmed as dozens of tiny explosions erupted from the damaged section of the Golgothic ship.

Finally.

"Reading power fluctuations from the ship, Admiral," said Mumford. "Their structural integrity is weakening."

"Good. Keep it up, Lieutenant."

Lieutenant Whitehorse coordinated the barrage with her targeting crew, and soon the entire ship shuddered with the response from the alien ship. "It's returning fire, Admiral!"

The viewscreen flashed with weapons fire. It seemed the other ship had finally decided the *Independence* was a threat, and instead of just the occasional rail-gun slug, it was letting loose with other energy weapons similar to the drilling beam. Four different spots on the ship erupted with purple-white beams lancing out towards the *Independence*.

The ship rumbled. "Those have some bite, Shelby," said Volz. "Decompression reported on decks five, ten, twelve, and sixteen, all starboard."

"Will laser countermeasures work against those beams?" she shouted out to anyone who could answer.

Mumford shook his head. "Unknown, Admiral. But we can try."

"Do it!"

Moments later the space in between them filled with rushing streams of silvery gas, each intersecting an enemy beam and composed of trillions of tiny micron-sized mirrors that would reflect and disperse incoming laser blasts.

An explosion ripped through the deck below them, which nearly threw Proctor out of her chair in spite of the restraints. "And?"

"Some effect, yes. Incident power reduced by fifty percent," said Mumford, the edge in his voice rising with each rumble of the deck.

She wondered if it would be enough. On the screen it was obvious the Golgothic's ship was taking considerable damage. Zivic's stunt had apparently weakened the ship enough to allow their rounds to penetrate the hull. She wondered what kind of technology had allowed the ship to essentially be immune to their weapons earlier. Solid-state plating? Smart-steel armor?

"Shelby, we're not going to make it," yelled Volz. "We're losing structural integrity past section eight."

On the screen the alien ship was taking a pounding. But not fast enough, not hard enough, dammit. "Riisa, port thrusters. Show them our other side."

The barrage continued. Explosions rang out below decks, above their heads, all along the hull and deep in its core, near the bridge. Proctor gripped her chair like it was a life raft. "Steady," she said. "Maintain fire. The bastard has to give eventually."

"Shelby! We're facing a core breach here. Rayna Scott is yelling in my ear to get the hell out or we're toast."

Proctor pounded the armrest. "No!" She pointed up at the screen and turned to face him. "We've got them right where we want them! Let's finish this, dammit!" *Finish this for Danny. Then go find him.*

Volz lowered his voice. "Shelby. Get us out of here, or we're dead. That thing will just keep doing its thing while we burn. We can come back. Fight another day. But we gain nothing by throwing away our lives."

She turned to Mumford. "Status of the Golgothics?"

"Widespread power fluctuations. Structural integrity damaged, but holding." He looked, shaking his head. "We're giving them a beating, but I'm afraid it's going to take a lot more to finish the job."

Dammit.

"Ensign Riisa, back us off. Full thrust. Get us around the limb of the atmosphere."

The inertial cancelers must have been damaged since the sudden change of velocity threw her back into the chair and to the side. But after a few seconds the rumbling and shaking dropped away as they escaped the incoming fire from the alien ship. Soon, the image of the other vessel, drilling relentlessly into Titan with its purple-white beam, disappeared behind the orange line of atmosphere on the limb of the moon.

She breathed deep and closed her eyes. "Volz. Damage report. Casualties."

"Heavy structural damage all over the ship from the enemy's rail-gun. Their energy beam didn't penetrate as deeply, but where it did hit they cut in at least a section or two. Life support out on about a quarter of the ship. Rayna's got the core under control, but the power couplers from the reactor are out so everything electrically powered is on batteries until they're back up. Casualties…." He shook his head. "Report still coming in. But estimates are at least eighty dead. Fifty plus are severely wounded. And … dozens missing."

Whitehorse cleared her throat. "And Admiral, not to pile it on, but the *ISS Vanguard* just q-jumped in. Mullins brought his fleet. Admiral Tigre too, with his ships."

Lieutenant Qwerty flagged her attention, speaking softly. "Admiral. General Mullins is calling for our surrender and for you to be arrested."

"What the hell is wrong with him? Is he blind?" She waved at the screen, where in place of the alien ship drilling into Titan, the IDF fleet now approached. "Can he not see we're under attack?"

Volz grunted. "Looks like he wants to prove to everyone he's not bought off by Shovik-Orion but is actually the knight in shining armor bringing in the vigilante."

Proctor chuckled a dark laugh. "So I'm a vigilante now, huh?"

"Incoming hail from Admiral Tigre, ma'am," said Qwerty. "Private channel. Wants to talk just to you."

"Patch him through to my terminal here." She motioned to her console next to her chair. It was private enough. She didn't have time to retreat to her ready room. And she'd already been through life and death with her bridge crew. She had nothing to hide from them.

"Shelby," he began as soon as his face appeared on her screen. "You need to be careful here. Half the government, half of IDF high command thinks you're in bed with GPC terrorists. President Quimby authorized General Mullins to bring you in for questioning."

"The President? Where the hell is Fleet Admiral Oppenheimer?"

"Still on Britannia." Tigre leaned in close to the screen.

"Shelby, the reason I'm here, I mean, besides the fact that I figured you'd want some backup against that ship … Shelby, I've heard from my team on Sangre de Cristo."

She felt her heart fall into her gut. "And?"

"They found Danny's remains. He fell through the atmosphere. Landed in a remote area. He didn't survive reentry. My people say he probably died very quickly once he hit the atmosphere. No suffering. I'm sorry, Shelby."

So, she'd failed. She'd failed before she even started.

Maybe it was just time to pack it in. Retire for good. Get the hell away from Mullins and politics and war, humanity be damned. If she couldn't even protect her own family….

"Thank you, Miguelito. It's … a relief to know the truth. Finally." She just realized her head had been cradled in her hands, and she looked up at him. "I'm done here, Miguel. I'm out. Will you get me a shuttle? I'm going back to Britannia. I'm going back home. For good this time."

"Shelby, I…."

"Don't try to convince me to stay. No. I resign. I came into this to find Danny. He's found. Now I'm going home. I've lived my life, done my part, fought my wars, and now I deserve a little peace."

Admiral Tigre squinted, grit his teeth. *Oh Miguel, don't try to stop me*. "Shelby, there's something else you should know. Danny's suit was *relatively* intact—at least, the data chips were. His camera was running the entire time from the point he put the suit on, to when he … hit."

"Miguel, it's done. I don't—"

Tigre held up a hand. "Shut up and listen, Shelby. My people have analyzed the video. Lots to tell you. In fact, you'll want to hear it, since Danny left you a heartfelt message right before he hit atmosphere. But the important part is what came before. Shelby, you remember the video feed from the satellite over Sangre de Cristo? The one Curiel broadcast? It's faked. Or doctored, at least."

She leaned forward. "How so?"

"The ship that intercepted the *Magdalena Issachar*. On the satellite imagery, it looked clean, with no hull markings. But on Danny's video feed, the markings are quite clear. In fact, on his feed, it's an entirely different ship. Whoever edited the satellite's video was very, very good."

"Which ship?" she whispered, fearing the answer, fearing the truth, fearing what it might do to her, what it would make her do. She'd been done. She thought it was over. But depending on Tigre's answer, it may only have just begun.

"The *ISS Vanguard*," said Tigre. "Mullins's ship."

It's only begun, she thought, her fists clenched.

"Do you have any idea what his end game is, Shelby?" said Admiral Tigre. "If he was responsible for the bomb at Sangre, *and* responsible for smuggling that other nuke onto your ship … the consequences are … terrifying."

"There's more. I don't have all the proof I need yet, but I think Shovik-Orion has developed a device—something we call a meta-space shunt. It was on both bombs, though the one over Earth was underpowered."

"What does it do?"

"So far? Our best guess is that it summons the alien ship. At least, that's what happened both times it was used."

Tigre shook his head. "Why in the world would Shovik-Orion, or Admiral Mullins for that matter, want to summon an alien force to invade our space?"

"*That*," said Proctor, "is an excellent question. I think we should ask him."

"Admiral," said Lieutenant Qwerty from behind her. "Just received a meta-space message from San Martin. El Amin has … exploded."

CHAPTER FIFTY-EIGHT

Terran Sector, Saturn System, Titan
Bridge, ISS Independence

"Exploded? What do you mean, exploded?" Proctor couldn't believe her ears.

Qwerty stared at his screen. "That's what they're saying, Admiral. First some gravitational instabilities, then a catastrophic pressure buildup in the mantle, then an explosion. The planet is mainly in several large fragments drifting away from each other, but they're projected to fall back down to the barycenter, crash, and basically throw out a huge rubble cloud over the coming weeks."

Proctor turned back to Tigre on her screen. "Did you hear?"

He nodded grimly. "We'd been watching it, keeping an eye on those instabilities. But this … this changes everything."

"Is San Martin at risk?" she said, thinking of the billions

of people back on the main populated planet of that system.

"No. Not for decades. El Amin is about as far away from San Martin as Pluto is from Earth. But still, Shelby, if that happens to Titan—"

She stood up, still looking down at him on her console. "I know. Millions of people here in the Saturn moon system alone. If Titan goes, they all die within weeks. And if Earth is next? Just think what an exploding moon could do to it."

"Seven horsemen of the apocalypse type stuff, no doubt," said Tigre. "End of times."

She bent over and leaned into the console, gripping both sides of it. "Miguel, are you with me? I need to know. The Mullins issue will have to wait. But this ship? We need to stop it. Now."

He nodded. "To the end, Shelby. I was a young man back during the Swarm War, but to me you were a hero. Still are. You weren't a step behind Granger—he just got all the glory. And the bullshit celebrity religion. Yeah, I'm with you—let's go save Earth again."

"Good. I'm about to make a fleet-wide announcement. Might be helpful for you to chime in afterward. That'd give the ship captains some cover to disobey Mullins and follow us in. And once we go in, target the weakened areas of the ship we've already hit. If we all bombard those spots together, we might just save our asses. And Earth's."

"Acknowledged. Tigre out."

His face disappeared and Proctor turned around to the comm. "Lieutenant Qwerty, open a broad channel to the whole fleet. Mullins's and Tigre's both."

A moment later, he nodded. "Open, Admiral."

Here goes nothing. Speeches. The part Granger always hated. Why couldn't everyone just know what the hell they should be doing without having a damn motivational speech thrown at them?

"This is Admiral Shelby Proctor, former fleet admiral of IDF. As you all know I've been called back into service by Fleet Admiral Oppenheimer to face this new alien threat. We've just received word from San Martin that the planet the alien ship already assaulted, El Amin, has exploded. If we don't act now, every inhabited moon in the Saturn system is at risk. And it won't end here. The alien ship could very well move on to Earth.

"I understand you've seen a lot of confusing things today, and heard possibly contradictory orders. You saw a nuclear weapon launch from my ship and nearly destroy Europe. You've seen my ship try to disable the weapon rather than immediately destroy it, and moved to block the *Vanguard* from destroying it as well. I assure you all there were very good reasons for these actions, and that I've acted for the survival of Earth and all of humanity in everything I've done. The *Independence* has even faced this alien ship three times now, and … failed … every time."

"I … I can't do this alone. That ship must be destroyed. Our survival depends on it. But I need your help. I'm going back in—all fleet captains, you're more than welcome to join me. It's now or never. Proctor out."

Volz grunted behind her. "Not bad."

She shot him a look.

"Not great. But … better than Granger ever did." He was almost smiling. But only in his eyes. The circumstances were too dire for anything more.

"Ma'am," Qwerty began, "Admiral Tigre is announcing his support to the fleet, and ordering his captains to follow us in … and from the sounds of it, several of the captains under Mullins are pledging their support."

Proctor sat back down and secured her restraints. "Battle stations. Lieutenant Qwerty, please pass along the instructions for generating the virtual meta-material hull shroud so the rest of the fleet can block the Golgothic's broadcast. Ensign Riisa, half thrusters back towards the Golgothic ship. Let's see who follows us."

A tense minute passed. They watched on the viewscreen as a handful of ships broke off from the main body of the fleet. Admiral Tigre's ships, followed by others that had come with General Mullins. But only a few. Lieutenant Whitehorse caught her attention. "We've got a total of fifteen, Admiral. Two heavy cruisers, a handful of light cruisers, and the rest missile frigates."

"It'll have to be enough. We ready, Ballsy?"

"All systems besides thrusters still on batteries. But weapons crews are ready. Ready as we'll ever be, under the circumstances."

On the viewscreen a battle schematic on one half showed the other ships flanking the *Independence* on either side. On the other half, the tiny dot of the alien ship was just becoming visible against the line of the horizon, the sparkling purple drilling beam a striking shaft of light against the drab brown-orange of the atmosphere.

"Proctor to fleet," she began, inclining her head toward her console to help the battle software understand who she was talking to. With a glance at the battle schematic she started rattling off names and instructions. "*Justice*, *Missouri*, *Paris*, *Dakota*, *Amsterdam*, *Janeiro*, *Sweigart*, form up into support and cover configuration Vickers Beta. Break off and come in from the north. *Jakarta*, *Weibo*, *Budapest*, *Orlando*, *San Diego*, *Manitos*, *Formidable*, and *Mumbai*, you're with the *Independence*. We'll descend ten kilometers and come at it from below. Support and cover formation Vickers Delta."

The attack wings sorted themselves into formation, and within two minutes they were in weapons range. The Golgothic ship loomed ahead of them and at a higher elevation, the drilling beam plunging down past them into the crust.

"Open fire."

CHAPTER FIFTY-NINE

Terran Sector, Saturn System, Titan
Bridge, ISS Independence

It had been thirty years since the last time Proctor had seen so many ships in a live fire situation, and while the rail gun slugs sailing past were undetectable to the eye, their effect on the alien ship was not. It sparked with dozens, then hundreds of explosions per second. She wondered what the hell was holding it together—even a Swarm carrier would never have withstood such a withering assault.

"Massive power fluctuations, Admiral," said Mumford. "The more the sensors read on this thing, the more I'm seeing that it's not only technologically advanced, ma'am, it's ... lightyears past our capabilities. It seems to have almost an organically distributed power system, with modest self-repair capabilities at the molecular level."

"You're saying it will regenerate?"

"If we let it, yes, it appears so."

"Well let's not let it. All ships, add in laser fire to the mix. Torpedoes if you got 'em."

The comm chattered with affirmatives. "The regeneration rate is far too slow to catch up, Admiral. And the other good news—I'm reading that the launch mechanism for those spheres is hopelessly damaged. Destroyed. That thing won't be launching anything down into that hole it's drilling."

Proctor nervously tapped her temple. "Then why is it drilling?" That didn't make any sense. The vessel was under attack, and destruction was imminent. Why was it still drilling when it could bring that weapon to bear on the ships attacking it?

"Admiral, the rest of the fleet is here. General Mullins is signaling for your surrender, quote, *as soon as the threat is neutralized*," said Qwerty.

"Like hell," Proctor mumbled under her breath. "Mumford, are you still not detecting any life signs on that thing?"

"None that I can recognize, Admiral. We still can't penetrate up into every single area of the ship, though. But at the moment it looks like the ship is AI-based. I'm not seeing any organic matter in there."

"No Golgothics, huh? Maybe we were a little premature to latch onto a name for them," she said, absentmindedly. She wanted to wait, to tell the ships to hold fire, to give her time to study this thing. To figure it out. Communicate with it. Try, one last time, to understand it before she was forced to kill it. Like she was ordered to kill the last dormant Swarm vessels. Like the Matriarch. *Mother-killer.* The epithet rang in her ears.

"Well this is odd—" began Mumford.

But before he could say any more, it exploded. The beam fluttered, pulsed in a seemingly random pattern, and disappeared. The ship cracked into several pieces. Several cheers rang across the bridge from the members of the crew watching the viewscreen.

The feeling was bittersweet, watching the broken pieces of the ship begin to fall from the spot where it had exploded, realizing she'd saved the day, but she'd killed without understanding. Humanity was safe, but another race was not. Was this an entire ship of AI beings? Had she killed an entire race? Was it a scout ship from another species that was looking for a new home? So many unanswered questions. She started to turn to Mumford to ask him what he'd found odd, but Lieutenant Whitehorse caught her attention.

"Admiral, the *Vanguard* is coming about," she said. "They're targeting us with rail-guns!"

"Bastard," she muttered. "All weapons crews, retarget. Set your sights on their guns only. We're going for neutralization of their weapons systems, nothing more—"

"Shelby! There's a shuttle leaving our shuttle bay," yelled Volz from across the bridge.

"Who?"

Before he could answer, Lieutenant Qwerty pointed up at the comm speakers. "They're transmitting, Admiral."

The comm speakers crackled on. "General Mullins, this is Lieutenant Ethan Zivic. I've got Admiral Proctor on board the shuttle. We're both turning ourselves in. Please send an approach vector and docking instructions. Zivic out."

Proctor stood up and paced toward the screen, watching

the shuttle arc wide around the *Independence*, against the backdrop of the huge chunks of Golgothic ship that were falling down through Titan's atmosphere. "What the hell is he playing at?" She turned to Volz, who's jaw was set tight. "Ballsy?"

"He's going to kill Mullins," he muttered. "Probably the whole ship. He's going to overload the reactor on the shuttle, and he's going to kill Mullins, along with the rest of the *Vanguard*. There's no other explanation."

"Is he out of his mind?"

Volz nodded slowly. "Mullins killed Batak. Ethan and her were getting to be good ... friends. And he's been on the edge anyway. Seeing her die in the blast when we were so close to getting her out of there...." He sighed. "Yeah, this is classic Ethan. When something doesn't go your way, you torpedo the whole thing."

"Open a channel," she said. "Ethan Zivic, this is Admiral Proctor. Get your ass back in our shuttle bay. Now. That's an order."

After a moment, Zivic answered. "Uh, ma'am, I was trying to give you a chance to get away."

"Bullshit. I'm not running from this situation, and neither are you. We're done running." She paused, mentally redirecting her attention to the rest of the fleet undoubtedly listening in. "Ethan, they found my nephew's body. His suit was intact. We've got *video evidence* of Admiral Mullins and the *ISS Vanguard* docking with the *Magdalena Issachar* minutes before its demise. It was Mullins all along. The new president of Shovik-Orion—yes, Ted, I know you're listening in, and yes, I have proof. You know," she paused, leaning back in her chair, propping a foot up on her bad knee, "when this all started a few days ago, I wanted nothing more than to get in, find my nephew, maybe save humanity, maybe not, but definitely go back to my beach house when it was all over and just kick back with a martini and an unflattering bathing suit. But you've convinced me, Ted. You've convinced me to come back and root out the cancer. This is your official notice. Assholes that threaten my family, and that threaten humanity and Earth and all its planets, have *me* to answer to. Understood?"

The comm was silent. Zivic didn't say a word, thankfully understanding that this wasn't about him, for once. Mullins didn't reply either, apparently sizing her up and wondering how much she was bluffing.

She prayed he called her bluff. She wanted nothing more than to beat the ever-living shit out of him.

To her surprise, Mullins's ship flickered, and disappeared. "Admiral, the *Vanguard* q-jumped away. Along with most of the ships in his fleet."

She sighed. "Damn. I was kind of hoping to teach him a lesson." She stood up and smiled at Volz. "At least him high-tailing it out of here basically validated my point. PR win, right?"

He nodded. "I think the next board meeting at Shovik-Orion will definitely be ... lively."

She tapped her finger against her temple, deep in thought. "What's your game, Ted Mullins?" She ran through the details. First he'd played the GPC to get those two missiles, then frame the GPC by making it look like the *Magdalena Issachar* had committed a false-flag operation and attacked its own people, ostensibly to generate sympathy and enthusiasm for the cause.

Now he was playing her and IDF, or rather, trying to get her out of the way and keep his influence within IDF. He'd probably arranged for the design of the meta-space shunt. Now that she thought about it, he'd probably arranged for both attempts on her life, too. And at San Martin he was probably trying to kill two birds with one stone. Kill her, *and* Secretary General Curiel.

But why? Power? He already had it. Money? It just didn't make sense yet. She needed more time to investigate. Time she didn't have.

Commander Mumford caught her attention. "Ma'am, I was trying to tell you earlier…."

"What is it?"

"Something I picked up on the sensors earlier. It didn't show up before, but the more the fleet's weapons penetrated into the ship, the deeper I was able to scan. The ship, Admiral. The ship is … well, let me just show you." He fiddled with his console, then pointed up at the front viewscreen. "This is a reconstructed image I put together from the most recent scan. It came from a piece of interior hull plating deep up inside the ship."

She turned back toward the screen. The image was grainy, but still easy to read. Letters.

"I … S … S … Vic…."

Her sweat went cold.

"ISS Vic?" said Volz. "That could be anything." He shook his head, as if trying to convince himself. "Impossible."

"No," said Proctor. "I'd recognize that until the day I die." She turned to Volz. "*ISS Victory*. That's the nameplate from her hull."

"What the *hell* is *Victory*'s nameplate doing inside an alien ship?" Volz waved his arms up in the air. "That's ... that's batshit crazy!"

Mumford cleared his throat. "Just to be sure, ma'am, I brought up an old materials analysis of the *ISS Victory* and compared it."

"Tungsten, right?"

"Right." He nodded, but pointed at the screen. "That's tungsten alright. But the isotopics are all wrong. It clearly does *not* have the same isotopic signature as the material used for the *Victory*'s hull."

"So what the hell is it then?" She watched the other side of the screen as the broken pieces of the ship continued to fall through the atmosphere.

Mumford swallowed hard. "The interesting thing is that, if you take the old isotopic signature, and step it forward in time by about, oh, thirteen *billion* years, then you get what we're reading now."

Impossible.

More than impossible. It was utterly crazy. Completely, utterly, batshit crazy, as Ballsy said. As the contractor, Sara Batak, would say, *it don't rain but it shitstorms.*

But the only thing she could say, as she collapsed into her chair, was a name.

"Tim."

CHAPTER SIXTY

Terran Sector, Saturn System, Titan
Bridge, ISS Independence

Mumford shook his head. "No, Admiral. I can basically scan the whole ship now, and I can confidently say there is no organic material anywhere over there. Captain Timothy Granger is not—"

"I know that! I'm not a friggin' Grangerite," she snapped. "But … but … still. The evidence is here. The data is … data. Could he have … could he have sent something back out of that black hole? How? Why?"

She wracked her brain, even as she watched the pieces of the ship fall down towards the hole it had carved on the surface of Titan.

"Replay the video. The moment it finally exploded." She waved at the screen.

The image of the piece of hull with the faded imprint of

"*ISS VIC*" disappeared, replaced by the video from the final moments of the battle. Hundreds of explosions peppered the surface of the alien ship. The drilling beam was still lancing out towards the surface. It fluttered erratically, then disappeared, and the ship exploded.

"Slow it down and repeat."

The video repeated, this time at a quarter speed.

The beam. The realization struck her, and she remembered how Rex had tapped out a pattern on that safe-house door. The code.

She watched it flutter, this time … in a pattern she recognized.

"Holy shit. Ballsy, are you seeing what I'm seeing?"

He shrugged. "A high-powered anti-matter drilling beam?"

She turned around. "Morse code. Mumford—slow it down. And Qwerty, please translate—I can't remember everything like I used to."

"Yes'm," he drawled.

The video repeated, slower this time, and the fact there was a pattern there was unmistakable. Qwerty finally looked over at her. "Coming."

Coming?

"That's it?" she said, though even as she said it she felt foolish. She'd finally made contact with the aliens behind the construction and operation of this ship, and all she could say was *that's it?*

"Just one word, ma'am," said Qwerty. "*Coming.*"

She shook her head. "No, that can't be it. There has to be more. Analyze the entire video sequence, from the moment it started the beam until the end."

Mumford worked, and she watched the pieces fall lower towards Titan. The data feed to the side of the live video indicted the debris was only a few dozen kilometers from crashing on the surface.

"Nothing. Just that one word at the end. And I checked all bands, all wavelengths."

Coming.

"Check the other videos. Ido. El Amin. Check those."

It took Mumford a minute to retrieve the files and display them on the viewscreen, but when Qwerty looked up at them, lips mumbling, she saw the answer bloom on his face. There was more.

"Lieutenant?"

He gulped. "It says, *Shelby, they're coming.*"

Shelby, they're coming.

CHAPTER SIXTY-ONE

Terran Sector, Saturn System, Titan
Bridge, ISS Independence

"Oh, my God," she breathed.

Volz bolted across the bridge and gripped her armrest as he bent low to her. "What does it mean?"

She didn't want to say the words. She didn't want to say them because they couldn't be true. They couldn't be.

She said them anyway. "It means ... that the Swarm is back."

The bridge, already quiet, fell to a dead silence.

"No," said Volz. His finger jabbed at the viewscreen, punctuating almost every word. "No. You killed the last of their ships. Granger piloted the *Victory* and a hundred anti-matter bombs into that black hole, and the Skiohra themselves confirmed that the meta-space link through that thing was shut. Permanently."

They all stared at the falling fragments.

Shelby, they're coming.

"Admiral! Reading a power surge from one of the pieces of the alien ship!" Whitehorse yelled from tactical.

"What is it doing?"

The video zoomed in on the falling pieces. One large chunk of the ship was pulling away from the rest, as if it had thrusters propelling it. "That's the central core section, Admiral," said Mumford. "It appears to … have its own thrusters."

"Shoot it down," she said. "Now."

Whitehorse shook her head. "Sorry, Admiral, it's at the bottom of the atmosphere now. Rail-gun slugs will never hit it, and lasers would be too dissipated at that distance."

She stood up and dashed to the helm. "Riisa, get us down there. Full thrusters. Now."

A hand on her shoulder. "Shelby, it's already gone," said Ballsy. "Look."

The roughly spherical chunk of the alien ship plunged lower and lower, accelerating, and with an anti-climactic puff of dust and debris, disappeared into the hole it had bored into the crust.

Moments later, the rest of the ship collided with the surface, landing with catastrophic force all around the hole, sending up huge billows of brown dust which plumed into a massive mushroom cloud, as if the area had been hit by a nuclear blast.

"Sensors reading that the impact of the rest of the ship on the surface has closed the hole up with rock and debris." Whitehorse looked up from tactical. "It's gone."

But she knew it wasn't gone. She knew it in her gut, deep down. It wasn't gone.

Shelby, they're coming.

Terran Sector, Earth
Elysium Fields Memorial Gardens, Nashville, Tennessee

For every funeral Shelby Proctor had even gone to, it had rained. Granger's funeral. Her sister's when she was young. All the friends she'd lost in the intervening years. Rain. Every single one.

Except, this one, and she found it ironic. The sun was shining on a glorious spring morning at the cemetery outside Nashville, completely out of place in her mind. Not only was her nephew dead, not only was Admiral Mullins still on the loose, not only was the mass of Titan slowly but perceptibly increasing just as Ido's and El Amin's had, not only was the GPC increasing in influence due to the Sangre incident, compounded by the recently exposed video from Danny's suit of the *ISS Vanguard* docking with the *Magdalena Issachar*, but in addition to all this, the message encoded in the alien ship's drilling beam never left her mind. Not for a moment.

Shelby, they're coming.
Shelby, they're coming.
Shelby, they're coming.

The words of warning repeated themselves in her mind

like a mantra. Like a dirge.

The sun shone anyway, oblivious to her dread.

Her brother squeezed her hand. He smiled at her, but it was a strained, hollow smile. He was putting on a good show for her. The priest had paused the service momentarily to drink from a water bottle, and her sister-in-law, standing on the other side of her brother, said, "It's so beautiful here." A cross rested on her chest. She was a believer, and from the peaceful look on her face it looked like she meant it.

It won't look so beautiful when the Swarm comes back, Proctor thought. In her mind's eye the tranquil scene of trees and grass and blue sky was overwritten with death and destruction—the only thing the Swarm had ever brought them.

Somehow, he'd come back to warn them.

But that was silly. That was Patriarch Huntsman talking. Tim was dead. The scientists were beyond sure. They even had video evidence of the old *ISS Victory* being stretched by the extreme tidal forces of the black hole, beyond what anyone could live through.

But somehow, against all probability, he, or someone, had sent her the warning. *Shelby, they're coming.* At least, she assumed the word *they* meant the Swarm, and *Shelby* meant that the message was for her, probably from someone close to her. Who else but Tim? And *coming*?

That meant soon. She felt it in her gut.

The priest continued, and concluded, and everyone lined up to throw soil on the coffin. The funeral officially over, she lingered by the grave, standing next to her brother who'd sat on the bench nearby. "Thank you, Shelby, for finding him."

The words felt hollow in her mouth. "I'm sorry I didn't

find him in time."

"There was nothing you could have done. He was dead before you even knew about Sangre." He sighed. "But it means a lot to me that you dropped everything to find him. To bring him back here."

She squeezed his shoulder. "Are you coming back to Britannia? I can give you a lift. I'm heading out that way on the *Independence* in a few days."

He shook his head. "Jess's family lives here in Nashville. I think we're going to move here to be closer to them. At least for now. She's more devastated than she lets on."

Proctor nodded. She bent low to hug him one last time, then made for the Marine transport she'd arrived in.

Fleet Admiral Oppenheimer was waiting for her.

"What do you want?" she said, starting to climb up into the car.

His face was ice. "I want you to retire. Disappear. Go lay on your beach. You've done your part, you've done what I asked of you, and now it's time to leave it alone."

She paused, and climbed back down to the ground. "You haven't talked to President Quimby yet, have you? Because he told me something quite the opposite this morning."

Oppenheimer grunted. "I'm well aware of your conversations with President Quimby. He's scared. Scared shitless. The alien ship striking so close to home, and the news about the *Victory*'s hull has him spooked. Of course he wants you to stay. He's deluded. He thinks you can save us from what's coming. When all that's coming is cleaning up the mess Mullins caused and getting a handle on the GPC political situation, which, frankly, is neither of our jobs. So I'm telling you again, leave. Go home. Go back to where you belong: a well-deserved retirement."

She stared at him for a moment, seeing the twitch in his eye. It was a tell. She knew he wanted nothing more than for her to disappear and get out of his hair. But it was clear he was hiding something. He wanted her gone for reasons other than his ego.

And she wasn't going to let him get away with it.

"See you on Britannia, Christian."

"Shelby, I'm—"

She stepped back up into the entrance hatch of the ground car. "I know you're serious, Christian, but so am I. I'm not leaving. You're stuck with me." She sat down in her seat, and before the waiting marine closed the door she smiled back up at the fleet admiral through the open window. "And I'm going to get to the bottom of it. All of it. It's what I do. I figure shit out." She motioned to the marine to shut the door. Through the window she could see Oppenheimer silently fuming.

Good. Let him fume. It wouldn't change her resolve to get to the bottom of Danny's death. Of Mullins's schemes, of Oppenheimer's possible involvement in those schemes.

It wouldn't change the fact that *they* were coming, whoever *they* were.

It wouldn't change the fact that, in spite of being dead, Tim Granger had sent her a message. Somehow, against all the laws of nature, he'd sent her a message from the center of a black hole.

A message that had taken thirteen billion years to reach her.

She waved to the driver.
"I'm ready."

Thank you for reading *Independence*.

Sign up to find out when *Defiance*, book 2 of *The Legacy Ship Trilogy*, is released: smarturl.it/nickwebblist

Contact information:

www.nickwebbwrites.com

facebook.com/authornickwebb

authornickwebb@gmail.com

NICK WEBB

365

Printed in Great Britain
by Amazon